SHAGOON

SHAGOON

VICTORIA VENTRIS SHEA

Enjoy!
V. Shea

Protection Island Trading Company

Dedicated to my beautiful children with Love,
Courtney and Nathan.
Thankful for the gift of being your mother.
and
Sitka Dancers, Sheet'ka Kwaan Naa Kahidi
who help their Tlingit culture live.

Contents

I

Ut-kart-ee (Root of a Tree) 1764

We are a forest on a mountainside,
a group of individual trees
strengthened by our interlocking roots.

Clarence Jackson, Tlingit
Listening to Our Ancestors, p. 163

Ut-kart-ee sits on an ice-covered rock, wrapped in
her deerskin—the one decorated with reflective shells
from her grandmother. It's cold, but the sun is shining,
sharp light dances off ice crystals in the snow. She
smiles at the red winter leaves with black round bear-
berries hugging the ground, then looks up to see a

*huge gray Wolf. He sits on his haunches across a small
clearing, fierce golden eyes attached to her, his prey.*

*Caught, she shudders, afraid to move, hoping
her timid stare might protect her. Wolf stands to his
fullest height, tall ears looking red in the penetrating
sunlight. He lowers his head to pick up something from
the white snow and stalks toward her, eyes locked on
hers as if to keep her in place.*

*Tight muscles quiver down her spine, telling
her legs to run, but she predicts the attack it would
provoke, the teeth, the tearing flesh. Her breath stops,
ready to fight. He lowers to a crawl and drops a black
Raven feather at her feet.*

She jerks awake, buried, gasping for air, pawing with bound
fingers at what covers her face, a tangle of her own filthy hair. A
Spirit Dream. *Her Spirit Dream,* yet she tenses for Wolf's bite . . .
and she can't escape, naked and trapped in her prison, her tiny
cell where she's to become a woman.

Finding breath, she wonders if it's day or night. No light escapes between hairy strips of cedar bark that keep her captive.
She hugs her knees to her chest, still frightened from Wolf's
stare and remembers that she can't feel because her fingers are
wrapped to keep her from scratching with her fingernails.
Grudgingly, she breathes her putrid air and tries to settle, coax
herself back into a state of submission.

"Privileged." She remembers her mother's word to describe
her cell within Hawk Clan longhouse rather than a hole under
the house, an easy way to die from the cold and wet.

"Find strength in silence. As niece of Wolf Clan leader, try to stay longer than the required four moons for your rite of puberty. Contribute to our status."

But it feels like punishment.

Tiny slivers of light arrive. She hears movement in the house and silently stands to stretch her legs, wondering what the black Raven feather could mean in her Spirit Dream. Wolf's stare returns, his hunting eyes causing her spine to tingle as though touched by Power. She imagines a new weave design to create in her baskets, tall red ears standing alert over the blazing golden eyes of Wolf.

Something to look forward to.

The day moves on without her. She battles her thoughts, imagining her normal time with her friends, collecting seafood, gathering wood, weaving baskets, cooking food. Food, she hasn't had food in days.

Don't think of food. Being weak helps me stay in this cage.

Her panic rises, choking her, and she rubs her forehead back and forth against the bark wall for distraction, something to do, the remembered power of choice. Soon, a wound is open, and the stinging wet oozes down her forehead, melting into her eyebrows. She lowers the mess to her knees to block it from her eyes, pushing hard to stop her gushing mind, to build a beaver dam there.

Be quiet . . . be invisible . . . be alone.

She sits, like a bear in a trap.

Darkness begins and her walls come closer, a tighter trap, tempting her to scream. She grabs the *ta-sate*, scratching rock that hangs from a cord around her neck and rubs it back and forth across her mouth until her lips are raw, teaching her mouth to be quiet.

Families come in for evening and cedar smoke surrounds her like a blanket, the aroma of roasting moose meat filling her nose, not her stomach.

In the middle of the night, the female slave Shouk (Robin) secrets her through the house under a long hood. She follows quietly in spite of the limp she was given at birth when her great aunt had dislocated one of her hips, opening her for later childbirth. Embers from the banked hearth fires make subtle red glows and shadows between the sleeping lumps of hides and blankets. They move past the slaves sleeping just inside the door and go outside past the bent cedarwood box of urine on the porch used for dying and cleaning, then away from the house.

Ut-kart-ee shivers against the cold night. It smells clean and sweet and spruce needles poke her feet with a lovely crunch. She hears the waves slam the beach, and the fine echo of pebbles rolling in retreat vibrates through her hollow skin. After wiping herself with moss and drinking water through a hollow goose-bone to keep the water away from her lips, she reluctantly follows Shouk back to her cell, forcing her feet to take each step.

Her mother Yake-see (Spirit's Voice) comes in a night with her first food, dried salmon and a small cake of dried huckle-berries in oil. Beyond hunger, Ut-kart-ee follows her outside and dutifully swallows it down. She will have no fresh seafood since her body must become dry, stable and strong like rock, not like water.

"I feel like a *ki yah hi*, a shadow," she whispers.

"The People will forget Ut-kart-ee, the child," Yake-see's copper labret in her lower lip reflects the moonlight. "One day they will meet the woman you will become." She gives Ut-kart-ee a large, smooth stone. "This is to keep you company. It will weigh you down, keep you grounded and strong."

Several days later her stomach tightens and cramps. She holds the stone against it like a shield, appreciating its weight, but her stomach grips cold and hard like the stone itself, and she pulls it harder to her body to keep from smashing it through her prison walls.

As days go by, Ut-kart-ee's loneliness fills her cage, and she feels useless, like a salmon unable to return to her spawning stream. Her mind begins to float, and her spirit begins to die. Her shallow breath stops, until a gulping gasp reminds her to breathe.

She has dreams, so many dreams, most forgotten. Dreams of longing, visions of her Tlingit village as if she sits in the bay, gazing back from a canoe on a bright, sunny day. The water is calm. Dots of dark islands protect her from behind. Just above the beach, small houses and smoke shacks cluster near big clan longhouses with their totem fronts, and thin, transparent salmon slices hang from racks to dry like floating red blossoms. To the right, the river crashes into the tide through a rocky outcropping, foaming like a soapberry treat; and to the left are the tiny grave houses and tall mortuary poles that hold the ashes of ancestors. Above the village stands the dense, silent forest, thick with hemlock, alder, spruce, and cedar gathered together with a base of berry bushes, devil's club and wild rose. Multiple layers of white icy peaks poke the sky above the forest like the spear points of great Tlingit warriors protecting their home. She dreams of the golden eyes of Wolf always on her.

She longs for her brother. Inseparable as children, the next time they're together, it must be with a chaperone. She won't be allowed to look at his face. He won't be allowed to offer her a gift except through her husband when she's married. Her heart tightens.

Her body changes as if it belongs to someone else. Soft hair grows with more flesh between her legs, her breasts get fuller and rounder, and fear of her future begins to lurk like dark shadows outside the safety of her cell.

She thinks about fear. When Raven brought light into the world, those who were afraid ran into the woods and into the sea. Those hiding in the woods became the animals. Those hiding in the sea became the fish. It was those who controlled their fear and stayed who became the People. She must control her fear.

When awake, she tries to remember clan songs and stories. Instead, she drifts into a trance, a floating fleck of ash.

She barely exists . . .

In the night, Yake-see brings a tiny rock carved into a wolf. "I found this on my sleeping furs. I believe it's meant for you."

Recognizing the craftsmanship of her brother, Ut-kart-ee holds it to her heart, knowing he wishes her to be strong, hard like rock.

Her grandmother arrives in the dark several nights later. Startled, Ut-kart-ee chokes back a sob as her grandmother grabs her wrist to hobble outside, their naked feet soundless in a dusting of new snow. Tiny flakes silently float, fall, and rise again, lighting the night world.

"The *kaa tlein* big man in the sky is busy chopping bits from his big block of ice," grandmother waves to the sky and to the snow at her feet. "I have missed you little S'ook (Barnacle). You must remember your strength. As soon as you got loose from your cradle, you went after things with no fear." The back of her gnarled fist wipes the tears that slide down Ut-kart-ee's face as she remembers her own puberty isolation, how her family needed to carry her out, nurse her back to health. The light driftwood labret in her lower lip moves up and down as she thinks. "Pray to Ke-an-kow (Spirit Above) little S'ook and to your guardian spirit."

Each night after her grandmother's visit, Shouk leads her further into the forest to work her legs, free her from her cocoon. She walks on her toes, thinking of crane's careful steps and squats like frog. She pumps her arms like hawk.

Each morning, she whispers prayers at first light: *"Watch over me, Spirit Above. Help me be honorable and without fear. Find me worthy of many children who will be strong and never die."*

The greatest gift of her confinement arrives one night on a full moon in a clear sky, lighting everything as if it were day, awakening her senses. The crisp Spirit shadows of trees and bushes stretch far into the woods like living ghosts. Looking through wide-open space towards the beach, she sees light bounce, dancing on water.

Everything lives!

The tawny-orange face of owl looks down at her from his tree limb. His call should signal misfortune, but over time, it's become the regular night voice of her friend. He's larger than she imagined, and she's glad to see him. "Hoo . . . hoo hoo," she calls. He blinks and ruffles his feathers but doesn't fly.

Day after day, her senses quiet.

She sleeps.

The door to her cell opens wide. She hears her mother's voice, "It's been eight moons, daughter, much longer than required. Surely, you're ready to be finished."

Ut-kart-ee's eyes stay closed, the light too bright. Words are far away, until they arrive with her full consciousness like a slap in the face.

2

Chark Cough-ye (Eagle Lowered from the Sky)

With the Wolf rock from her brother in her fist, she crawls from her cell, looking through a wild mop of hair. Her mother stands at a distance, tall, regal, alone in the big house, bracelets jangling as she motions for Ut-kart-ee to follow Shouk outside.

Do I smell so bad? Squinting against the light, she goes on shaky legs.

Outside, cold rain shocks her face, her shoulders, makes demanding tapping drips from the trees, igniting her senses. Spruce, hemlock, houses, everything pulsates with life. She stops, cautiously pushing her face into soft green buds of a young spruce tree, breathing in. Her breath shakes like the buds in front of her nose. *New life!*

Shouk sneaks her to the east end of the village, down to a bit of ocean shoreline near the mouth of the river, but she shrinks from the roaring chaos, ocean waves crashing against river water, the extreme opposite of her silent, static cell. As she stalls, tiny hermit crabs scuttle away from her feet.

Breath grabs with her first steps in, and she trembles as she moves forward, forgotten muscles cramping against the cold undulating water. Yellow and orange anemones wave from their rocks, calling her into deeper water, and she goes, distracted from the stinging saltwater. Shouk comes too, rubbing dead flesh from her sensitive skin with sand, and she grinds her teeth to keep from crying out. Swirling her hair through the surf, Shouk pulls her fingers through the long, dark tangle, tugging at her tender skull.

Shivering, they move to a quieter spot in the river to lather soapberry and pull a wooden comb through her hair revealing a reddish tinge, then pour blueberry juice to make it black. With Shouk's support and village dogs sniffing at her heels, she walks back wrapped in a blanket, cleaning her chattering teeth with a small spruce stick.

Inside Hawk Clan House, her enclosure is gone, the Shaman shaking his rattles and chanting to remove any remaining dark spirits. Her eyes bounce. Giant red and black Hawk stares menacingly at her from his wall at the back of the house--the house leader's space. Raven decorates corner posts while old mats, nets, stacked bent-wood boxes and overhead storage planks create separation between family spaces.

Am I the only change?

Her mother waits, spine straight, standing near their fire pit and sleeping platform. She motions for Ut-kart-ee to sit. "You've done well," she soothes, winding the long, damp hair into a club at the back of her head. She opens a pod from bladder-rack sea-weed, scooping out the gel to soothe onto sore spots, then re-veals a soft deerskin tunic fringed with tiny dentalium shells and painted with a Wolf crest.

Beautiful! Ut-kart-ee touches the softness with the back of her hand.

"Made by your Aunt Sarh Sar-tee (Hat Keeper), of course." She mixes warm spruce gum with suet to paint tall, red Wolf ears onto her daughter's face, starting at her chin and sliding up over her eyebrows. Then she pats a reddish-brown mixture of hem-lock fungus onto the pattern where it will harden. They hang her tiny Wolf rock on a braid of spruce root around her neck. Four earrings go in each ear, one of human hair for the aristocratic piercing at the top, a copper nose ring, jade bracelets, "and a new bracelet from your father, with the Hawk crest."

"Now for your crowning glory," her mother announces as she presents a beautiful hood rimmed in marten fur and matching robe.

Ut-kart-ee cries, covering her face. *Aatlein! too much!*

Yake-see's hand settles on her daughter's shoulder, waiting. "I'm sorry to tell you, but you must know . . . your friend Dis-yati (Young Moon) has gone into the forest with her ancestors. Their small house . . . She was in a pit under."

Ut-kart-ee folds in on herself, horrified, seeing the misery of her own isolation in a cold, muddy hole, so *alone*. Slaves begin to bring in food for the celebration, and she wipes her face, deter-mined to show dignity *and to sing the crying songs for Dis-yati after the feast.*

The meal is hosted by her father Al'ooni (Hunter) and her Aunt Sarh Sar-tee who are Hawk Clan of the Raven People, the opposite lineage of Ut-kart-ee, her mother and siblings who are Wolf Clan of the Wolf People, lineage coming through the mother's line.

Curious, hungry faces fill the longhouse with so many eyes *and nowhere to hide!* She looks to the floor, prominent cheekbones elevated on a square face, and sits motionless--the look of quiet obedience, pulling full lips into a calm smile as she has seen others do.

Young girls stare, in awe of her transformation, while Dis-yati's family is somber, haunted. She steals a glance at her uncle, Wolf Clan Leader Ka-uh-ish (Father of the Morning), the leader with greatest influence in the village. He wears his Wolf crest hat of twined spruce root and robe. Her brother A-kadi stands by his side, having lived at Wolf Clan House since he was eight years old to be trained by their uncle.

Quickly, she holds her Wolf token and smiles at him. He gives the slightest nod, showing the dimple on the right side of his face—the only talk they will have.

"*Goona cheesh, ach ho nay,* thank you friends and family for coming," her father begins.

Leader Ka-uh-ish thanks Hawk Clan for their hospitality and addresses his niece. "Ut-kart-ee, you have more than fulfilled expectations with dignity. I wish to release a slave in your honor because of your resilience. What slave will you name?"

Unable to shake the image of her dead friend, her words come uncontrolled. "I am well because," she raises her eyes, blatantly violating custom, "because I was able to stay *within* our clan house, not under, but Dis-yati." She hardens her face, swallowing. "I ask for something for the clan instead."

Shocked, her uncle dismisses her. "We all miss Dis-yati. She will return . . ."

". . . to have a building for families who need space for their daughter's rite of passage," she continues, "in Dis-yati's memory." She looks to her grandmother and sees her proud face.

"Time to eat," Ka-uh-ish announces gruffly, waving her words away like batting at flies. He grumbles something about the Council and following custom.

Trembling, she sits with her noisy family for the meal, enduring their fussing and touching, only picking at the rich salmon. When she feels as if she floats on water, she removes herself to sit alone in a corner, enjoying the comfort of her new garments. Her Aunt Sarh Sar-tee comes to join her, a short, square bundle of exuberance emerging from the crowd, "You look beautiful."

"Thanks to you," Ut-kart-ee smiles.

"I am pleased," she fluffs the marten fur around her niece's face. "Ready for your labret? sign of womanhood? readiness for marriage?"

"Not afraid," she whispers. "It seems a bother for eating, though." She touches her lip as if to prepare it. "Besides . . . why don't men have them?"

"Men don't cause fights and wars because of their gossip." She pokes her finger into Ut-kart-ee's chest, "You will learn it's better to have peace by controlling your mouth!"

"Men don't gossip, they insult," Ut-kart-ee counters. Her aunt grabs her lip, pinching, holding on while Ut-kart-ee continues to speak, "They still fight, provoked by words."

When her lip is numb, her aunt makes a small, horizontal slice with a sharpened bear claw and inserts a tiny bone plug which will stay for healing time. The bone will be enlarged several times, then replaced with a rounded labret. Blood rushes back to her lip, making it heavy. It begins to pulsate with her heartbeat.

"And now I have news!" Sarh Sar-tee's eyes sparkle. "Chark Cough-ye (Eagle Lowered from the Sky) the son of my cousin and nephew to Raven Clan leader! He will be your husband!"

Ut-kart-ee's heart jerks in spite of her exhaustion, "That angry bear?" She ignores the stab of pain in her stretched lip. "He's rude! already married to old Kaa-saagi (Fish Bones)! She probably died to be rid of him!"

"Shush! He was forced to marry the wife of his dead uncle when he was just a youth. Of course he's angry. Council hopes you help him calm down, put the needs of the People first." She dabs the incision with moss, soaking up a few new beads of blood, ". . . or you could marry Aas-daayi (Tree Bark). He needs a wife."

Shudders skip up Ut-kart-ee's spine.

"You'll be part of the two most powerful clans in the village! Be thankful."

Ut-kart-ee sees her father looking at her from across the room. His gleaming eyes say that he approves of the choice for husband, and he nods to her with one eyebrow raised, asking if she agrees. She considers curling the corners of her mouth into a smile like a good daughter but decides to protect her throbbing lip instead.

Chark Cough-ye's mother asks Yake-see for a marriage agreement, offering furs, copper, knives, a nine-year old slave boy. Yake-see accepts and in exchange gives sea otter pelts, blankets, and a few iron tools. They will be married in one year, as is custom.

Ut-kart-ee sees little of Chark Cough-ye except when he walks, long strides through the village to go fishing or hunting, the eagle feather twirling in his hair like the tail of a happy village dog. He creates wealth for her family, and it seems the men of her clan like him, maybe even respect him.

Her favorite time is picking berries with her friend Kla-oosh (Seaweed). Kla-oosh stops picking to straighten her back. "It feels like a fish swims in my belly." She stretches, looking up to the sky. "I should deliver soon. Are you prepared for married life, my friend?"

Ut-kart-ee shrugs, berry juice staining her lips, "How do you tame an angry bear?"

Kla-oosh grins, an upper tooth missing in a red mouth. "I doubt you'll have trouble with that! But living with him . . . I'm learning men are proud, like Wolf. Don't criticize. Try to treat him like the man you *wish* him to be."

She wavers like the tide between anxiety for her future and long, lovely periods of denial. On clear winter nights when the sky dances in sheets of greens, blue and violet, she thinks about the warriors up there who died in battle and are now lighting those sky fires. They warn the People of war or death. She wonders if she is seeing the death of her life as she has known it now that she will be married.

Several days before the joining ceremony, no food is eaten. Then face painted red, wrapped in a special Raven crest robe, Chark Cough-ye sits on a new mat in the place of honor in Hawk Clan House, facing the giant Hawk wall. Ut-kart-ee, in a ceremonial blanket decorated with fur, sits hidden in a corner under a woven spruce root hat that covers most of her face. Gifts are scattered on the floor in a pathway between them, and when a drum begins to beat, guests move together in a dance, chanting a song to call Ut-kart-ee to join her groom.

Awkwardly, she steps over the furs and other gifts with her head lowered, carrying a sheet of copper on her back, a special gift from her uncle Ka-uh-ish. As she approaches, Chark Cough-ye extends his hand to her, strong and rough. She forces her hand to move, putting it into his and lowers herself to the mat beside him, causing the room to explode in celebration. Embarrassed, she covers her mouth.

While the others eat, she steals a close-up peek at her husband and sees the angry bear—clenched jaw, shoulders broad, fierce, hungry looking. His light brown eyes glance at her, reflecting his copper nose ring.

"Are you hungry?" she asks.

Eagle down floats off his long, black hair as he turns toward her. "You think a little fast bothers me?"

"I'm good also. I did eight moons in confinement. I know self-discipline."

"Eight moons without talking?"

She nods.

"I wonder if you could keep that up when we're together," he gives her a serious, sideways glance.

"Funny," she answers, "I would be *happy* to not talk to you."

"That would be impressive," he looks directly at her, serious.

"I *am* impressive," she replies, looking right back.

Four moons since the marriage ceremony, the morning is motionless, so quiet, his breath is a disturbance. He listens to the Great Silence. Orange light lifts from behind the distant mountain peaks, illuminating the little round button islands that sit on the glass of the bay. The flat water mirrors the sky, turning pink now against the blue mountains. A hint of mist rises from the water undisturbed except by the wings of a lonely gull. A fog bank rolls up against the shore, telling Chark Cough-ye it's time to end his prayers and begin his journey.

Wearing his spruce root hat and fringed cape, he walks through the fog to claim his wife, gathering Raven Clan friends as he goes to help him carry a gift of firewood. Once he has started a fire outside Hawk Clan House, and his father and father-in-law come to warm their hands, he knows that he has their approval, and he goes inside to get Ut-kart-ee. She sits, weaving a basket of her Wolf design, her hair tied in a knot at the base of her neck.

"Time to go," he announces.

Her stomach tightens as she looks up, not moving. "Could we not live *here?*" her voice pleads, betraying her plan to hide her fear.

"You *know* the wife lives with her husband's clan, woman," his voice is strong, slightly irritated. He plops her hood onto her head and hands over her robe. She gathers a bundle of personal items and follows.

As they walk, he sees Raven land in a tree above them, *Ko-wulk-ulk-ulk*. "I remember when you sang to oysters and clams as a child."

"*You* used to brag about being the best hunter of the village! You were probably only twelve years old!"

"You were impressed, or you wouldn't remember." He sees Raven follow, flying from tree to tree as they leave Hawk Clan area. "Raven follows on our first walk. A good sign. Hey! Look, what's that building over there?" He nods with his head. "Is that new?"

"What *is* that?" she points. "Do you think it could be the girls' confinement house I asked for?"

He sees sparks of excitement in her eyes for the first time. "It *does* look like it's next to the women's house."

She looks at him, "How did I not know about this? I thought my request was forgotten long ago!"

"Maybe you were too busy singing in the berry patches to notice," he shrugs.

"So you've been keeping an eye on me!" she accuses. "Well, I *do* hope it is Dis-yati's House."

"Really? You want to have a space *for the unclean* named for her? What will she think when she comes back in her next life?" he sighs, shaking his head.

She punches his shoulder. "This house will save lives, you *kooshdaa*, river otter! Anyone would be *proud* to be associated with such a building!"

The fog turns to rain when they arrive at Raven Clan House.

A giant carved and painted Raven greets them at the front of the house forming the door hole with its mouth, but Chark Cough-ye does not stop. Instead, he increases his pace, his eagle feather fluttering as he continues down the row to a small house near the end and steps down into the oval doorway.

Her heartbeat quickens and she hurries to catch up in spite of her slight limp. *A separate home?* "Why not live in your clan house?" she asks as her eyes adjust inside. She sees weapons, fishing gear and nets hanging on the walls and a decorated post in each corner with a lower fire pit in the middle of the house, a smoke hole above.

He leans against a post. "I'll have you to myself . . . and be near my uncle, Raven Clan leader."

She tenses, not ready to be "had" by anyone, and she refuses to show fear, continuing to look about the room. "I see Raven shapes on the other posts. What's on this front post?" She slides her fingers over the images, hoping to look unafraid.

"A battle with the Haida," he explains casually. "They ambushed us, but we made them sorry." He removes a club that hangs on the same post, caressing its grip. "And this is my *chuck-har-nut*, right by me, always ready. It is Latseen (Power)." He whips it through the air in a menacing practice swing.

Her eyes enlarge at the threat and she notices mountain sheep hides on the floor near the fire pit topped with fur blankets of squirrel and marmot, another danger. He watches her face as he hangs his weapon back onto its post. Removing his hat and cape, he squats to start the fire.

Frozen like a frightened rabbit, she watches him twirl his spindle of red cedar back and forth, back and forth between his flattened hands, drawing her in with the promise of fire. Flames spit and crackle from pitch in the firewood, and she lowers herself to it. When warmth and golden light fill the house, he gazes at her and removes his otter skin covering from neck to knees. He enters the bedding, holding open a blanket for her.

She's become stone. He rests on one elbow with an expectant look, long black hair pillowed beneath his head. Trembling, she avoids his eyes as she removes her hood and robe and steps out of her tall moccasins. After fumbling with the marten fur tie at her waist, she slips out of her tunic which covered her from neck to ankles and quickly slides in.

His warm arm covers her, soft blanket fur-side down, and she wants to burrow into him for heat. Rough hands release her hair from its knot and begin to trace the young contours of her body causing her to stiffen, her flesh quivering. He whispers, warm breath near her ear, "Be without worry, my wife, I will always take care of you."

"Me too!" she whimpers. "Just never speak of old Kaa-saagi."

He pulls back, surprised, wanting to see her face.

She smells his musky scent and opens her mouth to breathe only to find his mouth on hers and his heat between her legs, forcing his way through, binding them together toward their new destiny.

Early the next morning before Raven calls, he rushes to join his Raven Clan in the icy water and submit to the daily beatings with switches. Just as she drifts happily back to sleep, she's startled awake by his cold, wet body and frantically tries to squirm away as he pulls her back to the furs, growling, fake bites on her neck as she shrieks.

When their day begins, he joins a hunting trip, and she rolls up the bedding and sweeps the floor with eagle wings. Fog swirls up from the beach and gulls work for their breakfast, dropping clams to break on the rocks. As she walks inland, carrying her baskets to the closest Wolf Clan berry patch, she finds Kla-oosh.

Kla-oosh is surprised to see her. "Well?"

"Maybe not such a *terribly angry* bear. He *does* growl though," she laughs. "Hey, do you know about the new building by the women's house? I hope it's a confinement house in Dis-yati's memory."

Kla-oosh looks confused, "Of course it is! Did you just find out?"

"Yes! Why am I the last to know when I'm the one who requested it?"

Kla-oosh grins, "Your husband wanted it to be a surprise, my friend. He's the one who built it."

3

Friar Riobo

On deck the Spanish frigate *Favorita*, Friar Riobo braces himself against the wind, grabbing his gray robe to control it, chestnut hair flying about his thin face. With 107 souls on board, it sails alongside its sister-ship, *Princessa*. As he watches Captain Bodega Quadra standing on the quarterdeck in dress uniform, powdered wig topped with a tri-corner hat, he's reminded that the expedition is to claim new territory in northern-most America for Spain even though his own hope is to win converts to Christianity.

The sky grows an ominous blue-black, and they are pommeled by a tremendous hurricane, separating the two ships. Forgetting their missions, they pray for survival. The storm continues for weeks until finally, *Favorita* drops anchor in a sheltered bay, narrowly missing an enormous rock in the night. Within a few hours, *Princessa* arrives in the same bay! Prayers of thanksgiving reverberate off the mainland's snow-covered peaks.

Friar Riobo joins Second Officer Maourelle and armed crew to go ashore to a village for fresh supplies. They walk through a littered beach past over-turned canoes. Racks of drying fish wave in front of small houses clustered near large plank buildings.

The People of An-ar-kark see a floating house invade their bay with great folded white wings, and they think it may be Yealth (Raven). After all, Raven was white before he was turned black from the smoke of a fire. Another enormous Yealth arrives, and since they can't remember a story of Yealth having a wife, the Shaman suggests they hide until they know what sits in their bay. When they see smaller boats coming to shore, a group of men gather their clubs, knives, bows with arrows and dress in wooden-slat armor and carved animal helmets to meet them.

The Spanish wait on the beach, appreciating solid ground. When natives come with a leader who carries a staff with a carved bird on top, Officer Maourelle attempts to ask for supplies, showing beads and fabric for trade while the friar walks a short distance and drops to his knees, praying aloud as he caresses his rosary beads, giving thanks for their survival and asking for forgiveness for these Innocents who do not know God.

Chark Cough-ye comes with his uncle Takl-eesh (Hammer Reef), leader of Raven Clan, and watches Gray Robe. "I think this Cloud-Face prays to Ke-an-kow and the spirit of his beads. I hope he prays for a good trade," he chuckles.

More people come out of hiding, and Riobo looks into their

faces, wondering how to connect with his new flock. He sees the women have labrets, nose and ear piercings, bracelets of wood, copper, and whalebone. The younger men have no facial hair, so he bends over like an old man with a hobbling walk and acts like he tries to tear out his beard.

The women begin to remove it with sharpened mussel shells, talking excitedly as they work, and the friar makes faces that make them laugh as the pain brings tears to his eyes. An elder spreads gel from seaweed onto his face, calming the sting. Her labret stretches her lower lip even tighter as she smiles at him and pats him on the head. Now he hopes he will be a friend.

A naked wild man comes before him with long, knotted hair, a frightening mask, and overwhelming odor. Riobo stares as the others back away. The Shaman wields his Power, shaking rattles and chanting secret messages to Spirit to send the Cloud-Face stranger away.

Hoping for good relations while grabbing new territory for Spain, Quadra approves additional trade. Natives bring fish, skins, arrows pointed with bone or copper, and spears to the ship hoping to trade for thin sheets of copper or anything iron. Others come from nearby villages and soon a hundred canoes compete, fighting to trade and stealing what they can until Quadra fires a cannon at an empty canoe. Frightened paddlers crash into each other, panicked to get away, some capsizing. He brings them on ship to provide food and cloth for warmth, but in the end, it's a public whipping that's required to regain order.

Yahaayi (Spirit Seen in Face) grinds his teeth like a beaver working tough wood. Losing at the sticks game for many days, he worries that he could lose everything. If he wins, he will gain status. He has prepared himself by fasting, a swallow of seawater and a bit of devil's club bark to gain spirit favor. When the game begins, the *naq,* bait stick, is slipped inside bundles of small painted sticks which are mixed, re-bundled, and hidden under a piece of cedar bark. Yahaayi tries to choose the bundle that includes the naq. He watches the movements, biting the inside of his mouth in concentration, and when it's over, and the shock of losing another game hits him, he turns in shame and wanders into the woods.

Squatting in his favorite quiet spot among the ferns of an alder forest, he wonders what to do next. The high breeze ruffles through the canopy above him causing large raindrops from the trees to splat onto his woven rain hat. He was good at the sticks game as a younger man. Now he's about to lose what little respect he has as well as all his belongings. Eventually, he reasons that his wife may not even *want* to be married to him anymore. He will return to the game. The bet will be his wife.

Ut-kart-ee's belly feels like a giant frog hops inside rather than a fish swimming. Her aunt Sarh Sar-tee supports her from behind as she squats in front of a young tree over soft moss which was prepared in a shallow hole. She grunts through her teeth, bearing down to give birth. A light rain cools her body for the hard work while her mind and spirit seem to wait at a distance, anxious to meet her child.

Wolf Clan Shaman dances around a fire beside her, causing

the puffin bills on the fringe of his *sun-kate* apron to clack. He chants through his painted mask as his long, knotted hair flies. The hardened pine resin in it crackles, and he whips his wooden crane rattle back and forth, swinging its ermine skins from side to side, keeping negative spirits away.

From the edge of the village, Chark Cough-ye anxiously listens and prays to Ke-an-kow for a healthy son, already imagining his role as father, the fishing and hunting they will share, their closeness together as father and son.

Ut-kart-ee's "geeee" of release announces the arrival of an unusually tiny baby to her aunt immediately followed by a second infant who slips onto the bed of moss. Her aunt freezes, shocked, not sure what to do. She uses a mussel shell knife to cut the umbilical cord of the first baby since it is a girl and passes that newborn to Yake-see. She uses a stone knife for the second baby where he lies in the moss. As she ties the cords with sinew thread, she asks herself if she should bother, but for the sake of her niece, she washes some of the birthing fluids away, and both babies manage to spit up mucus, grab breath, and mew their little cries.

Sarh Sar-tee gathers the afterbirth for the fire. She does not catch the first cries of the babies in a basket to be stepped on as is custom. "Two babies," she stammers. "Twins are *kush-tar-ka*, a sign of trouble and misfortune . . . We cannot anger the spirits."

Ut-kart-ee grabs her second-born from the moss and shrieks, "Do not touch these babies! They're mine! I've loved them since before I was pregnant, sang to them, talked to them, prayed for them! They're mine!" and she tries to also get ahold of the baby from her mother. But Yake-see quickly stands and hands the child to the Shaman who immediately takes her away into the forest.

Ut-kart-ee screams. Moss will be put into her first-born's mouth to stop her breath. She will be left to die, consumed by the forest creatures. Her screams continue as she clutches her baby boy.

"Niece," her aunt grabs her face, "your strength is through the clan. You must follow custom. Sometimes our sacrifices are great . . . this baby you hold must also go into the forest."

Frantic, Ut-kart-ee grips her son and looks to her mother who sits now, bent over, tears dropping to her lap. "Mother do something!" she wails, gasping for air. "If I can't keep both babies, you must help me keep one! How much pain am I expected to endure?"

"*Taok wu-qootz*, my heart breaks for you, daughter. I can't go against the clan. You will have other children, maybe these babies in the future, one at a time."

Ut-kart-ee sobs, cuddling her remaining child against her body as if to absorb him again, looking into his tiny, newborn face, kissing his tender, fuzzy head and cheeks, the tiny hands and feet. She begins to hum a song for baby boys, rocking back and forth, closing her eyes, imagining their future.

"The spirits test you," her mother continues, laying a heavy hand on her daughter's shoulder. "Don't become outcast. You must give him up."

Chark Cough-ye comes running at his wife's screams, his eagle feather flying. Her aunt meets him as he gets near. "Twins. She refuses to give up the second child, a boy. Convince her, for all our sakes."

A boy. His spirit grabs at the words, and he blocks his visions of fatherhood, knowing the Council will not allow him to keep his child. Quietly, he approaches his wife and squats down beside her, trying to not look at the baby in her arms, afraid of instant love. Gently, he wipes the tears from her face. "Ut," he whispers, cupping her chin with his hand, "will you give this newborn to me please?"

Slowly, she turns her head to face him, eyes black, piercing, and she spits her words like Wolf bites, "I will NEVER give up our child!"

Shocked, he stares at her, then looks to each of the women for an answer. "The baby is so tiny," he says to Sarh Sar-tee. "Do you think he will live? Maybe he will go into the forest on his own."

"Don't you make that mistake!" she points at his chest. "You will regret it!"

"I'll go to Council," he declares, unable to imagine forcing his wife to give up their child. Settling next to her, he wraps her in his arms, allowing himself to see his son for the first time, and he is in awe. The child's tough tiny fist is balled up at his mouth and he works to see his parents.

"Tiny but strong," he whispers privately, looking into Ut-kart-ee's desperate eyes.

She grabs his wrist with unusual strength. "Husband, promise me you will protect our child as you protect me."

His large, strong hand covers hers, "I'll do everything I can, my *chuck-har-nut*, right by me, always ready. You must also do something for me. Remember, you are not alone. Together we are strong, no matter what happens."

On his way back to the gambling game, Yahaayi sees Cloud-Face from the floating houses carry two young pine tree trunks up the base of the mountain. In front of the carved rock that names the area for the People of An-ar-kark (Village on the Shore), they plant one in the ground and cross the other over the first. Cannons fire, causing him to fall to the ground.

Captain Quadra is pleased with the Possession Ceremony to claim this place for the King of Spain. At the cannon sound, he and the officers and priests sign the Deed of Possession while a group of natives watch, unaware of its meaning.

Friar Riobo gathers the smaller children together from those who have come to watch the ceremony and uses a few Tlingit words to explain the love of Mother Mary. The children giggle at his antics and hurry home, confused, leaving him feeling frustrated, realizing that the greatest barrier to his work is language.

Yahaayi watches Riobo's storytelling and lingers, wondering if he might benefit from getting to know the Gray Robe. When the children have gone, he makes an introduction. "*Waa sa ituwatee?* How are you?"

Recognizing the greeting, the friar invites him to the ship. On board, Yahaayi sees several large, deck-mounted weapons that smoke. He is attracted to the iron rings on wooden barrels and iron nails in the ship and wonders how to get them.

As they attempt to talk, using bits of different languages including trade talk, Riobo realizes he must teach Spanish language along with catechism, easiest with young children, and he will need time. He asks Yahaayi if his people will trade for children. They will be returned in a few years, baptized and prepared to save souls.

Yahaayi hurries to tell Crane Clan leader, excited for the first time in years that he has purpose. Leader Gwalaa (Long Knife) does not hesitate, selling five children immediately, not letting on that they are slaves who come from other tribes. He hopes to raise his status and the status of Crane Clan above all others, and what he can gain in trade from the Cloud-Face Tribe could do it. He tells Yahaayi to keep it their secret.

As the leader's accomplice, Yahaayi vibrates with optimism. He returns to the gambling game, certain to win. The sticks are mixed, re-bundled, mixed again. His eyes work piercingly, like the eagle as he makes his choices, silently praying to his guardian spirit. His body tightens, realizing it before his mind does . . . It's over. He has nothing, no wealth, and no wife.

Pulling away from the game, he blindly wanders, plodding through the forest, overwhelmed with regret and shame. He hides in the dirt in dark shadow under tall salal bushes, not wanting to face anyone, especially himself. *This is where the worthless belong, among the slugs and worms.* How can he tell his wife that she belongs to someone else? He tries to numb his regret, empty his mind. Instead, his worst memory comes to haunt him.

> *He is a youth, hunting. He sees a deer and shoots his arrow, bringing it down, proud to be able to feed his family . . . but it's not a deer, it's a young Tsimshian hunter, killed.*
>
> *The Tsimshians insist that balance be restored—a life for a life of equal status, regardless that it was an accident, or the tribes will have war, hold*

a grudge for generations. His father doesn't have the wealth to buy his freedom, so he's to be shot with arrows until dead. He's afraid, even knowing he will return to the living one day, and he cannot make himself volunteer.

He hides for four days until his younger brother decides to wipe the shame from his family and clan and volunteers in his place. The Tsimshians respond quickly, fulfilling their duty of revenge. He hears his brother's rattling "fraaahnk" call of Crane Clan and sees the arrows fly, piercing his brother's body, his instant look of shock and pain as he falls . . . the mournful scream and incessant wailing of their mother.

That was the day that he began to hate himself, and his brother's scalp, wrapped in fox fur and stored inside a cedar box, is brought out at memorial potlatches by his mother and aunt to remind the clan of their brave warrior and lament his death. He needs no reminder, the memory haunts him like a flesh-eating parasite.

As he sits in his dark shadow, he sees Wolf Clan Shaman walk between spruce trees, something in his arms. He bends down, leaves what he carries on the ground, walks back the way he came.

Yahaayi waits until the Shaman is gone, then watchfully approaches the spot, knowing that no-one should ever interfere with a Shaman. A newborn lies on the ground with moss in its mouth. Assuming it's dead, he begins to turn away, but it moves an arm, eyes open as if looking directly at him. He gasps, wondering if Spirit speaks to him. He remembers Gray Robe's offer to trade for children, and despite overwhelming dread, he gingerly removes the moss. The baby breathes! *Ke-an-kow protect me!* Quickly, he scoops up the cold, naked body and sneaks to the beach for a secret trade, not knowing that Wolf watches from the shadows.

Ut-kart-ee keeps hold of her baby at the women's house as she's fitted with a tight band of woven bark around her stomach. She realizes that he is not getting normal attention. Her aunt doesn't pierce the baby's nose or ear lobes. She doesn't pull up the eyebrows as is custom. It's as if he doesn't exist.

She sings a clan song for baby boys, "Bring me my arrow, my bow and arrow . . ." The *t'ook*, spruce reed cradle made for her by her brother A-kadi is inviting, lined with fur and filled with soft moss, but she's afraid to let him out of her grasp. "You'll have a naming ceremony, my little one," she whispers with a kiss, "but I name you now. Your name is Do'ok (Solid, Closed, Impervious to Witchcraft). Now your name protects you, and your father and I protect you. Rest my baby boy. You are safe."

Exhausted, she continues her vigilance as protector of her son, blackening her face with charcoal from the fire and tearing out tiny tufts of her hair as she mourns the one she lost.

Friar Riobo thinks that the goats on board will provide enough milk for the children, including the newborn, if she lives. She's so tiny that he prays for a miracle. When he had asked Yahaayi for the baby's name, he had shrugged, "Tatook-yadi (Cave Child without a Father)."

Three boys ages 4, 5, and 10, and three girls ages 7, 8, and the newborn Tatook-yadi are put together in a small cabin below deck in the aft of the ship. As the ships pull away, Riobo turns on deck one last time to gaze with pride at the cross they erected. Instead, he sees it being removed and taken apart, probably for the nails. Even so, he knows that Captain Quadra has the Deed of Possession, and the children below deck are the hope for this tribe's salvation.

In An-ar-kark, baby Do'ok is still alive, rapidly gaining weight, his large, round eyes making him look like a hungry otter pup. Ut-kart-ee carves a tiny canoe with paddles, fishing hooks, and a spear to attach to his cradle so he will be a great hunter one day. At last, Chark Cough-ye receives the decision of Wolf Council. "Our son may live for now. If the spirits show displeasure, we must kill him ourselves."

"So when anything goes wrong, he'll be blamed," she sighs.

"They are afraid. The Shaman didn't agree with their decision," he mutters.

"Since he didn't get *his* way, he'll name our son a witch," tears drop from her eyes. "He'll be killed either way."

Chark Cough-ye puts a warm hand on her shoulder, then takes Do'ok in the little *t'ook* cradle to Raven Clan longhouse. Even without a warm welcome, he sets the cradle across the doorway as is custom, throwing ash over it to the outside, driving away any lingering spirits of the dead, clearing the way for his child to live.

Alone, Ut-kart-ee thinks of her infant girl, stolen away before she could be held, and anger gives her strength. "I saw you take breath, my daughter. You lived. I heard your cry. I name you She-ee (Limb of a Tree). You are mine, Ut-kart-ee (Root of a Tree). Do you hear me, ancestors? I claim her! She-ee is her name! and she was mine." She drifts between sleep and awake, wandering through the forest with She-ee safely in her arms. Wolf appears and drops a black Raven feather at her feet.

Baby girl Tatook-yadi cries. Having shared a womb with her brother for nine months, she feels abandoned, and in spite of the goat milk in her belly and the rocking of the ship, she needs to be held. Ten-year-old Ghan-ha (Abalone Shell), captured by the Tlingit from the Haida when he was five, reaches out to hold her hand to quiet her, but her cries increase, so he leans over and gingerly brings her into his arms. Her tiny fist curls around his little finger and to her mouth, then she settles down into the warmth of his body and relaxes with the thrum of his heartbeat.

4

⁐

Do'ok (Solid, Impervious to Witchcraft) 1780

Little Do'ok squeals held close in his father's arms as they dunk their naked bodies into the icy sea. He's wrapped in a warm fur, shivering, while Chark Cough-ye goes back for the beating with switches that he and the others will receive. At three years old, Do'ok is learning about the Tlingit custom of greeting each dawn.

Ut-kart-ee insists they train their son early so he can take care of himself since he is not treated like the other children. He's not welcome at fishing streams or on hunting trips, afraid he might scare away the fish and game.

Chark Cough-ye scoops up his bundled boy and runs toward home with Do'ok facing forward, arms out like Raven wings, stiff legs against his father's stomach—like the totem at the bow of a canoe. Little-boy grunts erupt with each jostling bounce.

Ut-kart-ee waits with hot fish stew to warm them up on this cold spring morning. She hears them clamor at the entrance and ladles the soup into alder bowls using her sheep horn spoon from an inland trade. Do'ok gobbles the hot chunks of clam, salmon, and black lily tubers, his one-year old sister watching from her cradleboard. His father takes only a few spoonsful of broth, "I want to continue my fast so our fishing trip will be good today."

"There's a naming ceremony tomorrow," Ut-kart-ee reminds. "Your sister Tinx (Kinnikinic) is planning another piercing for Do'ok at the ceremony."

He slurps more broth. "No more piercings than T'aay (Hot Spring), the Shaman's son."

"I know," she groans. "Must keep the Shaman happy."

"We just need to be cautious." He motions to Do'ok to finish his meal.

Ut-kart-ee holds up the small stone that hangs from Do'ok's neck. Dutifully, he rubs it on his lips as a reminder. "You must be better than village talk," she begins. "You must always be..."

"... be careful what I say and do," Do'ok finishes like a chant.

"Don't worry, my *lekwaa*, fighting spirit," Chark Cough-ye's big hand lands on his son's head. "Our boy is smart, in so many ways. The People will respect him one day."

"If they get to know him," she sighs, wrapping him in animal skins.

"Your brother A-kadi (Head of a Spear) will be with us. We'll be fine."

Before they leave, he helps her remove logs from the fish pit outside. She scoops out the candlefish which have been ripening for ten days and puts them into a bentwood box with water, boiling them with hot stones and stirring to separate the oil for trade, hoping their growing wealth will keep the Shaman at bay.

At the wide mouth of the river, the fishermen feel a sprinkle of rain in the ever-present wind. A thick forest of spruce and cedar sway on each bank, painting the sky in angry swirls while along the mouth, tortured trees with broken tops tell of previous windstorms.

Silvery clouds of candlefish work their way upstream to spawn. Gulls and eagles hunt them from above while seals and sea lions pursue them from below, creating explosions of fish. They keep their canoe broadside to the current and scoop with a long-handled net of woven nettle and sinew, feeling the tug of life and releasing the slippery mess into the boat.

Do'ok is delighted by the squirming show, but when he sees his reflection in the water, he can't look away, always obsessed with his image in puddles and from shadows, as if he has a friend there, his only friend. Now he hangs over the edge of the canoe to get a better look. His father grabs him, pulling him back to the center of the canoe, warning him of the Otter People.

His little body jerks, remembering the story. If they got him, he would become *Koushta-ka*, Land Otter Man, grow hair everywhere and a tail, lose his speech and walk on his knees and elbows! And if no one recognized him to save him, he would end up with the Spirits Below!

That evening at home, Chark Cough-ye tells a story in great detail as the fire crackles and snaps. It's about the beginning, when the only drinking water was from one spring guarded by a greedy, stingy man named Ganook. "Raven is very thirsty," he says, "so he distracts Ganook by making a big waste right on top of his head! When Ganook plunges himself into the sea to wash, Raven drinks and drinks from the spring until he's full. Then he flies away, dropping water everywhere—a big mouthful for a river, a little one for a fish stream."

"We were *at* the river today!" Do'ok squeals.

"Yes son, so now you know the story is true. We must be thankful to Raven and generous with others."

In the late summer of his fifth year, Do'ok and family are at summer camp, just like every summer. It's the camp of his father's Raven Clan, built of wind screens, smoke huts, and pole cabins covered with cedar bark.

Usually, Do'ok hauls water and helps at camp, sometimes carrying a large, dried salmon strapped to his back, hoping the extra weight will increase his stamina. Today he follows a deer path through the woods, striking at trees with a stick as he goes, hoping to build his arm strength. He's plotting his practice route to prepare for the running contest in three years, enjoying time away from his mother's constant worry. Ripe salmon berries squish in his mouth as he walks, lost in visions of winning the running contest. He wonders how to do that without calling attention to himself, something he's not supposed to do.

On he walks with his striking stick, lost in thought, whacking away when suddenly a cloud of bees attacks, stingers piercing his hands, back and face. He hits at them as they get thicker, more frantic, and he takes off toward camp, feet barely touching the ground over branches, around curves, between trees, running full-out. Gasping for air, he runs into his mother, burying his face into her soft skin apron, "Are they gone? Are they gone?"

"Is who gone?" she looks out, into the forest.

"Bees!"

Ut-kart-ee sees the welts beginning on his face, finding more on his back, neck, head. "How did this happen?"

"I hit 'em with a stick," he admits, feeling stupid. "An accident."

"Oh Do'ok, what does your father tell you every time you go into the woods?"

"Pay attention to your surroundings," he recites.

"What if there had been a bear or a wolf?"

"Sorry," he mutters, knowing he has worried his mother again, and he turns toward the stream to get mud for his stings.

"Do'ok," his mother calls, "just imagine that the bees are chasing you during the running contest and you are sure to win."

His frown turns upside down.

Do'ok is excited to go for the first time with his father for an inland trade. At dawn they travel upriver with candlefish oil, dried seaweed, fish, and various shells fitted into Ut-kart-ee's prized baskets and woven matting. With two dogs between them in the canoe, Do'ok paddles hard, working his muscles. At the trail that leads further northeast, they hide the canoe with brush and transfer the trade items into packs. Do'ok's small back is piled high with the lightest baskets, dwarfing him, and he's happy for the challenge.

They walk and camp several days, stopping on a level area with an outcropping of rock and burnt trees where they can see other mountains in the distance and the valley below. Do'ok gathers wood and lights a fire using a flint stone and dry grass from his tinder pouch as his father has taught him. Chark Cough-ye removes the packs from the dogs, and before he can get them tied, they get an uncommon whiff of something worth chasing and tear away in pursuit. Normally, he would be after them, but at the end of the long trip, he's tired and decides they will be back before nightfall. He's thankful that this small, pre-planned trade at the beginning of Mountain Berry-Picking Moon will be signaled by their small fire rather than a burning tree.

Do'ok practices shooting his arrows after dinner, striking closer and closer to a small stump from 20 feet. "I thought the Athabascans were not our friends, father."

His father sits, sharpening his new iron knife and ax on a stone. "For a good trade, everyone is our friend." He admires his weapons, gifts from his uncle, Raven Clan Leader Takl-eesh. "I've known Nalren (He is Thawed Out) since we were boys and our fathers traded."

The dimming light requires Do'ok to stop practicing and he lies back in his furs by the fire, examining the stars. The basket in the sky always reminds him of his mother, the basket-maker. His father says it's called Bear, a symbol of strength.

Chark Cough-ye hears the slow, heavy breathing of his son and relaxes to the sound of fire crackle. A nearby owl talks story to the darkened forest and bats flit here and there, filling their bellies with insects. Ominous waves of green light dance across the sky, the Gis'ook (Northern Lights) predicting war or death, and he falls asleep with the newly sharpened knife in his hand.

Do'ok wakes in the dark to heavy weight on his back holding him down so hard that he can't grab air. He thinks his back will break and feels hot, wet breath on the back of his neck. The stench tells him "Bear!" A squeak is the only sound he can make, using up the last of his breath, and he suffers arrow tips cutting into his hot, wet head as he is dragged like a salmon from a stream, away from the smoldering fire. In the next moment, he hears an increasing scream, louder than the deafening heartbeat in his head and he's dropped so the bear can stand tall to throw a ferocious roar.

A Raven scream from Chark Cough-ye gets the bear's attention, and now the reflection of the bear's eyes and teeth turn toward him. His knife comes up from below into its soft belly, and instantly, the bear swipes at Chark Cough-ye as it comes down to all fours, catching the side of his face and the length of his arm, leaving deep, ragged tears. Raven warrior stands firm, protecting his son. As the bear lifts his paw for another swipe, a gray wolf interferes, attacking at the side of the bear's neck below the jaw, fangs flashing. Adrenaline pumping, Chark Cough-ye grabs his ax and swings it down with all his force into the back of the bear's neck, cutting his spinal cord and sending the wolf away. The bear falls, unable to move.

Do'ok pulls his knees into a tight ball, trying to suck his head into his chest, hearing a violent commotion someplace far away. He feels his father's sticky hands all over his head, face, neck, and ribs. He seems covered in copper-smelling slime, and he opens his eyes in the moonlight to see a dim, distorted image of his father's face, dripping blood.

"You hurt, son?" his father demands.

"My head hurts . . . you're bleeding, father," Do'ok consoles gently.

"We can clean that off," he mumbles, unable to speak from one side of his ruined mouth. He puts his ax in his belt, ready in case a wolf pack waits in the shadows.

Together, they thank Tseek (Black Bear) for the meat and fur he will provide and for not sending them to the Land of the Dead. With a shaky hand, Do'ok follows his father's instructions to end the misery of the beast, inserting the knife for his first kill, and the bear's hot, sticky essence squirts across his face.

Chark Cough-ye quickly splashes water from the stream onto their wounds, feeling his adrenaline begin to wane and puts Do'ok in bed to the sound of chattering teeth. Using one hand to staunch the blood flow from his face, he throws wood on the fire and removes wrappings and sinew twine from their trade goods to wrap his arm. For his face, he grabs a handful of rose blossoms and settles against the wood pile, calming himself to slow his heartbeat, placing the petals over his wounds. He finds a long tear at the corner of his mouth and gently puts it in place, willing the thickening blood and rose petals to keep it there if he holds very still. He waits for dawn with knife in hand, praying for the return of his dogs, knowing that wolves will likely come back for the kill now that he's wounded, and the bear is easy food. As he rests, watching the sinister green lights in the sky, every heartbeat ripples pain across his face and arm.

Nalren comes in the morning with a slave and items for trade.

Turning in his beaded tunic and moccasin pants, he surveys the scene. "Hey my Tlingit friend. Playing with bears? Looks like a fight to remember."

"One ta furget," Chark Cough-ye slurs from one side of his mouth.

"Where are your dogs?"

"Took off 'fore I got 'em tied."

Do'ok sits hunched, not wanting to look at his father's face which is now textured in dark crusts of blood petals. "My son, Do'ok," he tells Nalren, lifting his good arm.

"Hi Do'ok. You've been taking care of your father," he smiles. "If you can increase the fire and boil some water, maybe we can patch him up."

Nalren pours water over the wounds. "Well, Bear Killer, you've got a story-telling scar there." He drops his smallest bone needle and a few strands of Chark Cough-ye's hair into the boiling water while the slave makes a soft meal and begins butchering the bear.

Do'ok sees his father harden against the pain of the stitching. When it's finished, he looks more himself, though discolored and swollen.

Covered in scratches, the dogs scoot on their bellies into camp knowing they're in trouble, and Do'ok rushes to tie them away from the butchering area.

"Looks like a lynx lured your dogs," Nalren reports. "Probably had it treed all night."

"No scuse. Sell 'em t' ya but need 'em to carry things to canoe."

That evening, when the bear hide has been stretched and the meat has been hung to drain, Nalren tells Athabascan stories to the delicious aroma of the roasting head and paws. Do'ok's favorite is about the Two Old Women who are left behind to die in the snow as their starving People search for food. The women do not die, they persevere, remembering the teaching of their ancestors and in the end, save the ones who left them behind. When Chark Cough-ye has had enough willow-bark tea to ease his pain and can enjoy the choice pieces, they eat, collecting the teeth and claws for special gifts and adornments, items of status.

They make their trade in the morning, and Chark Cough-ye's serious mood is lightened by his new copper, caribou hides, mountain goat wool and porcupine quills. He gives half the bear meat to Nalren, thanking him for his help.

"Bring better dogs next time, Bear Killer."

"Bring *your* son. Like t' meet him," he tilts his head toward Do'ok, "keep tradition."

In An-ar-kark several days later, Ut-kart-ee hears commotion at the beach, people gathered around a canoe, and she can see that her boys have returned. She sees the familiar eagle feather of her husband and something different. As she approaches, she notices a critical look on the Shaman's face and her husband's face, torn, bruised, and mended.

"It looks like you had *jinahaa* bad luck on your trip," the Shaman accuses, turning to stare at Do'ok.

"Scuffle with a black bear, no concern," Chark Cough-ye calmly replies, moving his mouth a little better now. He tells two slaves to unload the canoe and walks straight to Ut-kart-ee, putting his good arm around her. She grabs Do'ok and they continue walking to their house, away from the crowd. All the way,

Do'ok feels the stare of the Shaman on the back of his neck and down his spine like a slippery eel.

Ut-kart-ee wishes the event to be forgotten, even though the face of her husband is a constant reminder, but when Chark Cough-ye tells his brother that Do'ok killed the bear with a knife at the throat, and the brother tells his wife, the talk throughout the village becomes, *"Do'ok killed a bear with just a knife to protect his father when he was only five years old, without a mark on himself!"* and fear grows among the People, bringing whispers of witch-craft.

The competition of the eight-year-old boys brings the village together for an evening dance. Anxious to show his skills, Do'ok gets up with the others, his mother's wolf charm swinging from his neck. He hears the reverberation of his father's deep voice, chanting a song that belongs to Raven Clan and moves with it, stepping every other beat, to become the Raven. Inside his squir-rel-skin cape, he bends over with his arms out behind him like wings of Raven, each high footstep coming down to trigger a slight bounce of his head. He turns right, left, and a complete circle to the right, dropping to one knee. Upright again, he dances looking forward and cocks his head to one side and the other, praying the spirit of Raven will keep his dance true. He sees his mother watching, the reflection in her eyes moving with his every step.

The next day he readies his cedar paddle, waiting for the Raven shout. The spruce canoe of his father has Raven wings painted at the bow to help him fly through the water which is calm now. He notices dark clouds on the horizon, a storm coming. At the signal, his paddle instantly cuts the water and he pulls with all his might, moving cleanly across the bay and cutting through the cresting waves on the way back like *cheech* jumping porpoise. The muscles in his back strain and he hardens his stomach to provide more support. Controlling his breath into a rhythm to match his paddle, he pulls hard, focusing on the goal of the last stroke, getting the strokes in between out of the way.

The wind grows in the final stretch, splashing waves over the bow, wetting his face. Through the sea spray he sees T'aay frantically working beside him. Do'ok knows he can win, and he wants it as much as he wants air, but he hears the echo of his mother's voice, "Do not call attention to yourself," and lets up on his power, allowing T'aay to sneak ahead, a bitter ending.

Other competitions are a different matter. Unable to continue his self-restraint, he excels at arrow-shooting and out-runs all the others in the long-distance run by too many heartbeats to count.

That night there is talk about the advanced strength and skills of Do'ok, rekindling fear and reminding the villagers that he's different, he's the twin who lives. Clan leaders sit together at the awards ceremony, some wearing spruce root hats with rings on the top to show the number of potlatches they've given. Aristocratic men and women wear headdresses with masks of crest animals and white ermine skins hanging down the back. Wolf Clan Leader Ka-uh-ish makes the presentation, grinning with the toothless face of an elder.

"The purpose of these games is to develop strength

and skill in our young people, to keep our community strong and safe. We give attention now to reward consistent hard work. After talking with others, it's agreed that Do'ok is the winner, and he makes Wolf Clan proud."

Do'ok swallows hard, the focus of the entire village on him! Ka-uh-ish presents him with a high-status copper shield that he'll be able to wear as armor when he's an adult, and from his uncle A-kadi he receives an adult-sized bow made of yew wood, painted with Wolf ears and copper-pointed arrows, treasures more valuable than many adults can afford. He sees T'aay and his Shaman father standing with resentment on their faces, and his shyness turns to pride as he returns their stares.

Ut-kart-ee's spirit reaches out to her son with fear and pride. In the morning, he will go to live with A-kadi, and she can't imagine him going to Wolf Clan House without her. "We're proud of you son," she croons, admiring his awards, holding his arm, wanting to hang on.

Do'ok knows her thoughts. "You'll be okay, mother," he grins, patting her on the shoulder. "I won't be so far away." In truth, he's eager to move into Wolf Clan House with his uncle, away from the worries of his mother. He thinks about how different it will be to live in a big clan house, wondering if he might find a friend there.

That night everyone wears special clothing decorated with designs of their crest animals and embellished with collars or aprons, and jewelry. Men have their hair tied in knots on the top of their heads, covered with red ochre and fluffy white bird down while the women's hair flows freely. Beads, bits of copper and abalone shimmer from the dancers in the firelight, and no one looks as high-caste as Ut-kart-ee in her tunic, adorned with porcupine quills that wave with her movement. Keeping her eyes down, she dances to a sad love song, thinking of her lost daughter and the son that she's about to lose to her brother.

She worries to her husband, "Shouldn't we tell Do'ok that he's a twin before he goes off without us?"

His stomach tightens. "It might be too great a distraction right now . . . Let it go, your brother will take good care."

"I know," her throat tightens. "I thank Spirit Above for him."

Do'ok wakes to stormy weather and has his last dunk into frigid water with his father and Raven Clan. He says goodbye to his sister who is six and his two younger brothers. His mother holds him a long, long time. He makes himself be patient, not wanting to hurt her feelings by pulling away. When he finally says, "Goodbye, I love you," he quickly turns to leave, not wanting to show the reflection of his mother's tears on his own face.

Wearing his spruce-root hat and cedar-bark cape, he walks alone in the wind and rain through the village, not like the other boys who laugh together in groups. He's felt painfully alone all his life despite the love of his family, and he sees by the quick glances of others that they're uncomfortable near him. Even so, as he walks, he feels his mother's worry fall away and the beginning of optimism.

Tall Wolf totems look down at him when he arrives at Wolf Clan House, one on each side of the door. He thinks to look for A-kadi, but Wolf Clan Shaman steps out from the corner of the building with piercing black eyes, long, knotted hair flying in the brisk wind. He's naked except for a leather apron and necklace of bone pendants with bear teeth. A crown of goat horns sits on his head. He shakes his spirit rattle in one hand and holds a knife in the other, pushing it against Do'ok's neck, "I name you *Nakws'aati*, Witch!"

5

⚛

Miguel (Ghan-ha,
Abalone Shell) 1780

Fifteen-year-old Ghan-ha sits in his loincloth on a hillside outside the Spanish mission searching the massive night sky to find Bear, the Big Dipper, a symbol of strength. If he thinks and acts correctly for Jesu Christo, he will go to Paradise in Heaven in the Sky one day, a beautiful place where he can live forever. He wonders if Bear is a protector of Paradise in Heaven.

Taken from his Haida home at five years old and made a slave by the Tlingit, he became a non-person, unable to live after death. He could have been sold or killed at any time. Now with his new Christian name of Miguel, he's told that his soul can live on . . . confusing since the bodies of mission Natives are put into holes in the ground a distance from the church rather than burned into spirit.

He still *feels* like a slave, owned by the mission now in this land called New California, doing what the padres say to avoid their whippings. He doesn't mind the long hours of work, but why pull up grass and bushes that provide seeds and roots and berries to eat as well as homes for birds, rabbits and insects, which are also food?

Walking back in the dark, he can see the adobe wall that encloses the quadrangle of the mission and the intimidating white church standing inside. He steals back into the boys' quarters, a room with tule reed sleeping mats near the padres' room, thankful that no one noticed he'd been gone.

Morning is invaded by a thick fog which rolls in like a silent storm, and Miguel welcomes it as a remembrance of his home in the North. It creeps along the ground, obscuring the church up to its thatched roof. Inside, he kneels on the hard-packed ground for Mass, then goes to the *pozolera*, dining room to eat his morning *atole*, gruel of roasted corn and grain.

The other boys speak in their different languages, Ohlone, Miwok, Yokut and others as they walk to the fields for work. Some call to friends and family as they pass the native Mission Village just outside the mission wall where the married live with their young children.

Miguel and his younger "siblings" were purchased in the North by Spanish Friar Riobo. As the oldest, he's to teach Tlingit ways to them and use their Christian names, Rodrigo, Pedro, Teresa, Maria, and the youngest, Ana. Ana is his special sister. She was a newborn when they left their home in the North, and he has cared for her like a young father as much as possible within the mission.

Little Ana wakes angry in the loft. It's her recurring dream and earliest memory. Her eldest sister Teresa is in chains, dark hair hanging limp on each side of her face, a growing pool forming on the packed earth where her tears drip. She hears a cry from her middle sister, Maria, as she is slapped by Lucia, the Ohlone supervisor of the *monjerío,* the women's ward. "Stop interfering with your sister!" Lucia shouts. Being youngest at the mission, Ana is able to earn smiles from Lucia if she wishes, but when her sisters are in trouble, her intense devotion to them causes her to become fierce like a wolf, ready to fight.

She knows about Wolf and Raven from stories her family tell on Sunday afternoons: Raven, a trickster who brought light to the world, and Wolf, a great leader, with courage. Ana feels akin to Wolf since she dreams of him sometimes. He stares at her from shadows with golden eyes, and she doesn't feel afraid.

Now she gazes at the speck of light beginning to grow from the only small window, which is near the door. The mission bell will ring soon, and they will be ushered into Mass. At five years old, she's heard the first Catechism lesson for Natives so many times that she's memorized it:

"How many Gods?"

"One."

"Where is God?"

"Heaven, earth, everywhere."

"Recite the names of the Trinity," and the lesson continues with the Lord's Prayer.

The mission bell rings, and she hears the click of the door

to the monjerío being unlocked. Stepping down the ladder from the loft, she looks for Teresa, hoping they will avoid Lucia's wrath today.

To be in church, the women wear aprons of deer skin under the back of their tule reed skirts and lightweight capes of rough mission fabric. Teresa ties a short tule skirt around Ana's waist as Lucia prods them into line with her stick. The tattoo lines and dots on Lucia's chin make a funny round shape when she squishes her mouth into the "be quiet" face, and she escorts them into the chapel, ensuring that they cross themselves and stay to the left side, away from the boys. They wait on their knees, soldiers standing in the corners with sticks ready to poke misbehavers.

The padres use Latin, inviting God to come down from Heaven. One padre speaks in a sing-song chant, and when the other padre directs them to, some try to respond along with him by mimicking the sounds.

Ana kneels on the hard-packed earth, staring at her favorite painting which hangs above her. The padre calls it "Our Lady of Perpetual Help." The golden crowns on Mother Mary and baby Jesus reflect the light and draw Ana's first attention. It is the mother's caring, gentle hands holding the baby where Ana rests her eyes. Mother's head tilts toward baby's. They share a life. She's never felt a relationship like that and wonders what it would be like to have someone like a mother. A knot of longing grows in her stomach. She prays a private prayer to the Lady of Perpetual Help to someday know someone who treats her like her own.

This morning with Lucia, Ana collects kindling for the kiln. Her thick, black hair is tied, allowing the sun to toast her back, and although she can't see the big water, a light sea breeze floats in from the west to cool her. They return to the mission just before the bell which commands their days, and Ana joins her sisters for a lunch of more atole, then siesta in the loft.

"Josepha is teaching me how to make coiled baskets for cooking!" Maria whispers from her mat. "So different than the spruce root baskets at home. We used sedge root to stitch willow shoots into a spiral. She'll teach me twined baskets next . . . We can make new matting!"

"Good, you can teach us," Teresa bites a flea from her matting with her teeth. "It's time to burn these mats."

At two o'clock, the bell rings, and work continues for another four hours. This time, Ana helps Lucia pick peas and beans in a field until the bell rings for evening Mass. *Pozole* is served for the evening meal, a stew of meat, beans, and corn, the girls and boys eating separately. A person from each house in Mission Village just outside the wall comes with a water-tight basket to receive the portion to take to their house. When the bell announces time to Pray for the Dead and prepare for sleep, Ana doesn't know anyone who is dead, so she prays in earnest for her brothers and sisters and for her unknown parents, dead or alive, and especially for a person she hopes will be like a mother someday.

In the loft, she hears the click of the door being locked and lights are blown out. She lies on her mat, welcoming sleep because in her dreams, she is never alone. She is always with someone who makes her laugh and holds her hand. They seem to enjoy each other's company, and she wonders why she can never see the person's face.

The next morning, she knows it's Saturday because she hears

the scratchy, repetitive sweeping of the old men with their rush-grass brooms. Saturday means it's butchering day and there will be more meat in the stew, and the best thing about Saturday is that the next day will be Sunday and she will see her brothers.

On Sunday after Mass, Ana and her family meet together in the mission dining room since they don't have a home. Miguel is old enough to wear pants, and Pedro and Rodrigo, ages 10 and 11, still wear their waist cloths. They all sit together on a mat talking in their language from the North.

"Waa sa ituwatee?" "How are you?" Miguel asks, proudly handing Teresa some droopy star lilies. "We found these when we were out hunting."

Rodrigo leans forward, "We got a couple of rabbits, too!"

"Hey Miguel, I saw you looking at a girl in church again," Pedro accuses. "You'll get into trouble, my brother."

"How else will I find one to marry? Once I can marry and move to Mission Village, you girls will be able to join us there for visiting on Sundays and get a break from the monjerío."

"We'll still need a chaperone," Teresa complains.

Ana crosses her arms. "Why are we locked up anyway? Why can't we roam around like you boys, go hunting and everything?"

"The padres try to protect you, that's all," Miguel pats her on the head. "They don't know how fierce you are," he chuckles. "Your sisters will marry soon and will also be able to live in Mission Village with their husbands."

Ana's eyes grow wide, her mouth open.

"You'll still see them on Sunday," Rodrigo croons, seeing her alarm. "*You* can be married in . . . about eight years or so," he adds hesitantly.

"*Forever* from now!" Ana snaps, turning away. "I can't be without my sisters!"

Maria strokes her back, "We'll never abandon you, little *yush*, tadpole."

They try to console her, but Ana's arms remain crossed and she stares at the wall, tears running down her face.

Three years later, Ana is without her sisters. They're both married to Christian Natives and live in Mission Village on the other side of the wall. Teresa and Miguel each have babies and it is the delight of Ana's life to visit them on Sunday afternoons under the supervision of Catalina, the Christian Native wife of a Spanish soldier.

As they walk through Mission Village, she sees the houses made of young willow poles lashed together to create a rounded hut about six feet across, covered with tule, and a few are twenty feet to hold two families. Some also have shadows, woven willow bark roofs built on poles to provide shade for being outside.

She sees different tattoo designs on the chins of women, which Miguel has said shows their lineage, whether they are Bear People or Deer People, like the Wolf or Raven of the Tlingit. It helps others know who is proper to marry since they may not marry a person from their own lineage as passed through their father's line.

Miguel is also invited to the Ohlone village which is three miles away since his wife is from that village. He receives an invitation stick from the chief to visit their sweathouse. Walking through the Ohlone village, he sees steam rise from the ground as if the earth breathes where food is roasting, all kinds of food, even lizards and grasshoppers. Some women wear basket caps and men who wish to live as women wear them too. Miguel sees a smiling man with angry welts and scabs on his face and wonders if he has tangled with a bear.

He stops to watch children practice *shinny* in the games area. A player swings his stick hard, smacking a puck into the field, then runs, pushing, kicking, and tackling other players to strike the puck again. He knows it's not a "real" game because he sees no gambling.

Tule boats are pulled up on the river shore at the edge of the village. Ten feet long and three feet wide in the middle, they're made of three long bundles of tule reeds tied together, one for each side and one for the bottom. The sweathouse is beyond, built four feet into the earth with reed walls and partially covered with mud. The chief's messenger stands outside, *"Akkoy mak-warep, manne mak hiswi.* Welcome to our land, where we are born."

The tiny entrance requires him to crawl inside where he sees a standing pole decorated with feathers and long strips of rabbit skin, a sign of peace. Hit by the heat, he sits among spears, bows and arrows against a mud-coated wall. Men have thin sticks of wood or bone through their nose and earlobes. Some wear necklaces of beads and abalone shell pendants. Around the fire, clam shells are worked into beads and prayer sticks are created with tufts of eagle down. The man next to Miguel cuts around the inside of a green elderberry stick with an obsidian blade to remove its core. Tiny holes are burnt to make a flute.

Miguel accepts the chewing tobacco he's offered and feels

dizzy as he listens to origin stories of Coyote. The one about Coyote asking a beautiful woman to remove a thorn from his eye with her teeth so he can grab her and force her to have sex is shocking and embarrassing. An uncomfortable giggle erupts from him when the other men laugh. Hoping to change the subject, he asks about the man he saw in the village with wounds on his face. "Has he come upon a bear closely?"

Laughter erupts in the sweathouse. His neighbor grins broadly, "*Very* closely . . . It was a SHE-bear!" and the guffaws continue.

"On the wedding night," another explains, "a new wife is expected to scratch the face of her husband so everyone will know that she was very modest."

"Yeah!" the first neighbor cries, "even if she's a *well-experienced* bear!"

Miguel feels his face get hot, hoping it's no redder than other's from the fire.

He listens to their hunting adventures, enormous herds of antelope and elk, ducks and cormorants darkening the sky. Now they prepare for a deer hunt, having danced and fasted and prayed and avoided their wives and had daily sweat baths, this being their final push to the limit of endurance. They chant and play flutes, keeping time with split stick clappers and bird-bone whistles, passing the time as the fire gets hotter and hotter . . . until it's unbearable. Miguel is first to go, feeling sick and unable to breathe. Blindly, he crawls to the outside and lies on his back, gasping for cool air. Soon others join him and show him how to scrape sweat from his skin with a deer rib before dunking into the sanctity of the river.

To hunt, they will rub themselves with herbs to cover their smell and paint red clay with grease on their faces and bodies. They wear the skin and head of a deer to move into the herd, sometimes lying with their feet up so a deer will come to investigate.

At the mission, Ana is chosen with a few older students to be taught to read Spanish and Latin. She learns easily and tries to be a good pupil, what the padre calls "devout" and confesses her negative thoughts every week as she sits outside the opened confessional door while the padre sits on the other side. She admits that her anger can flare, that she is sometimes jealous of her sisters, and how she longs for a mother.

One night as she lies in the loft, missing her sisters, she feels desperate to get out, wishing she could squeeze through the rounded hole in the bottom of the door like the cat chasing after a rat. Her hands tighten into fists, fingernails digging her palms, heart racing. She bites her lips shut to keep from screaming out as panic rips inside her head.

Sometime before dawn, in troubled sleep, she's visited by Wolf. He's close and stares intently into her eyes. Eagle lands on his back, and a boy that looks like her stands next to Wolf, holding out his hand. The world begins to rumble. A roar fills her ears, louder and louder. Soon Ana is awake and being violently shaken, thrown out of the loft, hitting the dirt floor, crushing her shoulder. A sudden extreme jerk with deafening sounds of splintering wood and falling brick announces the loft itself as it crashes down on top of her.

The entire mission is rubble.

Shaken, Miguel sees to his family and hurries inside the wall to find that most of the buildings have fallen, injured and dead lying among the ruins. He finds his two brothers huddled together, afraid and crying, but unhurt. Ana, however, is another matter.

Unconscious, her head is rapidly swelling, eyes already blackened, her body covered with injuries. A padre kneels over her in the yard, anointing her with the Oil of the Sick and praying "May the Lord who frees you from sin save you and raise you up." When he sees Miguel, he shakes his head, "There is nothing more I can do."

Miguel kneels over the broken body of his little sister, the tiny person he has watched over since her birth. He looks at her misshapen face and sobs, gently taking her hand. Unable to let her go, he looks up at the padre. "Give her to me," he whispers hoarsely.

"No," the answer is firm. "Leave her with God."

"It's my *job* to take care of her!" His eyes bore into the padre's.

"I forbid it," he insists. "She belongs here."

Ignoring the padre, Miguel gently picks her up and carries her away, unconcerned about the punishment that will come.

Zesen sets her baskets right as the promise of day begins to lighten the horizon. Her tule house is still standing after the ground shook but will need repair. As medicine woman for the Ohlone, she knows that the energy from the Time of Creation still exists, and this shaking is an example. It also manifests as

Spirit and Power in all things and can be acquired by People through their respect. Everything is alive, everything is sacred.

She was told that the mission has been ruined, a sign that the Gray Robes shouldn't be there. She hopes they'll pay attention and leave. The People must continue the ways given to them by Coyote through their ancestors since Sacred Time. Whenever someone in her village thinks of going to the mission, she tries to stop them. Just as she finishes sweeping her floor matting and begins to feel like everything is in order, the chief comes to her door.

"Zesen, a Native man from the mission has come, carrying an injured girl child. He asks to see our healer. Will you see him?"

Miguel steps in, unable to wait, taking short, panicked breaths, terrified eyes pleading to her.

She motions to a mat, seeing that this man has run beyond the capacity of his lungs. The child's head is swollen. Her limbs hang in unnatural ways, but she is alive.

"I promise to pay you," he chokes. "Can you fix her?"

"I will try," she mumbles, already focused on her patient. "You need to go," and she waves him out the door.

In shock, Miguel stumbles the three miles back to the mission. In his disturbed state, he's confused to find the mission in wreckage, and he immediately begins to sort through the mess, trying to lift bricks back into place until a padre appears with a soldier.

Roughly, Miguel is pushed into the center of the yard and put into the pillory, leaving him bent over, head and hands protruding from the holes in the wooden frame, his bare back lit by the morning sun. "As your spiritual father, it is my duty to punish you with beatings," the padre says, taking a leather whip to Miguel's back. He grunts with the first, unexpected lash and comes to his senses, Haida and Tlingit roots returning, and he becomes hard as stone. Stoically, he endures ten strikes, leaving ten raised and bruised welts, followed by nothing but hot sun.

After days with no food and little water, the pain in his back and legs is so unbearable that he prays for unconsciousness. His younger brothers come to cry over him and sink to their knees, praying for God to change His mind.

Zesen sends a messenger for the dancing shaman and paints white stripes down her face and breasts. She hangs a raven wing and a red quartz crystal around her neck, adding eagle wings at her waist. Finally, she sings a soothing chant to her medicine bundle before daring to open it and puts it in a private place to ensure that its shadow will not touch her patient.

She makes a cut at the most swollen spot on the child's head. Singing to its powers to heal, she twirls a sharp obsidian point back and forth between her hands like making fire, back and forth, deeper and deeper until a hole is through the skull, letting blood and fluid ooze onto a pad. The pressure on Ana's brain reduced for the moment, doctor and unconscious patient take involuntary large breaths at the same time.

The dancing Shaman arrives to sing away negative spirits, burning herbs and waving smoke over the child with an eagle feather. Zesen is relieved for his abilities and her spirit dances with the ancient rhythm of his chant as she prepares to re-locate the little girl's shoulder and set her broken bones. She calls on the Power of the Spirits to calm and to heal and for the child to live and to be whole again.

6

A-kadi (Head of a Spear)

Yesterday the council named Ut-kart-ee's brother, A-kadi, as acting head of Wolf Clan House. It was a request from his uncle, Leader Ka-uh-ish, who said he himself was *shaan geeyi*, feeling the breeze from the old people's bay, and he wished to be replaced. Since Wolf Clan is the wealthiest in the village, A-kadi will have great influence, if he proves his worth. Ka-uh-ish agreed to continue as advisor, but this morning he is ill, and the Shaman has been with him since before dawn. That and the Cloud-Face Tribe trading in the bay cause A-kadi to pace back and forth inside the big house. He thinks he should be, *wants to be* with his People at the beach.

Carrying his small carvings in his sister's decorated baskets, he joins Wolf Clan as they load fresh fish and baskets of berries into their canoes and paddle out alongside the floating house, but as they bounce in the windy waves alongside the ship, they are turned away. Many of Crane Clan are already aboard, and the Cloud-Face hold up great armfuls of otter skins, showing what they want for trade. A-kadi wonders how Crane Clan had such an abundance of otter skins to trade since it's not custom to hunt so many.

Crane Clan returns to shore with Cloud-Face food that looks like tiny white maggots, something dry like tree fungus, and a dark, thick liquid like from the Village of the River Otters. A-kadi shakes his head, "I wouldn't eat that. Their food could weaken us. And how were you the first ones to trade, Gwalaa?" He notices Yahaayi, that hopeless gambler, shifting into the shadow of a smoke shack.

"Just lucky," Gwalaa smirks, not wanting A-kadi to know about his previous arrangement with this Cloud-Face Tribe.

A-kadi leans forward, angry, "Your clan seems to increase wealth at the expense of others in the village, Gwalaa. I wouldn't want your people to suffer because of *your* poor choices."

Gwalaa steps into A-kadi's face, chin lifted, "That sounds like a threat!"

Pulse racing, A-kadi opens his mouth to respond and his friend Kookenaa (Messenger) grabs his arm turning him around. "Let's go, my friend," he whispers. "Don't pick a fight as your first act as headman," and they walk together to Wolf Clan House.

Inside, he hears talk of vengeance among his People and knows that Kookenaa is right, violence within the village is not good leadership. "Wolf Clan Council approved a strike against the Haida," he announces to distract them. "We're to retrieve what they stole from us one moon ago, some totem items, a few slave children."

Instantly the planning begins. They agree to attack at the end of Big Moon when it will be cold and before the snow falls when tracks would show on the ground. The women will not be told. Too many families have kin with the Haida, and the women would want to warn them.

Squatting outside among the racks of drying salmon for a mid-day meal, A-kadi wonders why he hasn't seen his nephew Do'ok yet. He waits, bantering with friends when Crane Clan Shaman arrives.

Clearly agitated, the Shaman wears the crown of his trade, a rectangular hat with a woven crane figure in front. "You've threatened Crane Clan and now many are sick! What kind of witchery is this?" he growls.

A-kadi bristles, "Watch yourself, Shaman! I had nothing to do with it. Ka-uh-ish is also ill."

"You've bewitched him too!"

"Stop! There is no witchcraft here!" he warns. "I'll ask Wolf Clan Shaman to help with your sick, and there is no witchcraft," fear sneaking into his bones.

The Shaman's eyes become slits of suspicion, "Tell him to come to Crane Clan House, and if our people don't recover, I'll be back."

Inside Wolf Clan House, A-kadi allows himself a shaky moment. *Witchcraft* is a word that no one ever wants to hear. A person does not often escape the consequences.

Wolf Clan Shaman wonders how to overpower the invisible sickness. Maybe the red spots in mouths and on faces show that Do'ok is a stronger witch than he thought. He is a disciplined, well-prepared shaman who abstains from intimate relations, fasts, does not eat seafood, never cuts or cleans his hair, and drinks saltwater to ensure his spiritual strength. He spends time with his animal spirit helpers and seeks visions, following all the practices of a good shaman, and he knows that if he can't cure the sick, the only possible cause could be a witch at work.

He has suspected Do'ok for years. When Ut-kart-ee gave birth to twins, she made a serious mistake by keeping the boy, and he's felt somewhat responsible ever since, concerned that harm could come to the clan because of it. Now that he has Do'ok in his possession, maybe he can correct his earlier mistake. He'll need to get a confession, though. It's the only way to defeat him.

He pulls the boy up from the pit under his house by his arms which have been bound behind his back. It's a cumbersome task since his arms are also tied to his feet and to the bun on the back of his head, an effective method of torture as the constant pull on the back of his head stretches the front of his neck, making it difficult to breathe or swallow.

Do'ok groans, barely conscious, covered with angry welts and tiny barbs from devil's club beatings, eyes fluttering as shocks of pain shoot through his restrained body. His lack of oxygen and the poison of sea water in his belly cause his heart to beat in his ears, and he sees flashing lights and visions.

"Admit that you are a witch, twin!" He inserts a wooden peg into the boy's bun of hair and turns, twisting his head as far as he can to one side. Do'ok struggles for breath, thinking his neck will break. The Shaman holds tight.

In semi-consciousness, Do'ok sees Wolf who stands with a girl, and he can't look away from her, as though she's part of him, a hidden part separate from the torture, away from the pain, a safe place. "Admit you are a witch!" the Shaman spews. The boy's eyes roll.

As the Shaman unwraps his Knife of Clarity, preparing to cut the tender flesh from his young prisoner, A-kadi steps in. He comes to discuss the health of Ka-uh-ish, but when he sees Do'ok, his fist instantly meets the Shaman's face, sending him to the floor. Horrified, A-kadi unties his nephew's arms and legs and carries him to Wolf Clan House where he feels for dislocated and broken bones.

Do'ok is reluctant to leave the girl in his dream. Slowly, he realizes that it's his uncle's face he sees, and he gulps for air. "Why was he hurting me?" he whimpers, turning to fold himself into a curling leaf. "I'm not a witch . . . am I? What's a twin?" His eyes are attached to his uncle like a safe harbor. A-kadi shakes his head, wondering how to begin when both Shamans arrive, along with their helpers who carry rope for restraints.

"You are both accused of witchcraft!" Wolf Clan Shaman announces for everyone in the big house to hear. "Does it run in your family, A-kadi? We'll see. If your family punishes you, maybe kills you, suspicions against them will die. Otherwise . . ."

Ut-kart-ee and Chark Cough-ye move into Raven Clan House to be closer to his uncle and are preparing for the fall hunting season. She's always been interested in hunting, and her first hunt seems the only thing that might distract her from worry about Do'ok.

Satisfied with the springiness of their hemlock bows, they use whale sinew for bowstrings and check their whip slings and darts—the old standbys. Chark Cough-ye's whistle made of two small sticks bound together and slightly separated in the middle by a thin piece of cedar bark sounds like a fawn calling. A doe won't be able to resist.

"I can already smell fresh deer meat cooking on the fire," Ut-kart-ee chatters, arranging her arrows. "With me along, how will we ever get *all* the meat home?"

"We'll do our best, fierce hunter," he chuckles and sees Shouk running toward them.

"Shouk!" Ut-kart-ee chokes.

"Your mother sent me," she breathes. "Wolf Clan Shaman named Do'ok and A-kadi as witches! Both of them! She worries the whole family will be named if you're not willing to beat them to remove the bad spirits."

"What?" Ut-kart-ee takes her bow and arrows.

Chark Cough-ye grabs her by the arm. "Mother of Do'ok, sister of A-kadi, be smart," he says firmly. "Do not attack. The People fear the Shaman, respect him. He has Power. Be cautious, strategic now, like a good hunter."

She twists her arm away. "My mother worries about how we'll act toward our family rather than what I'll do to that weasel Shaman!?" Her face contorts, looking up to her husband, "Why did we let Do'ok go there alone? We *knew* this could happen!"

He puts his arm around her, "So he might have a *normal* life, remember?"

"That worm could be torturing them right now!" she panics, trying to pull away.

He holds her a moment longer. "Let's get the whole story and stay calm . . . keep Power on our side. *Then* we can decide what to do."

Eyes wild, she breaks away, headed for Wolf Clan.

He keeps hold of her elbow, slowing her down. "We need support. My uncle Takl-eesh will come. Also, your father and Hawk clan leader . . ."

They hurry through the village as more and more onlookers join them, having heard the story. Chark Cough-ye continues to strategize, but to Ut-kart-ee, everything is painted red, the color of blood that she wishes to see gushing from the face and heart of the Shaman.

A large crowd has gathered at the big house in front of the towering carved Wolves, the accused kneeling in the middle. Chark Cough-ye buries his thumb into his wife's elbow, telling her to be quiet. She freezes, her eyes boring into her son's to see if he's been injured.

"What are the accusations?" Chark Cough-ye demands.

The Shaman speaks loudly, "Sickness has come to Wolf Clan Leader Ka-uh-ish with the arrival of Do'ok at Wolf Clan House. Also, many at Crane Clan are ill after A-kadi threatened them on the beach. The sickness will not be sent away, so it must be witchcraft. Both are witches."

Gasps and murmurs roll as people step away from the accused family.

"*You* create an *excuse* for your lack of Power against the sickness!" Ut-kart-ee screeches.

Headman Takl-eesh of Raven Clan House holds up his carved Raven staff as he steps forward, silencing the group. "Why would Do'ok want Ka-uh-ish to be ill?"

"To clear the way for his uncle A-kadi to be new headman of Wolf Clan," the Shaman replies sharply.

"A-kadi was named leader *before* Ka-uh-ish became ill," Takl-eesh clarifies. He looks to Crane Clan Shaman, "When did your People become ill?"

"A few last night."

"*Before* any threats from A-kadi." Takl-eesh addresses the crowd, "These Shamans wish to save you all from illness, but there is something else at work here, not witchcraft. Maybe Raven is angry for some reason."

"The councils should talk," Hawk Clan leader advises, "including the Shamans."

Ut-kart-ee grabs her son. "Are you hurt?" she demands, seeing his red welts.

"I'm okay, mother," his soft reply.

She turns him away, "Come home with us now."

"The crisis is over," A-kadi intervenes. "I haven't been able to talk to my nephew yet. He hasn't spent one night here. Leave him alone, let him become a man someday."

Chark Cough-ye fondly squeezes his son's shoulder, then takes his wife's arm, drawing her away. "We have a hunting trip to take," he calls back. "If you need anything, call on Raven Clan or Hawk Clan for help." He directs his wife back to their canoe, telling her it is best, wooing her away with his promise that she can kill something.

The Cloud-Face Tribe bring their own sick to the beach, erecting large pieces of cloth for protection from rain. Crane Clan Shaman finds that they look the same as his own people, sores all over filled with pus. He hears the word "pox." The next day, the floating house is gone, their dead lying on the beach. In a week, when Crane Clan Shaman also succumbs to the illness, only eight remain, including Yahaayi. They wonder which clan might provide them a new home. Crane Clan of the Wolf People is no more.

Chark Cough-ye and Ut-kart-ee return from their hunting trip loaded with deer meat and hides, hurrying to Wolf Clan House to check on Do'ok, hoping all is well. They find him standing next to A-kadi, each with the same mischievous dimple, and they learn that leader Ka-uh-ish has recovered enough to be advisor.

"We're going to raid the Haida!" Do'ok bubbles.

A-kadi shushes him, looking sheepish.

"We?" Ut-kart-ee's eyes pierce her brother's.

Quickly, A-kadi explains, "I've told the Shaman that he can't come with us, although it's against custom and puts us all at risk. I can't leave Do'ok here with *him*! He can't go home with *you* or others will wonder about his readiness for training." His eyes slide over to Chark Cough-ye, "Come with us, brother! Then he will surely be safe!"

"A-kadi!" Ut-kart-ee points her finger into his chest, "This is your plot to get my husband involved in a Wolf Clan raid!"

Chark Cough-ye tightens. "Show respect for your brother, wife. He's a leader now."

"He was my *brother* before he became a leader! So, I stay here while my men face clubs, arrows, spears and daggers?" She sees Do'ok go pale. ". . . still, this family is smart . . . like Wolf and Raven, and strong like Bear," she clenches her jaw for a moment. "I will do my part," she mutters, grabbing Do'ok into a very unmanly embrace.

Surprised by her reaction, the two men slap each other on the back like winners in a race. Chark Cough-ye's enthusiasm stretches his misshapen face, "I'll speak with Takl-eesh and see if a few others from Raven Clan might come with us."

A suit of armor is made for Do'ok by his aunt Tinx. She uses their thick bear hide, cutting a piece large enough to go under his left arm with a hole for his head and pieces for leggings. Ut-kart-ee asks her father from Hawk Clan to create a wooden collar and helmet. He uses cedar, carving it down to a thin helmet that will not be too heavy. The collar comes up to just below the eyes, and the helmet, lined with fur, sits on the collar in the back, leaving the eyes exposed in the front. He paints it into a Wolf head and Ut-kart-ee supplies her own hair for finish, wanting to make him look fierce and to send some of herself with her son.

Four black war canoes with a red line across the rise of bow and stern are filled with 22 men each. Do'ok sits in front of A-kadi who is in the stern of Wolf Clan canoe as leader. Chark Cough-ye sits cross-legged in the middle of Raven Clan canoe as bowman. He must only look forward. As bowman, he will serve as scout when they reach the Haida.

Ut-kart-ee hurries to Raven Clan House where she uses rocks to create the shape of her husband's canoe. She blackens her face with charcoal and sits cross-legged in the same spot that he sits in his canoe, holding her scratching rock from around her neck. If she should forget and scratch herself with her fingers, her husband could receive a wound in that same spot. The women of all the men in war canoes will stay like this, being serious and somber all day, returning each morning and continuing each day until their men have come home.

The raiders laugh as they paddle because they raid the Haida in Haida-made canoes. Then they fall silent, focused on their task, paddles moving together as one. Do'ok feels important as he paddles along with the others. On the third afternoon, they're gifted with the cover of thick fog as they near their destination.

Silently, Chark Cough-ye moves through the damp forest, relieved that the breeze travels from the village toward him so the village dogs won't smell his scent. Then returning to A-dadi, he explains what he's seen, and they agree on a strategy of attack.

On foot in the pre-dawn, they steal toward a beach fire where young slaves guard red-cedar Haida canoes. One boy sleeps on his side against a driftwood log and the other dozes, drooping next to the first, cropped hair dangling from his forehead. Silently, the raiders each take a slave, hand over mouth and knife to throat. Then the entire raiding party comes to the beach.

Wordlessly they pull ten large Haida war canoes into the water and more than half of A-kadi's crew get into those canoes along with the two slaves who are tied, and they paddle them out to deep water. "Now slaves, wake your village," A-kadi demands.

Commotion erupts in the village and a chief in decorated robe makes his way to the beach, carrying his totem staff, followed by a group of men with full beards, followed by slaves with cropped hair.

A-kadi stands high on the tall prow of a stolen Haida canoe. His carved Wolf crest hat shakes as he shouts his oration of demands.

> *"We Wolf and Raven clans of the Tlingit are here to see that balance is regained. Two moons ago your people stole from us and we will have it back. We keep these two slave boys as part of your payment and these ten canoes if you do not talk with us. We will*

be on the beach across the water. Bring payment. If
not, we will take your war canoes and go. You have
a choice, but you must accept that this is a fair trade
and trouble us no more."

As they pull away, Do'ok sees frightening faces painted on tall totem poles in the Haida village. He feels the Spirit Power there and is glad to be leaving.

The Haida come across the water in various smaller canoes to negotiate, the chief riding in front, fringe from his tunic floating in the wind. His canoe is the only one allowed on shore. A-kadi trades for copper, hides, some carved totem items that were Tlingit in origin, the slave mother of one of the boys they already have and two of the canoes. Then he shouts an official statement for all to hear, "This feud is settled! We hope to trade again with the Haida another day!" He breathes a giant sigh of relief as they start for home and begins a chant of thanksgiving to Spirit Above as he feels the cloak of leadership settle more comfortably onto his shoulders.

At home, U-kart-ee keeps her reserve when her boys return, not wanting to embarrass her son. "May we stay home for a while now? No raids, no hunting trips?"

"It may be *necessary* to stay," Tinx says, joining them at the beach. "I heard that Ka-uh-ish is sick again. Shaman thinks he might die."

A dark shadow surrounds A-kadi as he drops his weapons and rushes to Wolf Clan House.

7

Ana of the Spanish Mission

Ana half-wakes in swirling confusion. Someone tells her, "Be still . . . rest . . .You are safe."

She sleeps.

For many days she drifts in and out between dreams and mist. Images of Wolf come and go. She sees the face of her dream friend, the one who laughs with her and knows her so well, but it looks like her own face, and it's confusing. She thinks that someone like a mother cares for her.

When the mist clears, Miguel is holding her hand. He looks older and much thinner, showing her a relieved, broad smile.

"Welcome back little Yush," he whispers in Tlingit. "You did not look so good."

"You took care of me," she mouths faintly in Spanish, still dazed, feeling pain everywhere, especially her head.

"Of course. I was your first mommy when we came on the ship. You wouldn't let go of me."

She tries to tighten her handhold in response.

"This is Zesen," he motions with his head. "She's been taking care of you."

Like a mother, her eyes move toward the woman. She's dressed in only a tule skirt, her long hair, which is just beginning to gray, mingles with clam shell beads that hang from her ears and from several wraps around her neck. She comes with a small basket of warm ground acorn porridge and begins to tuck small tastes into Ana's lower lip with a mussel shell.

Her mouth responds immediately, and the nourishment makes its way down her throat. As she eats, she follows the tattoo lines from each corner of Zesen's mouth, down over the woman's chin, neck and chest. Short cross lines connect between them like bird scratches on the ground. Ana looks at the kind eyes and calm, confident face.

"We owe her," Miguel continues, looking away.

"Don't worry, Miguel, everything will work out," Zesen assures, continuing to feed Ana. "I do not want padres or soldiers coming here. She needs time to heal."

At the mission, Miguel works in the warm afternoon sun wearing just his loincloth. The beating from the padre has left dark shadows and stiffness in his back. He thanks God for giving him the strength to take Ana to the Ohlone healer against the padres' wishes. As he fills a large trough with mud, straw, and manure to make adobe bricks, it seems that each ripe batch is heavier than the one before. He walks through the stiff mixture, lifting his feet, stepping back and forth in the trough until it's well-blended and uniform. Then he shovels it into wooden forms to create bricks. When that batch is left to dry, he removes the forms from yesterday's bricks and begins the process again.

Continuing to work, he sees a padre in his gray robe walking toward him. His grudge against the padre feels strong since his punishment, like a fire burning in his stomach.

"Miguel, how is Ana?"

"Barely alive," he bends down to examine his brick mixture.

"You are prolonging her suffering, Miguel. Bring her back to God where we can care for her," his voice sounds soothing.

Miguel stands to make eye contact, "She can't be moved. It would kill her."

"Then we will go to her." The padre stands squarely at Miguel, his eyes intense. "She belongs to God."

Miguel stiffens, "God is with her where she is," and he walks away.

Ana wakes to the comforting sound of women singing together. Their voices blend and move to a rhythm that sounds . . . gritty. Her eyes flutter, trying to see what is happening. Outside the doorway, each woman sits on matting, her own stone plate between her legs. In unison, they lift their stone rollers and drop them, rolling over something chunky. Lift, drop, roll forward and back. Clam shell and Olivella beads swing from the women's chests to the same rhythm. They are pounding acorns into fine, silky powder. It's a work song, and Ana has never heard anything so beautiful.

She sleeps.

Zesen brings willow bark tea and holds the back of her head as she sips. "It's acorn harvest," Zesen smiles, "the beginning of our new year, and the acorns are many this year." Ana sees the ceiling blackened by fire and deer-skin pouches hanging from the rafters. There are bundles of weaving materials, fishing nets, baskets stacked everywhere. She thinks she could fit three or four of herself, head to toe, across the center of the large house. When the tea dulls her pain, she drifts back to sleep.

She dreams of Wolf standing with her friend, his tail swishing playfully back and forth. She wants to join them, but the sound of ruckus brings her to consciousness, waking to see the back end of a furry animal, its haunches tightening and stretching as its front-end rummages through Zesen's baskets.

"Gaargh!" Ana yells with all her might, and the creature scampers away. Wanting to sit in case it comes back, she gently pushes herself up with her arms. She's dizzy and her head throbs, but she stays up, feeling better in time. She would like to straighten Zesen's baskets, clean up the mess but is unsure of how to accomplish it. Her left upper leg is tightly bound in a weave with sticks. Dragging herself to the baskets, she manages to scoop up some of the dried food with one hand.

"Straightening my baskets, are you?" Zesen has returned home.

"I hope you don't mind," she feels guilty for some reason. "I think it was a coyote."

"Good thing you were here to scare it away! How do you feel?"

"Thankful to be here," she smiles.

Zesen helps Ana return to her mat and finishes putting her baskets in order. "I was helping a new mother give birth. Unfortunately, it was *palichimin*, twins, two girl babies."

"Two? I've never heard of that!"

"That's because twins and deformed babies are not allowed to live. They carry negative spirits."

"So . . . they are dead?" Ana asks softly.

"We do not speak of the dead. Don't want them to attach to this place . . . or to us. They can be reborn if there are no ties with the living. We cry, singe our hair, scratch our faces, and when the body and *everything* is burned, even their house, we speak of them no more."

"Will people mourn twins?" she asks meekly.

"No, although the woman will need to heal. The husband has created a thick, warm bed of herbs on top of heated stones for her to lie on."

Zesen offers Ana a large clam shell of acorn and rabbit stew. "You're healing well and out of danger, I think. I'll keep you as long as I can. Just remember, one day a padre or soldiers will come. There is nothing that Miguel or I can do about that."

Ana sips the warm, thick broth, so unlike the daily atole she is used to. "Has the mission changed your lives very much?"

"We've lost many families to the mission," Zesen sighs. "The padres entice us with magical things like the box that makes music, and if we agree to belong to the church, we're not allowed to leave, like prisoners. Some sneak here to end pregnancies, not wanting to have babies born in the mission, but always, the soldiers come to take them back."

"When you feel ready," Zesen continues as she helps Ana lie back down, "you may help me prepare my medicines and maybe even help with patients when your leg is strong enough."

"Oh yes!" she grins, feeling the healing energy of a happy Spirit surge through her bones.

Ana wakes to shouts of joy. The men are greeting the sun as it rises, calling out words of encouragement.

Zesen is happy to see her up and asks if she would like to come to a nearby field. "You may use this staff," she holds up a smooth stick. "It will help support your leg."

"What will we do at the field?" Ana chirps.

"You'll see," she smiles, offering a breakfast of cormorant eggs and seed cake.

As they walk, Zesen explains how difficult it is to find enough of the wild seed they eat because the mission uses the ground for their crops and to graze their animals. "Our hunters must travel great distances now, sometimes into dangerous areas of other tribes because the animals we hunt travel farther to find their own food," she swings her arms wide as she talks.

Ana's discomfort with the mission grows, using up her strength. As they slowly make their way to the field, she sees sticks coming out of the ground at a turn in the path, feathers attached, they look like skinny birds.

"These are *iiot*, spirit sticks," Zesen explains, "to let us know this is a holy place, a place where the spirits speak loudly. Let's rest here, being respectful to not offend the spirits."

Quietly they sit. Tiny songbirds trill and the small ground

creatures rustle in the brush, and she feels the strength coming back into her limbs. When Zesen sees the glow of health return the color to Ana's face, they continue.

At the field, she sits to rest again, smelling the warm sweetness of harvest and seeing what remains of the grass as it grabs copper light from the sun.

"We've harvested the edible seeds from this field with our scoop baskets," Zesen explains. "Now we beat the bush to direct the rabbits and burn the field to ensure a good seed crop for next year."

They stand with others near a net that is stretched across an open area as fire burns toward them, a thrill of fear traveling Ana's spine. Soon, smoke billows high into the sky, and rabbits run this way and that, hopping straight up and down, all ending up in the net together, a big furry boil. Zesen holds up a rabbit by its feet and hits it on the back of the head with a stick to break its neck, then puts it into her carrying basket.

As they gather their catch from the net, Ana sees a young, fluffy bird getting trampled among the rabbits. She bends to scoop it up, and it settles down in her hands, seemingly thankful for protection. Zesen loads her basket onto her back with its strap across her forehead, and Ana tucks the bird into her skirt, tying the tule into a little hammock for their journey back.

In the Ohlone village, she's excited to see Miguel who's come to help with the butchering. She shows him the tiny bird nested in her skirt.

"A falcon! Very nice, little Yush. So you are a hunter after all," he teases.

The chief comes to see Ana's treasure. His hair is knotted on top of his head held by a wooden prong and long wooden ear plugs hang to his jaw. "Falcon is a spirit helper," his voice ruffles the colored feathers of his cape. "Be good to him. Our legends say that the falcon hero Kaknu, grandson of Coyote, saved the world from Body-of-Stone, the huge underground Lord who fed people to his servants. Falcon Kaknu shot arrows into Body-of-Stone breaking him into many pieces, destroying him. Just look at the ground to see the proof!"

Ana and Miguel look at the broken rock all around.

A messenger of the Ohlone chief arrives at Miguel's home with a knotted string and invitation stick to attend the celebration of the acorn harvest. He unties a knot each day and attends when the sun nears the horizon on the day of the last knot. A temporary fence of laurel branches is arranged into a large circle for the event. A messenger twirls a wooden paddle on twine over his head, a bull-roarer, to call everyone to listen and a speaker announces the chief.

The chief wears a long, sleeveless coat of many-colored feathers and carries a staff also decorated with feathers and long strips of white rabbit skin indicating peace. One side of his body is painted black, the other white, and his hair is knotted on top of his head under a coiled headdress which supports more feathers and porcupine quills, making him look bird-like. He speaks with an aristocratic accent.

> "Welcome to this celebration of the acorn. The spirits are generous this year, making it easy to be generous with each other.

We pay tribute to the acorn. The Acorn Tree Steward walks the ancient trails to feed each tree with admiration and thankfulness, praying for abundance.

We pay tribute to the acorn. From ancient times, Coyote taught the rain, the sun, and the ground to feed the acorn trees and therefore to feed the People.

We pay tribute to all acorns, valley oak, black oak, and live oak, and we dance to ensure balance and abundance, and to give back.

We dance to feel the Oneness.

We dance so the acorn tree and the land will feel good too."

Eight male dancers begin, bodies painted with charcoal, red clay and white chalk, some with white down glued to their skin. Footsteps match the beat of split sticks and bird-bone whistles. Dancing into a circle, black raven feathers fluff their aprons with each step as if to take flight and heads jerk from side to side, the movement of birds. Some have red woodpecker feathers arranged vertically across their foreheads and quail feathers stand from coiling on top of their heads, nodding with each beat.

Eight women follow, also adorned in paint and feathers. Ornaments of beads and pieces of abalone shell hang from their necks and arms and ankles and ears. Their circle surrounds the men, and they move together, stooping at the waist and stamping down with each beat.

The People chant, voices gaining power, sending their spirit to blend with the others. Their music, voices, feet, and the beat vibrate together into the rocks, into the trees, and into the air, repairing the world and making the acorn very happy.

Miguel watches, dipping his knees with the beat as he savors rich, sweetened acorn bread, chewy with crisp edges. He thinks of the feasts in the North when he was allowed to eat the leftovers as a slave, and he's grateful for his new status.

An argument erupts in the circle, voices raised, accusations flying. "The Miwok are getting too familiar with our women," a friend from the sweathouse explains. "They *know* to ask for a wife through the chief and parents. The idiots called for a line battle, but they won't get it."

Miguel looks to his friend, eyebrows raised.

"Only a chief can call for a line battle. It's when one or two men stand within range of the other side, hoping to move quickly enough to avoid arrows. It solves a dispute without war. Our chief will calm this down with words, though. The council will expect it."

Zesen's father, Chusen, comes with a gift for Ana's falcon, a small version of a tule house that swings from a handle at its top. He touches the young bird with one finger, knowing it will become a large falcon one day. The top of his head will be as dark as under his eyes. "He's a totem animal, Ana, a spirit ancestor. His Spirit will watch over you." Together, they feed him mice and grasshoppers several times a day and Chusen brings a small bird now and then. They laugh at Falcon with his food, and she enjoys Chusen's visits.

For four nights, she falls asleep to soothing Bird Songs, the men playing flutes and singing about the Sacred Time of Creation when spirits wandered the world, and she has never slept so well. In the morning, she stands outside with her staff to support her leg, gazing at the distant rolling hills which look like very pregnant women lying on their backs. She realizes that the bell of the mission has been a poor substitute for music and birdsong every day of her life, and she's thankful to be without it. Relishing her feeling of freedom, she inhales the sweet morning air. Falcon makes little *rehk, rehk* sounds, keeping her company.

The village becomes quiet, birdsong stops, everyone disappears into their houses. She looks around to see two soldiers, each on horseback and knows they've come for her. One glances at her falcon in its cage and says, "Ana, you're needed at the mission." He looks powerful sitting on the horse, wearing a sleeveless overcoat of layers of sheepskin to protect from arrows, and carrying an oval shield of cowhide layers painted gold, red and blue, the Spanish Royal House coat of arms. Each soldier has a long gun in a leather sheath and a belted cartridge pouch.

Ana's breath comes in shallow gulps, wanting to run. Then, slowly, her fear is overcome with great sadness, and she wishes that Zesen were there to say "goodbye." She tucks the soft deerskin medicine bundle that Zesen prepared for her under her arm. "May I please bring my falcon?"

One of the soldiers gets off his horse and lifts Ana up to sit in front of the other soldier, both legs on one side, being careful not to bump her injured leg. She has never been so high in the air except in her sleeping loft and has *never* sat on an animal before! He ties the falcon house to the back of his own saddle, and they are on their way.

The horse's head sways from side to side as it walks, and Ana stiffens, afraid of what it might do next. The soldier's arms hold the reins, keeping her from falling off. "My wife, Catalina, says that you are a good student and can read," the soldier comments, causing the horse's ears to turn.

Ana remembers Catalina, the woman who supervised her visits with her family at Mission Village. "Yes, sir. How is Catalina?"

"She's well . . . Did you know that in Spain there are people who practice falconry? You teach the bird to hunt and to bring its catch to you."

"That sounds difficult . . . I would like to be that close to my falcon." She turns her head for a last glimpse of the village, but they've descended down a slope and it's already out of sight.

Nearing the end of the three-mile trip, she's aware of her great distance from Zesen and the Ohlone village. Her breath becomes shallow again. She hears the call of the mission bell and bites her lip against an overwhelming sense of dread.

"You said that I was *needed* at the mission, sir. What did you mean?"

"There's an outbreak of sickness. The padres want you to help minister to the sick," he looks at her with serious, sorry eyes.

After several days of tending the sick, Ana cries and wipes a cool, damp cloth across her sister's dry-hot forehead. Teresa lies on her mat surrounded by family inside her small tule house within the Mission Village and exhales her final breath. Ana did everything she could, willow bark tea for fever and pain, balsam root for cough and runny nose, yerba santa for the red, blotchy rash, but Teresa was already weak from a difficult pregnancy. Her sister, Maria, keeps hold of Teresa's four-year-old son as Ana closes Teresa's eyes. Then her stomach lurches from deep inside, and she hears a wail erupt from her own mouth, uncontrolled, feeling the full impact of Death, and her brother Pedro puts his hand on Ana's shoulder, squeezing.

Painfully, she pulls her attention away, knowing there is more she must do. She tries to ignore her exhaustion and the agony of her leg, telling Pedro and Rodrigo to follow her as she pulls herself with her wooden staff to Miguel's house.

He and his whole family are sick. Miguel's wife sits against the wall, covered with red rash. Her head hangs from her shoulders as she holds her young daughter. Miguel and the older daughter sleep on mats. Together, Ana and her brothers give food and remedies.

"Miguel!" Ana is loud, wanting him to hear through his fever. "Teresa has left us to be with the Father. You may NOT abandon us! You must FIGHT, do you hear me, Miguel?"

"Yes sister." His voice is soft, and he returns to sleep.

She grabs him by the shoulders. "Think of your wife and children," she demands, waking him. "Fight HARD!"

Ana leaves extra tea and food and tells Pedro and Rodrigo to go to Zesen to ask for more medicine. "Tell her I will pay her back."

In the monjerío, Ana is surrounded by ailing women and girls. They lie everywhere in the nearly dark room. She knows she's been on her leg way too long and something more than exhaustion is overcoming her, but she must keep going. She sees two women who are recovering enough to be on their feet, and just as she is explaining how to use the medicines, the ground meets her face and her world goes dark.

As Ana regains consciousness from a dream about returning to the Ohlone village, her eyes meet the eyes of Zesen. "Like-a-mother," she smiles.

"You're better, Ana," Zesen soothes. "You're young and strong, but this is a tough way to stay off your leg!"

"I *had* to help," Ana's eyes fill with tears as she remembers Teresa's death.

Zesen takes her hand, "I know . . . you're a healer now. You will always help. Miguel and his wife are recovering, but they lost their youngest daughter. I'm sorry."

Ana sobs, "My poor Miguel." She imagines the tiny body wrapped in a blanket, buried in the dirt.

Zesen is quiet, touched by the young innocence on her wet face. "Death is part of life, dear Ana," she whispers, leaning forward. "Your brothers brought me here and the women snuck me in . . . maybe they can sneak me out again?" she raises her eyebrows.

Ana's mouth turns down, "I will miss you again."

Zesen squeezes her hand, "My love is attached to you forever, little falcon girl."

When Ana gets better, like so many others, she covers her face in pitch and ash and singes her hair and scratches her face, and the padres become angry, saying that the baptized are in Heaven with God and they should be happy about that. Even so, bodies are stolen by loved ones and burned on a pyre before the Church can get them into the ground.

For the first time, she's glad that she is Tlingit because unlike the Ohlone, she can talk about Teresa and remember her, and maybe see her again in the birth of a new baby someday.

Unexpectedly, the world of Power takes notice of Ana. She is confined to a corner of the monjerío where the unmarried Ohlone women talk to her about her life change and explain that she is becoming a woman. They tell her that she should fast and not eat meat or fish or salt or drink cold water. ". . . and do not scratch yourself with your fingernails," one tells her, giving her a scratching stick. "It's bad luck."

In the evening, the women quietly chant and dance for her, honoring the Power that has entered her body, and they share a meal, a new sisterhood. Wistfully, they tell her that if they were in the Ohlone village, there would be a great feast and she would receive her tattoos.

On Sunday afternoon at Miguel's house, her family cooks a special meal and gifts her an apron of deerskin. When she also receives a light-weight cape that was created by Teresa before her death, an unpredicted sob erupts from her mouth. She realizes that her family has been preparing for this moment for a long time.

"If we were in the North, there would be a great feast," Miguel remembers. "You would be getting a small bone or wooden labret put into your lower lip today . . . unless you are a slave. Then you'd get nothing. I always forget that you could have been a slave, like the rest of us. Anyway, a labret is a sign that you're of age to be married, just like a chin tattoo is here."

"Married!" Ana blurts, her heart racing. "I waited so many years and then forgot all about marriage! I can get out of the monjerío!"

"Whoa, little sister!" Miguel holds up both hands. "With all the reading and writing lessons the padres give you, they may have some special plans we don't know about . . . and they might not include marriage."

"WHAT?"

8

Ka-uh-ish (Father of the Morning)

In An-ar-kark, there is no more work performed by Wolf People at the death of great Leader Ka-uh-ish. His brothers-in-law of the Raven People take care of everything so Wolf Clan are free to mourn. As the Shaman dances, the body is carefully wrapped in furs and he is set up against the decorated back wall inside Wolf Clan House to preside over his own funeral, his handsome Wolf crest robe draped across his chest.

Great respect is used with every action so the spirits will give generous treatment to their leader in the Land of the Dead. Ut-kart-ee's father, Al'ooni of Hawk Clan, speaks to Ka-uh-ish as he gently lifts the stiffened hands into his deerskin mittens, inserting a stone to prevent a ghost from taking anyone else. Al'ooni pulls moccasins up over the feet. "These will help you over the rocky path to the Afterworld . . . and you must take your weapons," he says, fitting his knife and spear into the leader's hands. He places the woven conical hat with a stack of seven cedar rings, the number of potlatches that Ka-uh-ish hosted in his long life, upon his head. "You have done well in this life, my brother. Come back to us soon."

Chark Cough-ye helps arrange the leader's treasures around his body: his carved Wolf hat topped with sea lion whiskers, several copper shields, furs, tools, some with iron, and fishing gear. Widow Kageet (Loon) arrives crying with her face blackened and hair singed short, and he helps her take her place among the items of wealth, tucking her in with warm furs. She sits, hoping to sense the soul of her husband while Chark Cough-ye and other men of the Raven People stand guard against witches and thieves and watch over her.

Ut-kart-ee and her family wait in Hawk Clan House with blackened faces and cut hair. She thinks of how Ka-uh-ish has been her good uncle and the leader of her clan all her life. In her grief, she relives the loss of her first-born and the memory of her Spirit Dream returns, Wolf dropping the black Raven feather at her feet, as if it relates to these deaths, but she can get no closer to understanding its meaning.

The dark, drooling day is just beginning to present a bit of light when great booms from the big box drum of Wolf Clan House vibrate off the mountains, announcing that Ka-uh-ish is ready to receive his People. Ut-kart-ee arrives in time to hear her brother A-kadi speak to the spirit of their uncle:

"Uncle and teacher, I love you so much, I
would have died in your place. You taught me well

and gave me a happy heart. You will be remembered
as we remember Raven, and I will listen for your
counsel at the end of each day."

Relatives from other villages arrive and the wailing of female mourners which sounds like the call of many loons from a distance transforms into the crying songs of their clans. Inside Wolf Clan House, men beat wooden staffs held straight up and down onto the floor while women stand together, swaying side-to-side, their cropped hair flowing back and forth with the beat like floating seaweed in the tide. Ut-kart-ee sings her lament, a Wolf Clan song, low and slow, tears designing tiny gray streams through the charcoal on her cheeks.

At night, men of the family tuck a bit of their traditional tobacco mixed with ash and ground horse clam shell into their lips. A-kadi sprinkles a portion for Ka-uh-ish into the north, south, east, and west corners of the fire, saying "Ka-uh-ish" each time so he can enjoy it in spirit form. Then they break their fasts with a nibble of moose meat, his favorite food, adding it and some water into the fire as well.

On the eighth morning, the in-laws make a hole in the back wall of Wolf Clan House by removing some planks and carefully take his wrapped body out through the hole, then reverently place him on a pyre of hard wood and candlefish oil. Chark Cough-ye puts charcoal inside each corner of the house to deter ghosts from staying and throws ashes out the hole. He protects the children from wandering spirits by wedging charcoal into split sticks and hanging them open-side-up over their sleeping mats.

Personal items of Ka-uh-ish and food are added to the pyre

along with the bodies of two elderly slaves, killed by restricting their breath by a ceremonial log pressed against the neck. One had volunteered saying, "I have served Ka-uh-ish all my life and I would be honored to serve him in the next." They will serve their master in the Land of the Dead with no injuries and more importantly, earn themselves time in the Afterlife, otherwise unattainable for a slave.

Carefully, the brothers-in-law remove his scalp under the supervision of the Shaman. It will be dried, wrapped in marten fur and stored in a carved cedar box to be shown on special occasions. A-kadi reassures the mourners:

> "His spirit has left his body, but his soul is
> unaffected. We light this fire to keep him warm in the
> Land of the Dead. The ancestors have taught us there
> is no difference between life and death; it just looks
> like there is. His soul will continue, and we will have
> him back one day."

The pyre is lit. Blazing flames immediately lick the sky, causing mourners to step back, and the crying songs of the men follow the beat of a box drum as the women, who sit further away, join in. Ut-kart-ee sits with her aunt, the widow Kageet, who trembles so violently that Ut-kart-ee wraps her arms around her, afraid she might jump into the fire.

Kageet turns to her niece. "Ut-kart-ee, my husband asked that you deliver him back to the People in his next life." She presses a tiny pouch into her niece's hand and pulls it open to show bits of fingernail and hair. "He thought it would be a good joke to be nephew to A-kadi after A-kadi was nephew to *him*," she forces a hopeful smile, "and he knew you would be a good mother."

Ut-kart-ee squeezes her aunt's hand and hangs the pouch from her waist. Then arm-in-arm, they walk around the pyre eight times and Ut-kart-ee squats low near the fire, lifting her tunic and calling "Ka-uh-ish" as she urinates, connecting his soul to hers.

A-kadi watches the fire, feeling the heartbreak of his family, realizing his full responsibility as leader and the enormous role his uncle played in his life. He speaks to the group as the fire dies down.

> *"Our lament will be heard as clearly as Eagle calls his mate. To honor the great life of Ka-uh-ish, I wish to free the female slave Shouk who has served my family all my life. If she wishes to stay with us, I will adopt her as a member of Wolf Clan with a place at our fire."*

When the fire cools, the sisters-in-law reverently gather the bones and ash from the fire, wrap them in furs, and put them into a Wolf totem cedar box to be attached to the top of a mortuary pole when it is prepared.

A-kadi's mind is jumbled with preparations for the memorial potlatch along with his general responsibilities as a leader and the clear knowledge that he must prove himself worthy to keep his position. He is reminded of this every time he feels the eyes of the Shaman on him.

He walks beside a clear, fast-running stream, wondering what to do first. His duties seem without end. He has taken his aunt, widow Kageet, as his second wife in order to support her, which is custom, but Kiyanee (Land Flower) his first wife, and Kageet seem to bicker day and night, which requires all the patience he can find. Now he will have access to the berry patches and fishing and hunting areas of Wolf Clan and both wives' clans of the Raven People, and he needs as much wealth as he can find for the memorial potlatch, but he doesn't know where to begin. He paces along the stream like a trapped wolf, back and forth.

A bird flies in front of him, diving into the water. It's the dipper bird "old woman sunk." She walks underwater on the bottom of the streambed with struggle, head bent into the current, pulling herself forward with her stubby wings and grasping at rocks with her bird toes to find the little fish and under-water insects to eat.

Intrigued, A-kadi watches her labor, thinking that the potlatch could be the most important work of his life and it's like his head is underwater, making it difficult to think. The "old woman" bird pops to the surface and flies away to her nest. When she trills a happy call, he realizes that he's been walking alone, underwater against the current long enough. He will pull his head out and speak with his Council at home. That is where to begin.

Wolf Clan Council proves helpful, and he realizes that asking for counsel is sometimes a sign of strength for a leader. They recommend that Do'ok prepare to be storyteller for the potlatch by visiting as many clan houses as he can to learn their stories and get permission to retell them. Also, they agree to contribute to the planning and the gifts for the potlatch, causing the weight on A-kadi's shoulders to roll off his back. He suggests they create a memorial pole like those he saw at the Haida village, and they begin to discuss who would be the right carvers to hire from the Raven People.

Preparations begin. A-kadi arranges extra fishing and hunting parties. Ut-kart-ee hires her friend Kla-oosh to help make baskets in exchange for teaching her the unique Wolf pattern that she developed which is now the property of Wolf Clan. Chark Cough-ye introduces A-kadi's friend, Kookenaa, to his trading friend Nalren for extra Athabascan trade.

A-kadi and Do'ok work fast in the spring when the herring come to spawn and the water splashes with flashing fish. The fish move together like a current, sinking to avoid gulls, swimming up to avoid salmon and seals below. The fishermen sweep spruce rakes studded with sharpened bones through the water, bringing up a load of fish with each sweep and dumping them into the boat. The chaos in the water is matched with that of the sky as the gulls scream, plummeting for fish, swallowing their catch whole in mid-flight, and often fighting other gulls during the act. Time and again, A-kadi and Do'ok dodge the gulls as they bring their catch to An-ar-kark for drying and processing and go out again.

Gulls land on squirming fish in shallow water, poking their bellies with their beaks to get at the eggs while Ut-kart-ee works with her children and other women of Wolf Clan to lay hemlock boughs onto the beach. Fish will deposit their eggs on the boughs during high tide. Then the boughs and seaweed, moss, anything covered with fish eggs will be collected at the next low tide and hung to dry. Ut-kart-ee sings with the others in celebration of their abundance as the village becomes crowded with drying racks and the air ripens with the processing of fish and fish eggs.

On her last morning of fish-egg collection, Ut-kart-ee sees a spiky piece of driftwood wagging back and forth with the waves in the surf. Wading out, she can see that it's embedded with spikes of iron! *A gift from the Spirits!* Her face fattens into a greedy smile as she thinks of all the tools and weapons that can be made, and quickly, she calls for help to roll it up onto the beach.

When Wolf Clan accumulates enough wealth to host the memorial potlatch, A-kadi sends messengers to clans in other villages, inviting Raven People who are relatives and who helped with the funeral and anyone else who should be paid. The potlatch will be held at the end of Digging Moon when animals dig their winter nests. Each clan practice their songs and dances in preparation. Several moons in advance, all of Wolf Clan begin to fast and avoid intimate relations to ensure the success of the potlatch.

The memorial potlatch begins more than a year after the death of Wolf Clan Leader Ka-uh-ish. Gull Clan of the Wolf People and Frog Clan of the Raven People, both from Naakee-ann (North Village) paddle south to camp overnight near An-ar-kark. They arrive in the morning in a stately show of seven large war canoes lashed together side by side, a richly dressed leader standing in the bow of each.

They sing their arriving song from the water and A-kadi, wearing his carved Wolf hat and holding his carved totem staff, joins with Wolf Clan to sing their greeting song. After songs of peace are exchanged, there are statements of clan lineage.

I am A-kadi, Leader of Wolf Clan of the

Wolf People, nephew of Ka-uh-ish, son of Yake-see and Al'ooni of Hawk Clan of the Raven People . . . Do you see the Wolf Crest on my head? Why are you here?

Frog Clan leader replies:

"Wooshkitan, we have been invited to your party! In memory of great leader Ka-uh-ish, we wish to be with you while the sun passes behind the clouds and to help you breathe life into the ancestors."

All of Wolf Clan hurry into the water to carry their guests and canoes to the beach. White eagle down is sprinkled into the breeze and it takes flight, floating onto the water and up into the trees to signal peace as the guests are welcomed into Wolf Clan homes.

Approaching Wolf Clan House, they see the new life-size carved Wolf twelve feet in the sky behind the big house, held up by four carved posts. Wolf's ears point up and his teeth show in his partly open mouth. His claws carry the carved, bentwood cedar box that holds the bones and ashes of Ka-uh-ish. It's a mortuary pole and a perfect example of the honor the People wish to give their beloved leader.

Additional guests arrive over four days amid feasting and entertainment, storytelling, and singing and dancing competitions. Do'ok shines as Storyteller after learning from different clans. He remembers looking into unknown faces at many firesides as a learner, and now it's the face of one teacher's daughter that he seeks. She sits on the other side of the fire, giving him all her attention with shining eyes. Her name is K'aan-at-shi (Dolphin Song). He shows her his best smile and family dimple that he hopes will touch her heart.

At the main fire, he retells his favorite story about the great flood when Raven created a new race of people made of leaves rather than rock so they would become more flexible, lighter and faster. It was the time when people became mortal. He gives all the detail and uses the correct voice and the perfect timing, and as he looks into the eyes of his listeners, he sees approval, and he publicly thanks his teachers for their good teaching at the end of the story.

The main Memorial Potlatch ceremonies last two days. Wolf Clan is dressed in the ceremonial clothing of their ancestors and their faces are painted black by the Raven People. They gather in the big house to view the regalia of Ka-uh-ish arranged in front of the crest wall along with his spruce root hat, many carved treasures and marten furs. Two slaves stand in front of the crest wall, each holding a copper shield which reflects the golden light from the fire.

A-kadi steps out from behind the wall in a ceremonial robe, the inlaid teeth of his Wolf crest hat glimmer as if the spirits reside there. His arms open wide as he welcomes the group. Widow Kageet and sister Yake-see reverently lift the scalp of Ka-uh-ish from its ornate box for all to see the long gray hair, and the wailing begins.

People sing songs of lament during the taking up of the drum. A-kadi leads everyone outside to the front of the house where large cedar mats are removed to reveal a carved and painted, 65-foot memorial pole. The bottom portion lies in a 20-foot long, slanted trench in the ground. The trench is much deeper at the bottom of the pole than midway, and a hole has been dug at the base. He explains:

"Our beloved leader Ka-uh-ish should be remembered in a way that is solid like this memorial pole. May he and the ancestors be proud. Who will help me raise it?"

Most step forward, but the men do the heavy work. Together, they lift the top end and put a short log roller under the pole. The log is rolled toward the bottom of the pole as the pole is lifted again and again. Scissor supports are added, and pikes are used to push the pole into the air. Finally, lines which were previously attached are pulled, righting the pole as it slides into the hole.

The memorial pole stands, impressive in front of the snowy peaks of blue mountains in the distance. *"It's called 'Morning Light,'"* A-kadi explains.

"It is a story of Loon, which represents Kageet, the wife of Ka-uh-ish. From his arms at the top, she calls down to a lost canoe that is captured by Fog Woman. Raven, creator of all things, sits at the base of the pole. He holds up Wolf, the spirit guide of our clan. Next above, the wispy arms of Fog Woman surround a lost canoe of wolf pups, but they are able to follow Loon's call up to the morning sunlight and return home to Ka-uh-ish, the Father of the Morning."

The people stand in awe. Some have not seen such a decorated pole before. They go through the story again with each other to ensure they will remember it and can retell it at home, bringing more status to themselves with the retelling.

That evening Wolf Clan also grieves for other relatives who have died since the last potlatch. When their voices grow quiet with sacred songs and their feet move like heavy chunks of wet wood, they expel any remaining sadness from their bodies saying "uuuuu" "uuuuu" "uuuuu" "uuuuu." It's the final mourning and lament, the end of suffering for those left behind.

Blackened faces are cleaned and replaced with red, the color of peace, and the attitudes are changed from sorrow to joy as the feast begins. Carved alder bowls with abalone inlay and sheep horn bowls are set before the guests containing dried foods mixed in candlefish oil: salmon, berries, seaweed with herring eggs, and more. Everyone eats heartily, giving honor to A-kadi and Wolf Clan.

Wolf Clan members are invited to name ancestors who have perished since the last potlatch while sprinkling food into the fire, providing sustenance to the deceased soul of their family member. Then Wolf Clan performs dances and songs for entertainment.

The gift giving begins--furs, moose and deer skins, slaves, large pieces of Native copper, copper shields, spikes of iron, adornments, preserved foods, and Ut-kart-ee's Wolf designs on baskets. The greatest gifts go to those who helped at the funeral and potlatch, the carvers and the house leaders. Each Wolf Clan member, even the children, contribute something, a song or a speech.

That evening the rose-colored sunset reflects A-kadi's mood and he feels proud. Through the potlatch, all Raven People who helped with the rituals of Ka-uh-ish's death are thanked and compensated, strengthening relations between many clans. The resulting goodwill will protect his clan and their children long into the future. Also, the stories and memories and music bring them the strength and security of their traditions. Wolf Clan was able to increase status, and most importantly, A-kadi has created a long-term positive effect on Wolf Clan's *shagoon,* its origin, heritage, and destiny, as begun by his ancestors. He hopes this potlatch will be remembered for generations as he understands that protecting and enhancing Wolf Clan's shagoon is his greatest responsibility.

As A-kadi steps forward to close the ceremony, Takl-eesh unexpectedly presents him with a conical Wolf hat adorned with a cedar ring at the top for his first potlatch. A-kadi smiles, proudly putting it on his head and delivers the closing speech.

> *"Our ancestors remain as constant in our lives as*
> *the tide. Balance has been restored and we will mourn*
> *no more. The Naming Ceremony is our final gift."*

For the Naming Ceremony, each house leader announces the new names within his household, some because a child has been born or has gotten older or because of a special event, and guests repeat each new name four times. Ut-kart-ee and Chark Cough-ye come forward with their son, alive for six moons, and he laughs a big slobbery laugh. "This child is always happy," Chark Cough-ye explains, "and your faces show that it is contagious. Remember how Ka-uh-ish loved to make us laugh?"

"Ka-uh-ish thought it would be funny to be nephew to A-kadi," Ut-kart-ee continues, looking to her brother, "and asked to be reborn through me so that could happen . . . and he would think it a good joke to attend his own potlatch." Smiling broadly, she announces, "We name this child Ka-uh-ish!"

Surprised, everyone laughs, repeating his name four times,

"Ka-uh-ish, Ka-uh-ish, Ka-uh-ish, Ka-uh-ish," creating a potlatch to be remembered forever.

9

Captain George Vancouver

At the mission, Ana wears her cape for warmth on a chilly afternoon as she cuts cakes of soap from the tallow pot. Lucia comes to tell her that the padre wishes her to meet a visitor. Entering the dining room, she sees a man standing in a dark-blue uniform wearing a white wig above his long face. He holds a triangular shaped hat at chest level.

"Captain George Vancouver," the padre says, "may I present our little miracle, Ana."

"Pleased to meet you sir," she performs her best curtsy accompanied by the soft rustle of her tule skirt.

"Miss Ana," Vancouver responds, lowering his long sloping nose in her direction and speaking in Spanish. "The padre has given me to understand that you know several languages and can read Latin and Spanish."

"Yes sir, the padres have been good to teach me."

"I am compelled to tell you that I am impressed by your achievements. Surely those honorable skills will promote agreeable results for you regarding your purposes in the North," Vancouver says encouragingly.

Ana is confused, and her eyebrows come together as her lips form a tiny circle. She hears the padre's clock tick in the silence as she turns to him, "The North?"

"Ana, you've been groomed all your life to take Christianity to the heathens in the North. When Friar Riobo took you on Captain Quadra's ship as a newborn, you were so small that he did not expect you to live. But you did live. That is why he called you "his miracle." He brought you here 14 years ago along with the other five children with the agreement that at least one of you would return to your homeland to spread the word of God."

She is stunned and stands mute. When Captain Vancouver sees her become pale, he suggests that perhaps she should sit down.

"That is why I have taught you so many lessons and why Miguel has been careful to teach you the Tlingit language," the padre continues. "The time for you to return has come with this visit from Captain Vancouver here of the British Royal Navy. He will transport you on his ship *Discovery.*"

Ana immediately sinks to the dirt floor.

The padre sees that she will need time to recover and he waves her away with the wide, gray sleeve of his habit. "You're excused, Ana. Be ready to leave in three days."

Her legs don't seem to work correctly as she wobbles to her sleeping mat, a dark, safe, quiet place where she can block her mind and pretend that nothing has changed. It feels as if she's suffered a blow, another great injury like when the loft fell. She feels hollow and wounded, and when her breathing slows, her mind betrays her. "Three days!" begins to repeat in her head and her panic erupts.

She goes to find Miguel, hoping he will help her do whatever is needed to stay with her family. The longer it takes her to walk to the field where he is plowing, the angrier she becomes. Lucia follows with her walking stick as quickly as she can.

"Miguel!" Ana cries as she approaches. "I can't believe you didn't *tell* me!" She feels like hitting him.

"Tell you what, little sister?" Miguel turns toward her with eyebrows raised.

"That I'm going back! You've *abandoned* me!"

"Going back where?"

"To our homeland in the North! and you knew it all along!" Her hands ball into fists.

"There was a *chance* that you might go back. I honestly didn't think it would ever happen."

"Well it *IS* happening, in three days!" she cries, "unless you can get me away, sneak me into the mountains! *Save* me Miguel!" she sobs, falling into him, her big brother.

He holds her up, feeling her tremble. "*Lo siento mucho*, I'm so sorry my darling sister," he whispers in her ear. "Your life has not been easy so far, maybe it will be better in the North."

"I will be a *slave* in the North!" she chokes.

Miguel pulls back to see her fear. "They won't know *who* you are, and when they find that you speak many languages, including their own, and are able to *read!* They'll never treat you as a slave, *trust me.*" He gives her shoulders a little shake.

"I don't *want* to go. I'm not even *married!* Why am I not married, Miguel?" Her tears flow, blurring her vision. "Why must I go *alone?*"

"I know. It was hard when I came on the ship at ten years old. It worked out okay."

"What about Zesen and Chusen? I can't leave without saying goodbye to *them!*" she cries.

"I'll take care of that, don't worry, little Yush," he pats her on the head.

She knocks his hand away. "Don't *do* that! I'm not a child anymore!" Anger feels better than sadness and better than fear.

Wandering back into the quiet shadows of the church, the smooth earth feeling like home on the bottoms of her feet, she sees her surroundings through blurred vision, like a memory of the last time, and the tears flow. She looks to the alter and kneels below her favorite painting, "Our Lady of Perpetual Help." Mary's face is kind, and for the first time, Ana realizes that it is also a strong face. Mary would do anything to protect her child. She wonders if she, herself, had been loved in the North, and if there is someone like Mary who would have fought fiercely to protect *her*. She remains on the ground beneath the mother and child, trying to make sense of this enormous shift in her life.

"Have faith, Ana," the padre stands behind her, bending to lay a reassuring hand on her shoulder. "Sometimes change is for a good purpose, one that we can't see in the beginning. Have faith that God's purpose for you will be revealed and that you will know Him better because of it. To help you with that, we want to give you this Bible." He presents one of the few treasures from the mission. "Use it well."

Shocked, Ana slowly holds out her hands to receive the Book. Carefully, she feels the cool, brown leather cover and the weight of it in her hands. She's never imagined herself as having anything in her life so valuable as a Bible and continues to hold it out in front of her as if it sits on a tabletop.

"I guess I don't need to tell you to be careful with it," he chuckles. "Now get your chores done. Enjoy a few days of normal life."

She feels less angry and slightly less afraid carrying the Bible. It makes her feel stronger somehow, important, and despite her heavy sadness, her panic begins to quiet, for now.

Dressed in her new bodice with sleeves and her tule, deerskin skirt, 14-year-old Ana stands on deck of the square-rigged, three-masted ship *Discovery* as it leaves the giant, marsh-rimmed bay near the Spanish mission for open water. The chaos of everything new wrapped in a completely unknown world is truly overwhelming. She's never seen a ship before. She thought it was a floating forest when she first saw it, and the deck spans nearly a hundred feet of length below her, the bowsprit extending far beyond. The immense expanse of water around her is also new and shocking, even though she's lived near the bay all her life.

She grips the rail in a tight fist, standing exactly where Captain Vancouver directed her to stand. Amid the harried activity and shouts of officers and crew and the flurry of gulls, she keeps her eyes attached to the shoreline and tells herself to breathe. In her mind, she sees herself back on shore, a safer place where she belongs. She relives Miguel and the soldier coaxing her onto the smaller boat to take her out to the ship. She could not *believe* what they were asking her to do! She froze into stone, and they had to load her onto the ship like a new calf, swinging her from ropes through the air over the water! She thought she would drown or die of fright!

Her body is so tense as the ship moves away with the morning tide that it hurts. People on shore become smaller and smaller until they are tiny dots, and she gulps back her tears, working to resist the dread that threatens to overwhelm her. She hears Zesen's voice in her ear. *"Your thoughts can be more dangerous than your worst enemy, little falcon girl. Learn to control your thoughts, and if you don't know what to think, find something to be thankful for."*

"I'm thankful I'm not dead, I think," she says aloud, her voice drowned by laughter of the gulls. She keeps her focus on the shoreline but as they move further away, the beach becomes difficult to see, and she is forced to concentrate on the rolling hills behind. She remembers the tears on Miguel's face and Zesen and Chusen holding hands as they stood on shore to say goodbye, strained faces with forced smiles. There was love in their eyes. She looks down at the medicine bundle tied around her waist and the elderberry flute that Chusen made which hangs from her neck. She grabs it now, squeezing tightly.

The hills become smaller. Eventually, the gulls begin to diminish, and the sea breeze picks up, causing her to notice the coolness on her wet face. She stays in her spot, eyes attached to home, until it disappears, and she feels the floor beneath her feet rise and fall with the larger swells of open sea. She hears the wind humming in the sails, and the cooler air creeps into her clothing so that her trembling from shock is joined with shivers from chill. Swallowing hard, she forces her hands to let go of the railing and turn around.

Her eyes are met with a full view of the village-size ship, busy with crew and uniformed officers. Big white sails flutter and fill with air, surrounded by an enormous world of dark water. It rolls and runs in bottomless hills all around her, erupting into white foam. It takes her breath away. Her chest hardens and she can only grab little gulps of air. Specks of light fill her vision and she hears roaring in her ears. The closest sail unfurls right in front of her with an enormous snap and her world goes black.

Thirty-six-year-old Commander George Vancouver of the British Royal Navy stands on deck, taking stock of his ship and crew. The ship looks clean and trim, the livestock having been neatly stowed in the hold. The crew seem to be able seamen and work well together despite being from many nations. As they head toward The Sandwich Islands, he feels fortunate to have talented officers with him such as Lieutenant Peter Puget, Lieutenant Joseph Baker, and Master Joseph Whidbey, as well as Dr. Archibald Menzies, a Scottish botanist and surgeon.

Accompanying *Discovery* is the armed ship *Chatham* under the command of Lieutenant Broughton and the supply ship *Daedalus*. Vancouver's commission is to finish the surveying and mapping of the Sandwich Islands which he began with Captain

Cook 14 years before. Then he is to do the same along the north coast of America and continue the search for a northwest passage, eventually proceeding to the far north of the continent to survey and report any settlements of other nations that he encounters.

Also, there are passengers for transport: Sixteen-year old Kualelo returning home to Molokai after three years of employment on British ships and receiving education while in England, two girls previously captive on an American ship also returning home to the Sandwich Islands, and Ana, a 14-year old Tlingit from a Spanish mission to be taken to the North as a Catholic missionary.

Ana wakes in a dark, cramped room with two girls close to her age. She's reminded of the hungry coyote in Zesen's house when she sees them going through her things underneath her narrow berth. "Hey!" she yells. Surprised, both girls jump, and sit together on the only other bed in the room, which fills the tiny space. They wear fabric tunics to their knees. She notices the feeling of movement beneath her and grips her bed, realizing that the ship rocks on the waves, and she remembers the immense water that swallows her. The girls seem unconcerned.

"Saludo," Ana says.

They look at her, eyes crimped in confusion.

"How do you do?" the younger girl says.

Ana assumes that the words are a greeting and points at herself, saying "Ana."

The younger girl points to herself, saying "Lili," then to the other, more mature girl and says, "Kawena."

The three girls share a smile and Ana looks for Falcon. He moves in his cage at the foot of her berth, fidgeting, wanting to get out. She sees a candle burning on a tiny desk attached to the wall, creating their bit of light. The ceiling is low and she's unsure if she'll be able to stand up fully. She checks the bundle of deerskin clothing that Miguel had created to keep her warm in the North and sees the Bible. Everything is wrapped in a rabbit-skin blanket that Maria, Lucia and Catalina provided to her as a gift. She runs her hand over the soft fur. Immediately, Lili and Kawena join her, petting the luxurious skins and talking excitedly between them.

Ana hears the ship's bell ring three times. There's a knock on the door, and a smiling, curly haired steward presents himself. "Miss Ana," he states, awkwardly trying the bit of Spanish he's learned, "Encontrar capitán por favor?"

"Si!" she says, anxious to get out of the stuffy room and see the only person she knows. She glares at the girls and uses hand motions to tell them to stay out of her things, then follows the steward. He stops in front of a door, opens it, and announces her to the captain.

Vancouver stands in his cabin dressed in uniform of white leggings and dark breeches and vest, covered by a navy jacket with decorated lapels. He does not smile but seems purposed on business rather than a social visit. Maps are open across a table which stands in front of a wall of windows in the stern of the ship. He coughs and clears his throat before inviting Ana to sit down. She sits in one of two armchairs, noticing a Bible on the table next to her.

"Miss Ana," he says and continues in Spanish, "the circumstances of the ship demand that you will be required to inhabit a small cabin with two girls from the Sandwich Islands. They were kidnapped by the crew of an American merchant ship and their captain requested they be returned to their home on our indirect route to the North. I am afraid that the cramped quarters are unavoidable, and perhaps you can create an agreeable situation there. Nevertheless, the arrangement is only temporary."

"Thank you, Captain Vancouver. I appreciate your taking time to speak with me."

"Now, is there anything you need or questions you may have?"

She grips the chair, feeling movement beneath her. "I wonder if I might bring my falcon on deck for fresh air and to practice using his wings."

"Only if the seas and weather are favorable," he smiles at last. "Otherwise, the open deck is a most dangerous place," he lowers his forehead at her to emphasize the seriousness of his statement. "This requirement is an element of protection with which I must be unwavering in that your welfare is of concern."

"Yes sir."

"Also, many languages are spoken on this ship, Ana. Perhaps this voyage will afford you the opportunity to add another language or two to your repertoire. If you find that you have need of some essential service, please request the attention of my steward, Mr. Bonner."

As Mr. Bonner leads Ana back to her room, she is still aware of the rocking of the ship and a growing headache. She tries to distract herself by focusing on the copper curls that float on the back of his collar. Grateful to return to her bed, she's overwhelmed by the constant movement and its effect on her stomach. The creaking and groaning of the wooden hull add voice to the rolling and swaying and her hand flies to her mouth.

Lili and Kawena take care of Ana for the next four days as she is sick. Despite her misery, she learns some English from the bits her roommates have gained while on the American ship. They tell her that the bells give notice to the crew when they must work on a "Watch." On the fifth day, Lili offers Ana some black tea, and it tastes good. Her stomach has calmed, and she's ready for a ship's biscuit.

Ana ventures to midship deck with her falcon in the afternoon. He fidgets as they go, even more anxious than Ana to get into fresh air. The ship cuts cleanly through the sea before a steady wind which fills the sails, and she realizes how quickly they're moving. Cautiously, she lets Falcon out of his cage, hoping he will stay low within the ship.

Once loose, Falcon flutters about and eventually manages to fly to the edge of the quarterdeck. She puts a piece of leather on her left arm that she received from the soldier at the mission, and with her right hand, holds up an injured mouse by its tail. Falcon flies to her arm and grabs the mouse in his beak. Surprised by the bird's quick response, she puts him and mouse into the cage and realizes that the ship will be a perfect place to train her bird.

"How do you do?" A crew member looks down from the rigging. His bare feet land nimbly onto the deck in front of her. He's a tall, native-looking young man dressed like an English gentleman in a double-breasted gray jacket and gray breeches, his bare feet being the only evidence of having been in the rigging. "My name is Kualelo," he smiles, bending from the waist. His endearing, friendly face is framed by black, shiny hair tied at the back of his neck.

"My name is Ana." She feels a little flutter in her chest at the sight of him and attempts a simple curtsy.

"I'm pleased to meet you," he bows again, slightly awkward. "I read about falconry in England," he motions to the bird. "How did you learn it?"

"Spanish . . . friend . . . told me," she replies in rough English, seeing light sparkles swimming in his dark eyes. "Please . . . where you are from?"

"The Sandwich Islands, our next stop. I help Dr. Menzies with plants from each port and draw pictures of them. I also interpret Polynesian languages."

"You return home?"

"Yes! You will *love* the islands," he steps closer, wanting to tell her about his home.

She steps back, holding a hand up, palm out. She knows that her conversation with this young man is inappropriate in many cultures, including Tlingit and the Spanish mission, and she won't know him long. "I will not stay. I will go north. Plants from the mission, I can help."

"Yes!" Kualelo's enthusiasm is contagious. "I would introduce you to Dr. Menzies."

Returning to her cabin, Ana realizes that her tense shoulders have loosened, she's relaxed for the first time since coming on ship, and she feels better.

The following afternoon she returns to the deck with her falcon to find that the ship has slowed, the air thick and stagnant, the sails sag. Unfiltered sun beats on deck, reflecting off the glistening back of a crewman who is strapped face-down against a rowboat that stands on its side. Red bloody welts rise on his back in ridges as he is flogged, and his groans become more like cries with each strike. It's not a new sight for Ana as it is something she saw at the mission from time to time, and the sound of each crack of the whip causes her breath to catch. She sees Mr. Bonner witnessing the punishment and asks him if she might be told what offense has been committed.

"This time, it's for disobeying orders. The crew was told to stay away from you three young ladies. Evidently, he had relations with Miss Kawena last night."

"Oh!" Ana puts her hand to her mouth with embarrassment.

"No one should come to your cabin except the captain, Dr. Menzies, or me," Mr. Bonner explains. "If anyone else tries, report it to me. It's the only way to keep order on a ship."

Ana returns to her cabin and reaches for her Bible for the first time. She prays for Kawena and Lili as well as for Captain Vancouver and Mr. Bonner and Kualelo, and everyone at home causing her to feel dreary and tearful, missing her family and friends. She holds the small wooden cross that hangs from her neck—a gift from the padre. "It will help you know that you are never alone," he had promised.

Ana is impatient for afternoon to arrive. Even so, she tries to concentrate on her task when she goes on deck, using mice from the hold of the ship for Falcon to hunt, not allowing herself to look for Kualelo. When she sees him watching, her heart flutters like a loose sail.

"Your falcon makes progress."

The smooth tenor of his voice washes over her, caressing her neck, and she shows him the dimple on her right cheek.

"I think," Kualelo continues, "the goal is to have the bird bring its catch to *you*, for *your* food."

She removes a lock of her hair that's blown across her face. "I'm just teaching him how to hunt, like a mother. I want him to be free one day, when he's ready. I hope he'll always be my friend."

Kualelo leans against the railing. "Our People believe that animal spirits are messengers."

"The People of my birth also believe we can learn from them." The nearness of him makes her feel giddy. "Would you like to hold him?"

"If he won't mind." Kualelo keeps his eyes on Ana rather than on the bird.

Ana transfers the leather arm-cover and Falcon to Kualelo's arm. The bird is uneasy, moving his weight from one foot to the other. Ana smells Kualelo's scent and it lights up her body like full moon ripples on the crests of a chilly stream, something she's never felt before. "He trusts you," she whispers.

"I'm a very trustworthy person," he murmurs, searching her eyes.

A cough alerts Ana of an audience, and she turns to see Captain Vancouver. "Miss Ana, Dr. Menzies would appreciate your attendance in his cabin to assist him in identifying a few plants from your Spanish mission. May I introduce you?"

Face flushed, she lowers her eyes and curtsies, "Of course, captain."

Kualelo stands in the crow's nest high above deck, his toes curl over the edge of the platform as it sways back and forth in the setting sun. He has smelled home the past few days, the richness of earth, the sweetness of growing things, the perfume of plumeria. This morning he saw a hibiscus blossom floating.

The descending sunlight glitters off the water, creating a golden path for the ship to travel. He looks beyond to the western horizon, hoping for home and waiting for the green flash that will appear with the final moment of light. At the flash, he sees the top of the volcano Mauna Kea (White Mountain) just under 14,000 feet.

"Home!" he shouts, "Home! Land Ahoy!" and he scrambles back down the rigging to find Ana.

10

Goots-kay-yu Kwan (Cloud-Face Tribe)

A rough, dirty hand covers Ut-kart-ee's mouth, stifling her scream. She bites hard to stop his member from ramming into her insides between her legs.

"Oche! Ye bitch!" He knocks her out with his fist.

"Hell, Hughes. Why din't ya get a young one like I told ya? They don't fight so much, and now this one's damaged."

"This one was handy and she din't have one of those flapping-plate things in her mouth. Next time get yer own. Let me finish, will ya?" Hughes carries on, wishing she'd been younger.

When Lee enters her for his turn, Ut-kart-ee comes to. She plays dead, slipping her hand behind her back as he lifts his hips for another plunge. She pulls the knife from the back of her waist and opens her eyes as she buries it into the man's side. Looking into his startled eyes, she pulls the knife deep through his flesh toward the front of his belly as he jerks away.

"Aargh, she gut me!"

Ut-kart-ee rolls away and growls like Wolf as she sprints through the bushes and into the woods to get away. She will not be followed home to Raven Clan House.

Lee's exertion pushes his hot innards out through his cut belly like a baby being born. It steams on the ground, and the foul stench sends Hughes racing through the berry bushes. He hears Lee moan behind him, "Oh God, I'm dead" and begin to cry.

Hughes sees his ship's first mate on the beach and cries out, "Lee's been killed!"

They slash through the bush to find Lee still alive, lying in a pool of blood and mess, looking gray.

"I told you men to keep it in your pants!"

"Just hav'n a little fun," Hughes mumbles to his shoes.

The first-mate squats between Lee's face and his destroyed gut and holds his hand. "At least you can die among your own people," he consoles. "Two of you," he motions to the crew, "stay with him until he's done and stay alert; and you, Hughes, you stay too. You're partly responsible for this. Fire your weapon if there's trouble."

Ut-kart-ee hides, blending into the forest, huddled in the safety of tall salal bushes. She rubs her face on the wet, waxy leaves, trying to rid herself of the foreigner's stench and uses her own urine to erase their venom. It's only when she remembers the alarmed look on the face of her attacker when she cut him and the feel of the knife cutting through his flesh that she feels better, stronger, not such a victim, and she's able to quiet herself.

At dusk, on still-trembling legs, she sneaks to the stream to wash. When she reaches Raven Clan House, she tells a slave to secretly bring her husband outside.

Chark Cough-ye gives her an immediate hug, feeling her shiver. "Your clothes are wet! Where were you?"

"I was attacked by Cloud-Face," she whispers, her face a tight grimace. "Two raped me. I cut one, but the other will talk. I think we're in trouble," she begins to cry.

"Whaaat?" he growls.

"Shush! I don't want others to know!"

"How hurt are you?" he looks at the swollen side of her face.

She whimpers, moving her hand to her face, wanting him to hold her, warm her, keep her from collapsing.

"Where did it happen?"

"Wolf Clan huckleberry patch. Maybe I shouldn't have been there alone."

"On Wolf Clan property? You go inside to the fire and the children."

Later in the night, Chark Cough-ye, A-kadi, and Kookenaa move silently through the woods and simultaneously from behind, cut the throats of the three men standing guard, returning to their homes, a small amount of balance restored.

People are just beginning their day when a deafening *"kerboom!"* sounds, and a wall of Raven Clan House is crushed, sending debris into the air. The screams of a mother are heard as she carries her baby, unmoving, from the wreckage. At first people think that Thunderbird has arrived, then realize it has come from the ship in the bay.

Three small boats, ten sailors in each, come ashore, firearms at the ready, and stand on the beach, waiting.

Leaders Takl-eesh of Raven Clan and A-kadi of Wolf Clan come to meet them. They are dressed in their armor decorated in clan crests and carry their weapons of war, bows with arrows, spears, daggers and clubs. Fifty men walk behind each of them, also with weapons, followed by nephews and about thirty slaves.

"You are not welcome here," A-kadi announces menacingly, staring through his Wolf mask. He leans forward with his spear as if poised to attack, his long, double-edged dagger glistening at his waist.

"Four of my men are dead," the first mate accuses.

"They had no permission to be here."

"I want the ones who did the killing."

Takl-eesh speaks up. "As you were told, you are not welcome here. Come back at dusk and we will talk."

The first mate sees that the crowd of natives continues to grow, getting close to a hundred and more still come. He decides to return later.

Emergency Council is called, and discussion is mixed. "We can't win against their weapons and if we don't trade with Cloud-Face Tribes," a Hawk Clan leader advises "we will lose our wealth, become vulnerable to other clans."

"Would you have us be *used* by these Cloud-Face?" A-kadi drives his spear into the ground. "Stand up to them! There are others more trustworthy than these foul slime! They have no honor!"

At dusk, every able man in An-ar-kark wears his fiercest looking war-armor garments with wooden mask or hat in the shape of a menacing animal, many with embedded teeth and hair. Each carries weapons and walks with determination behind the clan leaders to meet the Cloud-Face Tribe.

"I want the female who was in the Wolf Clan huckleberry patch yesterday to pay for my man who died by her knife," the first mate declares, "and I want three of your men killed in exchange for my three whose throats were cut."

Seeing both A-kadi and Chark Cough-ye bristle, Takl-eesh asks, "Who told you it was a Wolf Clan berry patch?"

The first mate's eyes glance at Yahaayi, the gambler.

Frustrated with the talk, A-kadi steps forward. "We give you four men for the four who were killed." He motions and four Wolf Clan slaves come forward. "Do what you will with them, but it seems they would benefit you more through work rather than by dying. Now how will you compensate us for the death of a child, the rape of a woman, and the damage to Raven Clan House?"

The first mate looks taken aback while the People are encouraged, looking strong. Power is felt among them and the murmurs begin, moving the crowd forward. "I must talk with the captain," he stammers.

"The agreement was to talk now!" A-kadi roars. "You will give us two hands of your iron weapons that smoke in exchange for the wrongs done to our People!" His eyes are on their weapons that smoke.

"I must ask the captain," the first mate repeats, then backs away, returning to ship.

That night in their furs, Chark Cough-ye tries to hold his

wife and she hardens herself, moving away, fighting against the memory of her violators, their stink, foul breathe, hard hands, the abuse. Chark Cough-ye wrestles with what he should do and decides to give her more time. "I'm here if you need me," he whispers.

By morning, the ship is gone. The People will remember the unpaid debt. For the sake of balance, a Raven Clan man takes the first mate's name for his own so that each time his name "First Mate" is spoken, the unpaid debt will be remembered, and the offender will be shamed.

Chark Cough-ye carries furs and leads Ut-kart-ee into the dense woods below a dark-emerald canopy. It's silent, the forest creatures unsure of the intruders' intent. He extends his warm, familiar hand, "Come to me."

"I can't," she whispers, looking away.

He moves slowly, as if she's a deer that might spook and stands in front of her. Gently he wraps his arms around her, touching her just lightly. She tenses, and he remains, unmoving. Taking his time, he gradually closes his embrace to hold her tightly. Her breath becomes ragged, still he is unyielding and patient. The tears begin and she sobs and screams and pounds out her rage using her fists onto his chest, releasing the fury that she has held back since her abuse. When she tires and stops, he continues to hold her, steady like rock. Her senses fill with the warmth of his first touch, she feels his steady heartbeat, smells his familiar scent, and gradually, she relaxes into him.

They move to the furs and he kisses her bruised face. His hands touch her tenderly like butterfly wings, like a misty rain. He finds more bruises and softly kisses each one. Looking into her eyes, he sees that her pain is further away, and he kisses her tears. "I love you. I will always love you. You are safe." As they come together, she cries; she loves him, and she is so thankful for him.

He listens to her breathing. Slowly, it deepens into sleep, and he sleeps. The forest creatures resume their daily tasks and happy talk. With a jerk and a gasp, she wakes, having stabbed her abuser in her dream. When she realizes where she is, she snuggles into her husband, his chest warm against her backbone. He hears her sigh.

"Are you better?"

"Yes." She turns to kiss his mouth.

He lifts his head, "Would you know my thoughts right now?" She looks at his face, waiting.

"Ow!" he rubs his chest. "If you need comfort in the future, let me put on my armor first!" Then he receives the beautiful smile and dimple that he was hoping to see.

As she drifts back to sleep, her heartbeat slows, blending with the pulse of the earth, and her strength is slowly renewed.

Sparkling spots of sunlight travel the water with Do'ok. Where the clouds part, the light brightens the red Wolf ears and Black Bear claws painted on the side of his canoe. He paddles toward Naakee-ann to learn about the Cloud-Face Tribe there, and he also hopes to see K'aan-at-shi at Frog Clan House. After he arrives and settles in with his in-laws at the main fire that night, he sees her. She smiles at him over one shoulder, and he thanks the spirits for her.

The next morning, clan leaders tell him that the Cloud-Face Tribes are becoming disrespectful. One of the house leaders was held captive on a ship until Frog Clan could provide enough sea otter skins to buy him back. Also, there is a camp further north near the Aleut. All the young Aleut women are penned together as prisoners while the men are forced to hunt sea otter all day under the threat of their daughters being hurt. They treat people like slaves, even their own people.

"I have spoken to Baranov, the Russian Cloud-Face leader," Gull Clan leader explains, "and have told him the location of the fishing and hunting areas of our People. He still sends his Aleut slaves everywhere to kill the sea otter and to fish and hunt in *our* areas."

In An-ar-kark, clan leaders discuss what to do. Word has come from the south that some clans and tribes there, including the Haida, are beginning to attack and kill the invaders, take their weapons that smoke, because of their disrespect.

"If we don't compete through trade," Takl-eesh begins, "we'll need to go on raids to protect ourselves economically. That will generate more raids on us."

"The Cloud-Face want sea otter skins," A-kadi says, "and we need weapons that smoke to protect ourselves. Our only choice is to hunt the otters."

"Otter is a powerful spirit animal," Wolf Clan Shaman offers. "Magic is easy for it, which also makes it dangerous to hunt. I can perform spells to protect you, but my wife won't like it since I'll need to stay out of her bed."

"Maybe she won't mind all that much," A-kadi smirks.

Prepared with sea otter skins, A-kadi leads other clans to meet a new ship that waits in the bay. He stands in his long war canoe stretching his hands to the sky, asking Spirit Above to protect him and guide him in trade with this Cloud-Face Tribe. He calls out an elaborate speech, telling the captain that Wolf Clan is ferocious and fair, and he shows good faith by sharing a song from his ancestors. Trade continues for several days.

On the last day, a warm, sun-filled afternoon, some Cloud-Face lie on the beach, nearly naked, their washed laundry moving in the breeze. As the rum flows freely, young Tlingit boys move silently around them, and when the sun gets lower and the air chills, the Cloud-Face stir from their slumber and look for their clothes.

On ship, the captain sees no humor in their story. "Did you think you were in your own yard back home? You idiots should have had a sentry standing guard!" As he heads toward the shore boats and they follow, he stops them. "Not *you!* I'm not taking *you*, stark-naked and shivering! I want men with clothes! Men who stayed on ship!"

Once organized, they hurry down the beach, storm into the largest house in An-ar-kark, and grab A-kadi. Weapons drawn, the captain announces, "We take this chief in exchange for the clothes that were stolen. If they are not returned quickly, he will become our slave . . . or killed."

A gun pointed at A-kadi's head, Wolf Clan is afraid to act, and he is taken. The young offenders come running, laundry in their arms, crying, "It was to be a joke!" and the clothes are immediately taken to the ship by canoe. It's too late, A-kadi is already aboard.

The captain is angry and wants the natives to know that he and his kind are superior, so while the laundry sits in a canoe next to the ship, A-kadi is put into chains. "Put him on the quarterdeck where everyone can see," the captain orders. His arms and legs are stretched wide, and he is whipped with the cat-of-nine-tails, nine lengths of rope tied together, each two feet long, each knotted three times, hardened and sharpened in dried tar and fitted with musket balls, bruising and cutting with each stroke, ten times.

A-kadi endures, like rock, earning honor for himself and his ancestors. Ridged welts and vertical, ragged tears cause his back to run red as if a mountain lion has cleaned its claws there. Crew members stand back to avoid tiny shreds of flesh and blood as it flies, so engaged with the vengeful show that they don't notice large war canoes surrounding them.

Not satisfied, the captain grabs his knife planning to shame him by cutting A-kadi's hair. At that moment, a torn, scarred face comes up from over the side of the ship, a knife between his teeth.

Warrior Chark Cough-ye climbs up over the side, his club Latseen at his waist, and others follow. The captain is killed with a knife to the throat, and many of his crew are killed or wounded before A-kadi can be released from his chains. Women and younger nephews who have been minding the war canoes retrieve the wounded and dying who fall into the water. Chark Cough-ye helps A-kadi to a canoe and signals with a Raven call for the others to follow as bullets continue to attack them.

The first mate and remaining able crew stand guard on ship throughout the night to put out flaming arrows that fly at them from the darkness. They shoot back, but never see their target. In the morning, they leave at high tide, looking for a new, friendlier bay or a companion ship to help them recover.

Two moons later, to the amazement of the People, the same ship returns, reinforced with new crew. Accompanying them is another ship, the ship of the "First Mate," the one with the debt to pay. This time, canoes do not visit the ships in search of trade. Instead, men put on their armor for war and paint their faces black, while women hide their children and grab their own weapons.

A ship's cannon fires, sending sand and debris exploding into the air as four small boats of Cloud-Face Tribe with guns arrive on the beach.

"Give us Claw Face," First Mate demands, pointing at Chark Cough-ye.

A-kadi's hand grips his knife. "What makes you think we would give you *anyone or anything*?" he spits. "You *owe* us weapons that smoke."

"Claw Face was involved when our men were killed in the berry patch," First Mate declares.

"And he led the attack on our ship, killing the captain and eighteen of the crew," the new captain adds. "Or we will blast this village into ruin and all of you with it. Turn him over and we'll think about letting the rest go."

A-kadi looks at the big weapons on the ship pointed at his village and the hand-held ones pointed at himself and his People. He feels the still-tender thickness of new flesh growing on his back.

Chark Cough-ye wonders how to protect the village and especially his family and clan. He lovingly smiles at Ut-kart-ee and Do'ok who stand behind him, then steps forward.

"Brother, No!" A-kadi gasps, grabbing ahold of Ut-kart-ee.

Instantly, Chark Cough-ye's hands are tied behind his back and he's put into a small boat. As he's being transported to a ship, he remembers when A-kadi was also taken to a ship and the many lives that were lost as a result. He cannot allow that to happen again.

Before they get half-way, he pushes off with his feet from the bottom of the boat and dives over the side into the sea, swimming underwater with his legs, his hands still tied behind his back. When his head breaks the surface for air, he sees canoes entering the water and hears bullets whiz nearby. He swims downward again and toward the canoes with all his strength.

The next time he comes up for breath, canoes are creating a barrier for him. His People sit on the sides of their canoes so the bottoms are up, protecting them from bullets. They cut Chark Cough-ye's bindings and together, reach the beach before anyone is hurt or killed.

Chark Cough-ye runs into the woods, away from the village, hoping to draw the danger to himself and away from his People. As he waits inside the tree line to see if he will be followed, he's joined by others, including A-kadi, Do'ok, Kookenaa, and Ut-kart-ee, there to fight with him. Ut-kart-ee looks fierce, her eyes ablaze. She holds her bow in hand and her hunting knife is at her waist.

"No, wife! You cannot be here!" Chark Cough-ye grabs her arm.

"I *must* be here!" she shrieks, "Where *else* could I be? If I lose you, my life is over."

He puts his face in front of hers, nose to nose, eyes to eyes, "If you ever listen to me, hear me now! Your *duty* is to raise our family. Mine is to protect *you!*"

She throws her arms around his neck, *"I will not . . .!"*

"What of our son, Do'ok? Will you have him die trying to protect you?"

"Then we all die together!" she argues, readying her bow.

"You stay behind that group of trees," he points, "and watch over Do'ok!" To his friends, "This fight cannot be won against their weapons! Protect yourselves! Go back to the village! Hide! Do not fight!" and he runs into the forest.

As the Cloud-Face Tribe enters the forest, they hear Chark Cough-ye's call of the Raven telling them which way to go and they continue their pursuit. He runs and ducks behind trees, wanting them to follow. He leads them far into the deep woods and across a river, away from the village, thinking that if he can get them spread out enough behind him, he may be able to circle back undetected and deal with them individually.

He reaches the base of the mountains and discovers that a rockslide has removed the brush that he had planned to use as cover. Nowhere to hide, he falls under a torrent of bullets and grabs at the mud beneath him. He slithers to a fallen log and burrows beneath it out of sight, but when he hears the screams and shrieks of his People nearby and knows they didn't hide like he told them to, he can't stay while they are being attacked. His

Warrior-self rises to the fight, knife in hand to defend his People. Six bullets immediately plunge into his chest and back, yet he charges his nearest enemy and they fall together, Chark Cough-ye's knife turning through flesh.

Left by his pursuers to die, the actions around him begin to slow and fade into the distance. He gazes at his beautiful world and wonders if he has already passed into spirit. It is perfect here. The dark-green tree limbs wave in the breeze, and he listens to the forest tell its stories in the tittering tweets of its creatures. He knows that his soul, as Warrior, will go directly to the sky before cremation, and he will light the fires of the Northern Lights and watch over his People to warn them of war. He is glad that he is a Warrior if he must die. He hears an eagle call in the distance. Slowly, his eyes close on his vision of Ut-kart-ee's and Do'ok's tearful faces, and even the wailing of his wife cannot keep his heart beating.

An-ar-kark is in turmoil. Ut-kart-ee moves numbly and methodically through her days as if in a trance, hanging onto her husband's last words, "Your duty is to care for our family." She clings to the vision she creates in her mind of him holding their first-born daughter in his arms in the Land of the Dead and smiling down into her tiny baby face. She refuses to cry, knowing that her tears would make a wet trail for her husband, and she wants him to have an easy, dry path, the only gift she can give him now.

At night, she watches the sky, singing her heart song to him, the breath of her spirit rising to meet his. When at last she sees the rays of iridescent green and blue, she knows that he has climbed the rainbow to his Warrior Home and is lighting the fires there. In time, her grief expands, and her life spirit dissolves like a drop of blueberry juice in the sea.

Tinx brings a bentwood cedar box and opens it to pull a shimmering, full-length white robe out by its shoulders, hoping it will bring Ut-kart-ee comfort. "My brother ordered this for you before he died," Tinx explains. "He wanted it to be white to show his love and to remind you of your strength, not anyone can wear an all-white robe after all . . . The eagle feathers are to remind you of him."

"Killed by Cloud-Face." Ut-kart-ee slurs as if distracted, "He flies now . . . in the sky." Her fingers gently stroke down the length of white swan feathers, across several horizontal rows of brown eagle feathers, with fluffy, white down sewn between, and her eyes cloud with tears. When her fingers stop, Tinx carefully returns the robe to its box.

Do'ok comes the next morning. Ut-kart-ee has become so consumed by her loss that she has trouble focusing on his face. She knows that he also suffers from the death of his father.

"Mother," Do'ok speaks quietly. "I need to know what it means to be a twin. The Shaman called me a twin, and I'm afraid to ask him or anyone else what it means."

Ut-kart-ee can hear the fear in his voice. "It means, my dear son, that when I gave birth to you, I gave birth to another at the same time. The baby was a girl, your sister," she blinks through watery eyes. "She was put into the forest when she was born, against my will. They would take you too, but I would not let go of you."

Do'ok is silent, trying to understand. "I was not supposed to live?"

"I'm sorry, son. I wish I could save you from this knowledge forever," she reaches for his hand.

Do'ok pulls away. "Am I *kush-tar-ka*, bad luck?"

"I do not believe that."

"Is this why we lived in the small house instead of Raven Clan House? Was it to keep me away from others? To *protect them* from me?" His dread grows as he gains understanding. "Is this why you and father worked harder and created more wealth than any other family? To keep the People from challenging your decision to keep me alive?"

"Do'ok, you are strong and smart and worth every breath. I would do it all again many bundles of times if I needed to, just to be able to know you. Your father was, we are proud of who you are."

He stands, looking at the floor, weaving together this new understanding with the memory of his childhood, his isolation, the discomfort he seemed to cause other children, even adults, his treatment by the Shaman, and he realizes that everyone knew except him!

As he suffers with this new awareness, she feels powerless to help him fight the battle. "You are loved," is the best she can offer.

"I'm sorry, mother. I'm sorry for everything . . . maybe you should have let me die too."

11

Chief Kamehameha, The Lonely One, 1794

A conch is blown in Kealakekua Bay, announcing the arrival of a massive, double-hull canoe which streaks around *Discovery* like a fast-swimming shark, 25 paddlers pulling in quick, rhythmic motion, overturning many smaller canoes in its way. Chief Kamehameha stands tall on the platform in the middle of the canoe, yellow feathers of his long royal cloak and matching feathered helmet ruffle with the breeze. Braced in front of him stands a tall guard holding upright his eight-foot royal standard of feathers, also yellow, that designates Kamehameha as *ali'i nui*, the highest chief of the island Hawai'i, largest of the Sandwich Islands.

In her own canoe, Queen Ka'ahumanu, endures the chaos of his wake and waits as Kamehameha's seven-foot frame ascends

Discovery's ladder without waiting for permission to board. She sees him stand proudly on deck, towering above the foreigners as some of his priests dressed in white, lesser chiefs in red and yellow capes, and guards and attendants in loincloths parade up the ladder to join him.

Captain Vancouver alerts his officers to have guns secretly ready and greets the chief warmly. "Kamehameha, welcome to *Discovery*. It is good to see you again. We are honored by your visit," he bows slightly to the much taller man. "Your royal cloak is stunning."

"*E Komo Mai*," he replies, relaxing his face into a dignified smile. "Welcome to the waters of my Island of Hawai'i. I am happy that you return, Vancouver. You are welcome here as long as you and your men follow our *kapus*, taboos. Do not leave the ship without my permission. I believe your country is one we can trust, and I wish to know you as friends."

He takes Vancouver's hand and leads him to the leeward side of the ship. "See that I bring you many hogs, fresh food and water. You will not want to trade with anyone else since I have all that you desire."

Vancouver sees ten large canoes filled with fat hogs happily munching taro root and many additional canoes loaded with produce and large gourds of drinking water. "*Mahalo*, Chief Kamehameha. This is most generous of you. We are grateful for your welcome and friendly attention. I also have gifts for you, and may I say that your English is excellent!"

"I have been learning from my interpreter here, John Young," he grins, indicating the Englishman behind him.

"Mr. Young?" Vancouver extends his hand wondering about his story.

Kamehameha motions to his favorite wife in her canoe. She comes slowly at first, showing that she's perturbed at being left behind. Gracefully, she steps onto the deck, and all on ship become silent, impressed with her six-foot beauty. She wears a skirt of multiple layers of *tapa* cloth reserved for royalty, made from beaten paper mulberry tree bark. It's dyed orange and wrapped around her waist several times, draping down to her knees. A royal necklace "Speaks with Authority" is thick around her neck, thousands of strands of braided human hair with a whale tooth protruding from its center.

The necklace reminds Kamehameha of her fierceness as an eight-year-old when her father wore the same necklace handed down through generations of royalty. He was taken captive by a cousin. She came to his aid on the back of the warrior servant, Pahia, arriving the same time as Kamehameha, just as the attacker was about to cut her father's throat. He hesitated, not wanting to get blood on the sacred necklace which gave Pahia time to throw a stone from his sling and knock the attacker back, allowing her father to cut his attacker's throat instead.

"This is Ka'ahumanu," he announces with pride, "my *ku'u 'i'ini*, my heart's desire."

"Welcome to *Discovery*, Queen Ka'ahumanu. It is a privilege to meet you."

Ana is miserable, standing in the shadow of the stairs that lead to her cabin, watching. Normally, she would be enchanted by the dress and dignity of the people she sees, but she's numb, cloaked in the memory and loss of Kualelo, gone to his home on

Molokai. She remembers when he kissed each of her hands and held them together against his chest, feeling his dark eyes penetrate hers when he had asked her to come with him. She knew that Captain Vancouver would forbid it. He would remind her of her duty, his obligation to deliver her to the North. Her grief is stronger than her curiosity.

As the conversations with islanders continue on ship, the sun descends towards the horizon, painting the sea in golden strokes of light. With a reminder of kapu at dusk, they rush to their canoes, many diving overboard to get home in time.

Kamehameha speaks to Vancouver just before he leaves. "It is the season of Lono, the god of fertility and the Makahiki Harvest Festival. Life now is all about games, no work, no war, but we do have war *games*," he grins broadly, reminding Vancouver of the twenty-year old he met years before. "The priests have collected taxes, so now it is play, hula, sports, and feasting. I will take you to the games tomorrow. You will like it."

Ana peers over the side when the islanders leave, watching naked swimmers climb into outrigger canoes. She sees Queen Ka'ahumanu turn in the canoe to look at her. Ana immediately looks away, intimidated by her regal manner.

Kamehameha arrives in the morning dressed in loincloth and a red and yellow feather cape and helmet to preside over the games. Vancouver presents him with five cows, two ewes and a ram and asks that a kapu be placed on butchering for ten years to give the animals a chance to reproduce, and that in ten years' time, the meat would also be available to women. After some thought, Kamehameha agrees, but says that women will still not be allowed to eat pork or to eat in the same room or from the same *imu* underground oven as men. He uses his canoes to deliver the animals to the beach. They bolt wildly into the crowd as the islanders scream and run and the crew roll in laughter.

At the games, spectators line the field. Kamehameha is joined by other chiefs and he introduces Vancouver to his cousin, Kamanawa, and then to the identical twin, Kame'eiamoku. "Kame'eiamoku is the one who brought us my interpreter Mr. Young," he explains. "These twin brothers are called *ni'aupi'o*, sacred twins, because their parents are brother and sister which keeps their royal bloodline pure."

Vancouver is aware of European royals who marry their siblings to keep a pure bloodline, so is not surprised.

One hundred fifty men along with a few women gather on a large field, separated into two armies. Kamehameha calls out prayers to war god Ku and reminds his warriors of their training: "Be brave, be strong and able, be lithe and quick, use the power of Ku! Stare fiercely and show the whites of your eyes!"

Ooro, one of Kamehameha's officers, steps forward snarling and showing teeth like an angry shark as if to demonstrate the words of his chief. He stomps to the middle of the field in a loin cloth with thick matting as armor around his torso and a short red-feather cape over his left shoulder for protection. A feathered helmet raised above his skull provides protection from sling stones. His chest is tattooed above his body armor, looking like smiling mouths. Dots and lines decorate his chin, right eye and forehead. He wears a necklace of shark teeth, bringing the spirit of Shark with him.

Carrying a heavy, five-foot long spear, he bulges his eyes, showing the whites. His muscles quiver as he lifts the weapon over his shoulder and throws it with such power that it sings, whirring through the air like an arrow from a bow. His opponents are able to dodge it and knock it away, and more spears are returned. The war has begun, spears flying in both directions, warriors dip and spin.

Kamehameha explains that if it were a real battle, Ku would require a human sacrifice and the ferocious wooden image of Ku, with a mouthful of dog teeth, would be carried onto the battlefield.

As more and more bloody injuries maim the fighters, Vancouver becomes concerned. Suddenly, Kamehameha stands, strips to his loincloth and runs into the middle of the battle, showing the whites of his eyes. Instantly, six spears fly directly at him with full force. He dances away from three, catches two, using one to knock the next spear away, and turns the other around to send it flying back to the other side. Kamehameha is clearly comfortable on the battlefield.

Vancouver is surprised that fighters throw spears at their leader, but Young tells him that they also ambush him sometimes. It helps him keep his skills sharp.

They wait for hula to begin and Vancouver visits with the two Americans, Isaac Davis and John Young. He learns that Davis is the sole survivor of the trading schooner *Fair American*. "The rest were killed by Chief Kame'eiamoku over there," Davis says nodding toward one of the twins. "Our captain was only 18 years old. It was his father, captain of the *Eleanor*, who got it started. He killed a hundred islanders because they stole a skiff, and Chief Kame'eiamoku put a stop to it. I was injured, nearly died, but Kamehameha honored my bravery and had me nursed back to health. Young here," he looks to his friend the interpreter, "he was the bosun, senior crewman on the *Eleanor*. "They left him behind in such a hurry to get away."

"I became Kamehameha's artillery trainer," Young joins in. "We stopped trying to escape a while ago. Actually," he looks toward the chief, "he treats us well. I have property now and two high-status wives to keep me happy," he grins. "In fact, one of them is his niece!"

"I am glad you're here," Vancouver replies. "He has the qualities of a great leader. If he could get the chiefs of each island to talk together, he could provide stability and even prosperity for all the islands. They could stop killing each other."

Two hundred women and men kneel, dressed in a variety of dance regalia, ready to perform hula. Chants begin, voices without music, rhythm provided by a wooden dance drum. Another drummer joins with two gourds glued together, sides tapped alternately with fingers and palm and then pounding down onto folded tapa on the ground. Torsos sway, an ocean of four hundred arms float gracefully above shoulders, hands undulating like the seaweed in water, making waves in the air.

Kamehameha explains that hula is to tell a story or honor a god or a chief. "This hula is to honor 'The Captive Princess.' She is my sacred wife, Keopuolani, who is of the purest blood line and highest lineage in the islands, a direct descendent from the gods. She was captive because when she was eleven, I kidnapped her and her grandmother and hid them until she was old enough for me to marry. Her royal grandmother thought I would be *ali'i nui,* high chief, someday, and so she gave her blessing to our marriage before she died. I removed my teeth to mourn her death," he smiles large, showing holes where his eye teeth used to be in an otherwise perfect mouth.

At least he didn't take an eye out, Vancouver thinks to himself, having also seen that result from an act of mourning during his previous visit.

Sixteen dancers wearing golden tapa skirts stand to perform for entertainment. They wear green fern *leis* around their necks and on their heads and hold gourd rattles decorated in short white and long red feathers. The dancers' legs are wrapped in netting of white feathers below their knees. Drums begin and hips sway back and forth slowly, smoothly, invitingly, as they dance. They shake their rattles as they step and turn, step and turn, causing the long red feathers to take flight, flowing with each turn. Hips dip and roll voluptuously, enticingly, like a rolling wave, ankles and knees bend and twist, white leg feathers fluff. Suddenly, drumbeats grow louder and faster, more excited. Smooth moves become rapid vibrations and violent jerks. Again and again grass skirts turn, feathers ripple, hips seem unhinged, the beat is frantic . . . Suddenly, it stops. Looking slightly flushed, Vancouver stands to applaud.

The before-sunset feast for men, cooked by men in their underground *imu* ovens, is delicious, kalua pork, roasted fish, sweet potato, poi, bananas, coconuts. They relax to talk story as the sun melts into the horizon, announcing the arrival of a blue moon, the second full moon of the month. The intensity of wave action explodes, causing tremendous crashing on beaches and rocks, and crimson light streaks the sky.

"Will you tell me why you were known as 'The Lonely One'

when you were a boy?" Vancouver asks. "Someone as charming and intelligent as you must have had many friends."

Kamehameha smiles. "I was taken at birth and lived alone where my father thought I would be safe, thus, 'the lonely one.' You see, there was a prophecy that a child would be born to unite the islands, and when I was born, a great star soared over my birthplace. So they thought I might be the one." He pauses, looking at Vancouver intently, "I *am* the one, you know . . . Then my uncle began training me as a warrior chief of Ku. There were 800 of us in training, so not lonely anymore," he laughs. "And a few years ago when my cousin brought an army to take my land, Madame Pele intervened. She erupted Kilauea and killed them, so I *am* the one. Madame Pele has spoken."

"And your cousin? He died in the volcano?"

"He survived the volcano. Queen Ka'ahumanu's father killed him for me."

From the ship, Ana marvels at the islanders who ride boards on the waves. She's never imagined such a playground, having lived a life of constant work and prayer. She breathes the warm fragrant air and continues to watch.

"Ana." She turns to see Captain Vancouver standing behind her. "I imagine you would like to get off ship for at least a short time."

"I'm not sure, captain," her eyes fill with tears. "It's more and more difficult to say goodbye to people."

"It might be good for you to have a job to do and walk on solid ground. You still have a long voyage ahead. Dr. Menzies will be onshore to work with plant samples, and you could help him, especially since Kualelo is no longer with us."

Her heart pinches at '*Kualelo*.'

Flashes of morning sun bounce off waves, momentarily blinding her as she and Mr. Whidbey are rowed to shore. He laughs, motioning toward people standing near shore, beating the water with vines of morning glory. "They are hoping the water spirits will make waves for their surfing," he shakes his head. "It's too flat for them today, but *we* like it that way . . . flat as flat could be works best for me," he smiles, using the same tempo as the crew's rowing.

Ana steps on shore and finds she can't walk properly. Her feet and legs expect the ground to move with the up and down of the ocean, and she tries to walk on steps of air, putting out her hands in case she should fall.

Dr. Menzies comes to meet them and chuckles. "It will come in time, lass."

She follows along the beach to the left of the village of rectangular houses that are thatched in clusters of skinny pili grass. They continue to the observatory of several tents and shelters created by Mr. Whidbey. He tells her they are not allowed to go into the village and their observatory is kapu to the villagers.

As she works, she learns that Dr. Menzies was the botanist for the laird of the Menzies Clan in Scotland before he earned his medical degree as a surgeon. "Do you miss home?" she asks. A breeze comes up, causing a tired orange blossom from the nearest kou tree to plop onto the ground.

"There's plenty of time ta go home, see'n the world's the thing for me. You?"

"I'm not sure where home is. I grew up in the mission but felt connected to the Ohlone People," she says wistfully, thinking of Sezen and Chusen.

Dr. Menzies assigns each specimen a number and writes its information into his field book, then Ana prepares it for the wood-frame plant press. "Flat, wee samples go straight into the folded paper to take out the moisture," Dr. Menzies instructs. "Fold or cut the others or slice it if it's too thick." She enjoys the precision of his sharp slicing knives and grows content with her work as the warm breeze caresses her skin and the rhythm of the surf calms her heart.

That evening on ship, she asks the steward Mr. Bonner if he might assist her in obtaining a local skirt since her deerskin-tule skirt is too warm. In the morning, he presents her with a skirt made of ti leaves attached to a braided line for her waist. "They believe the ti plant keeps evil spirits away," he grins. She likes the green scent of the thick layers of leaves and continues to wear her bodice, having learned modesty at the mission.

Ana brings Falcon to the beach, and children gather at a distance to see the curiosity. She lets him hunt, flying higher and higher, circling overhead, and diving a U shape several times before killing the rat she releases. The children talk among themselves as they walk away, looking back over their shoulders at her.

Dr. Menzies bends over his specimens. "They might think you're a witch."

"A what!?"

He straightens up. "Because lass, to them, the only reason t' have a bird in a cage would be for its pretty feathers, for making royal garments and such, and it looks like you've mind control over a bird, so their best explanation would be witchcraft. Try to get the next samples set for the press 'fore they start ta rot."

Ana stares at him. "So much to learn," she mumbles, thinking of her mission in the North.

From then on, Falcon hunts each evening from the ship. His talons grip the leather on her arm as he pushes off and strokes the air to gain elevation. Each time he flies, he travels slightly longer distances and his wings gain strength. Eventually, he flies further over land, sometimes finding his own rat or small bird and always returning to the only home he knows.

Ana arrives on shore one morning to work with Dr. Menzies, and someone is already there to help him. Her heart sinks, thinking she's been replaced, and as she gets closer, she sees who it is. "Kualelo!" she cries, throwing her arms around him, feeling the strength of his body.

"Ana," he breathes into her hair. "How I've missed you."

"What are you doing here?" She sees that he wears only a loincloth, his skin darker than hers now.

He smiles broadly. "I was asked to come and work here on behalf of Dr. Menzies while he goes on a trek up the Mauna Loa (Long Mountain) volcano. Also, there's terrible famine on my island, so I hope to be of use to Chief Kamehameha now that he's high chief and friends with Captain Vancouver."

"We get to work together?" she squeaks.

"Looks that way," he laughs squeezing her to his chest.

Dr. Menzies and Lieutenant Joseph Baker join a parade of more than a hundred men, mostly Hawaiian porters, and they begin their trek, each wearing a palm-leaf hat to hide from the sun. As they travel through an old lava field, Dr. Menzies notes an unusual flock of geese feeding on young grass shoots, short tufts of white feathers in stiff ridges on black necks.

"They're called Ne Ne because of the sound they make," a porter tells him. "They never leave this island and can grow very old."

At 2,000 feet, they meet the Ainapo Trail, used for sacrifices to Pele, the volcano goddess of fire, and continue their climb. Dr. Menzies stops frequently to gather plant samples and rest at several rock shelters along the way, realizing that his ship's legs are not used to climbing.

They continue through heavy, wet clouds at the mountain's mid-section where he sees one of the quarries where the adzes are created. The enormous wound in the mountainside has supplied material for tools and weapons for hundreds of years. He's thankful that they camp here and that he's brought enough Scotch to put his muscles to sleep for the night.

At the 13,000-foot summit, he breathes like a runner in a race searching for oxygen and wears everything he can for warmth. He looks out over the immense expanse of dry, barren rock of the volcano, seeing steam as it escapes between fields of snow.

Ana and Kualelo work together like two hands of the same person, rarely speaking, and the closer their bodies work, the more magnetism grows between them. Ever so gently, he brushes against her, again and again, like the warm, tropical air, making the tiny hairs on her arm stand up. It causes her breath to become more and more shallow. Clouds arriving on a new wind ruffle the plant samples and make Ana think they are the perfect example of the chaos brewing inside her as she attempts to focus on her work while craving Kualelo.

He hovers behind her, beginning to caress her waist, his warm breath on the back of her neck. She trembles, unable to work, overpowered by his attention. As her body turns itself around to press against him and he wraps his arms around her, they're interrupted by a frantic messenger who calls to them.

The runner stumbles, sucking breath as he chokes out his words.

"We're to prepare for surgery!" Kualelo interprets. "Dr. Menzies is coming with a wounded man who will need his foot amputated. We need to prepare."

Ana rips her mind from his body.

By the time they assemble the needed supplies and tools on a clean table, Dr. Menzies arrives, red-faced from sun and exertion and focused on his task. The injured man is carried on a litter, moaning, looking exhausted.

"Foot's been crushed, torn in a rockslide," Dr. Menzies breathes.

Ana grimaces at the man's foot, broken into an unusual shape more than twice its normal size, blue and purple with jagged tears down its length, oozing blood and mucous.

Kualelo gives him a large dose of rum, talking to him while it takes effect, and a crowd forms, keeping their distance because of the kapu. Ana sees a strap tied tightly above the injured foot and knows from Zesen's teaching that it's to restrict the blood flow. Dr. Menzies washes his hands and pours rum over his scalpels and the saw he will use.

"Good lad to bring the rum instead o' my prime Scottish whiskey, or we'd be forced to let the poor wee bugger go," Dr. Menzies jokes and drinks a swig, trying to steady his hand and lighten the mood. He motions to four Hawaiians who accompanied him on the trip to hold the man steady and pours rum over the ankle and into the open wounds. While the patient screams, he slices quickly with his largest scalpel around the ankle and begins to saw bone. Eventually, unconsciousness allows everyone to breathe a sigh of relief, onlookers standing in silent shock.

To the Hawaiians, Dr. Menzies becomes "the red-faced man who collects grass and cuts off limbs," and Ana becomes "the girl who talks to falcons."

12

Alexander Baranov, Russian America

In An-ar-kark, Do'ok's mind swims with the knowledge that he is a twin and should not be alive. Now he understands the reason for his isolation and his parents' drive to bring wealth to Wolf Clan. It was to encourage the Council to let him live! The idea that his People did not, do not, have never wanted him permeates his air, making it hard to breathe.

Having fasted, he takes himself into the seclusion of the forest, the only place he's ever felt comfort. Surrounded by the camouflage of trees and brush, he begins with the prayer to Ke-an-kow that he learned from his mother: "Watch over me, my Spirit Above. Help me move beyond my beginning as a twin to become worthy of Wolf Clan." He sings a song to Chark Cough-ye, his warrior father in the sky, then sits in silence.

Evening grows and the forest sounds change over to those of the night creatures as he becomes surrounded by peace. He feels the strength of this living forest and his acceptance within it. The presence of his ancestors and his father surround him like a warm blanket, and he sees the loving face of his mother who needs *his* strength now. He knows he's only alive because she demanded it, committed her life to it. The image of K'aan-at-shi appears, hair glistening in firelight. She's the one he hopes to spend his life with, and she's the one who causes him to begin to imagine a future.

He looks up to the night sky before sleep to see Bear and remembers the warrior power of his father as he fought the bear, willing that strength for himself and vowing to be honorable like he was when he saved their village from the Cloud-Face Tribe. He realizes that the teachings of his ancestors through his family and his isolated childhood have actually worked together to make him solid and strong, like rock, and he will thank his mother for her gift of life and her many sacrifices that have kept him alive.

After returning to Wolf Clan House and hearing stories of Russian Cloud-Face abuse, he slips through the tide toward Frog Clan to check on K'aan-at-shi. He's known the urge to search for someone like K'aan-at-shi all his life. Now he wonders if it was the spirit of his twin that called him. As his canoe moves silently through the water, he sees a large gray wolf loping along the shoreline, looking in his direction, and he remembers Wolf's protection during the bear attack. It causes him to think of his father.

"Will you come with me, father? So I am not alone? Mother

would *never* let me go if she knew." He watches the drips drop from the end of his paddle and the shore becomes a blur as he listens to the silence inside the ocean talk, receiving a vision of himself as Wolf, still and silent, invisible in the camouflage of the forest. It leaves him feeling cautious.

The village is quiet. He's not greeted by his in-laws when he arrives at Naakee-ann, and he wonders if they are captives . . . or dead, eventually finding some elders with small children inside a home. "Grandfather, where are your people?"

"Our young were stolen from our berry patches and fishing areas, taken by the Russian Cloud-Face," Grandfather sighs, shaking his head. "We were poking at their nest, scaring away sea otter before the Aleut slaves could hunt them in their skin boats."

"They say we can get our children back if we stop," Grandmother whispers.

"The others are at summer camps, discussing what to do. They can't stay forever." The wrinkles of his face deepen, "There's fishing and processing to do, the weather's getting colder."

Do'ok thinks of what his father would do or would want *him* to do, but it doesn't stop him from going to the Russian Cloud-Face camp to have a look. He will be cautious and invisible like Wolf and go through the forest to avoid the Aleut skin boats.

When he smells the sour scents of people imprisoned and hears human sounds, he blends with his surroundings, crawling on his belly to a ridgeline where he can see. A click at his head, the firing end of a weapon that smokes, his arm is grabbed, and he instantly twists, breaking the grip. He's about to run when a crushing blow slams him to the ground.

K'aan-at-shi feels his head through his hair where he lies in the mud, and when her fingers find a tender lump, he jerks awake, seeing her face. "Are you okay?" he asks.

"Yes! But what about you? And why are you here?"

"I was looking for *you*," he admits, touching his tender head. Slowly, he rises to look around, thinking he should have done a better job of that *before* he got caught. He counts thirty young Tlingit and a few Aleut inside their enclosed area, the Aleut keeping their distance against the wall. Outside the wall is mostly Aleut with several small groups of armed Russians. The camp consists of several lean-to's, a few rough plank buildings, and a large rain shelter where skins hang to dry.

Ut-kart-ee has left Raven Clan longhouse and moved with her children back into the little house that she shared with her husband in the beginning. She works herself to exhaustion every day, knowing that she is now expected to provide for her family alone since she refuses to re-marry. Huddled on the floor in a shadowed corner of her home, she moves as if numb, using spruce root strands dyed in cranberries for the red wolf ears on a small basket.

"Sister," A-kadi arrives and squats in front of her to get her attention. "Do'ok has not come back from his visit to Frog Clan. He went to scout the Russian Cloud-Face camp and has not returned."

Ut-kart-ee stops weaving and stares at the floor. Through her sluggish mind she hears A-kadi's words but has trouble making sense of them.

"Do'ok's gone?"

"I'll take a group to get him back." He lays a hand on her shoulder, waiting for a reply, and when she doesn't speak, he leaves.

Ut-kart-ee works to clear her mind. "Do'ok's gone," she repeats. Suddenly, when her understanding comes, a gasp chokes her throat and she jolts up like a salmon leaping up-stream. She stands fixed in the middle of the room, panicked, unsure of what to do until A-kadi's words, 'I will get him back,' come to her, and she prepares to go too.

Quickly, she paints tall, red Wolf ears from her cheekbones to the top of her forehead and wears all her jewelry, abalone and shark tooth bangles from each ear, many bracelets, the proud bear-claw necklace that her husband wore for special ceremonies. She opens the bentwood cedar box for the untouched gift, stroking its white iridescent feathers. "Come with me, my husband," she murmurs as she gingerly inserts her arms, lifting it onto her shoulders, feeling stronger and secure under its weight. She puts her bow and pouch of arrows over her shoulder and tucks Chark Cough-ye's iron knife into her waistband against her back and her smaller berry knife into the flap in the bottom of her tunic.

As she walks to the canoes, she remembers how her husband used to call her the same name as his club, "my *chuck-har-nut*, right by me, always ready," and a tiny smile lightens her face for the first time. *This is why I'm here, to fight for my children in place of their father.* The war canoes are being loaded with Wolf Clan and Raven Clan men who carry weapons of spears and bows and arrows, hatchets, knives and clubs. A few have guns. Many are dressed in armor and carry copper shields.

Ut-kart-ee gets into the Wolf Clan canoe next to her brother's and sits at the front as a leader would do. Her shimmering robe and the severe look on her face allow no one to question her place, especially since her son has been captured so soon after the death of her husband. She has always been a woman to be wary of and now she carries weapons.

Paddles slice in various rhythms through the waves as Ut-kart-ee gains strength from the wind and sea spray. She feels Power turning her hard like rock. Her gaze pierces the shadows on shore where she sees the reflection of Wolf's golden eyes. "Watch over Do'ok," she says quietly and begins to chant a Wolf Clan war song, the others joining in. In time, all paddles move together as one to the beat of the chant.

Ut-kart-ee and the clans from An-ar-kark arrive at Naakee-ann and leaders gather at the same fire, sharing stories of mistreatment from the Russian Cloud-Face. Most say they have endured enough aggressiveness from the invaders, and now that their children are imprisoned, they are ready to end it. Leaders roam fire to fire, "Be prepared to fight."

In the morning, they apply black and red powder in severe designs on faces and wrap their bodies in wooden armor and thick hide. Sharp Wolf teeth on masks reveal the fierceness of the People, and long, pointed Raven beaks on helmets glide over the water, pointing the way. Three hundred paddles from ten large war canoes dig into the water, pulling north through the waves toward the foreign encampment. As they travel, excited Raven calls and Wolf yips punctuate the chanting.

They see a three-masted ship at anchor as they approach the Russian camp and stop offshore. Clan leaders stand in the bows of their canoes, menacing, continuing to chant the messages from their ancestors. Light reflects off copper shields in flashes and glares like sky messages while they wait for a Russian Cloud-Face leader to appear.

Alexander Baranov, governor of Russian America, is determined to keep his camp whatever it takes, despite the fierceness of the Tlingit. When he imprisoned 200 Aleut daughters in his previous settlement to keep their fathers busy hunting sea otters, it worked very nicely. *Why shouldn't I expect the same tactic to work here? All 180 kayaks are out there hunting sea otter for the profit of Russia right now, and I need to keep them there!*

Warriors brace when a cannon is fired to announce the imminent arrival of a leader to the beach. He is short, backed by armed guards as he makes his way down the slope. Drips of rain splash onto his smooth head and roll down his face.

Tlingit leaders come ashore together, followed by their people with weapons. The few with muskets stand in front while expert bowmen stand in the canoes, arrows ready.

Ut-kart-ee takes her place next to A-kadi, shimmering in the iridescence of her robe, curved bear claws standing out from her neck. On A-kadi's other side stands tall leader Takl-eesh of Raven Clan along with Frog Clan and Gull Clan leaders. They stand proudly as Cloud-Face eyes flit nervously from leader to leader and to Tlingit guns and arrows.

Baranov feels a shiver of cold sweat run down his spine inside the protective steel mail he wears under his clothing as he stands to face the ferociously masked natives, obviously ready to fight.

If they had decided on war, they would have already attacked, he assures himself.

A-kadi remembers the beating he received on the Cloud-Face ship, how his people were killed to get him away, the rape of his sister, the murder of Chark Cough-ye. Now with the imprisonment of Do'ok, he vibrates with fury. Moving his jaw stiffly as if made from iron, he makes a formal introduction of himself as leader from Wolf Clan and tells Baranov that he would be wise to release the Tlingit prisoners.

Baranov is silent, then replies in a calm, strong voice through an Aleut interpreter. "These prisoners are my assurance that their people will stop interfering with my hunters while they are simply doing their jobs . . . Your people are not being hurt."

Ut-kart-ee feels the knife burn her back at her waist where it rests, wanting to be used. The invisible arms of her husband seem to restrain her.

"Do you have the mind of a clam?" A-kadi growls. "Did you not notice the sea of Tlingit standing behind us? Their spears and blades and fire weapons and arrows? And what do you mean by 'the prisoners are not being hurt'? You know *nothing* about us!" He spits his words with disgust. "We will *never* live in a cage! *Never* be slaves. We will live with our families around our fires and hunt and fish in *these* territories which belong to *us,* as always."

"You and your thief-hunters are in *our* territory," Gull Clan leader growls. "You are *intruders* here. You take *our* furs without permission. These are *our* hunting grounds and waters. You must go!"

Baranov knows that trade might help although he has nothing to trade to the Tlingit other than their own children. Heaven knows he could use supplies. Mother Russia is not even sending provisions for their survival. If it were not for Aleut hunters, they would not have enough to eat. His wits are often the only ammunition he has to work with, and he doesn't want to trade away what little power he has. Knowing he must show strength, he looks at each leader.

"This land and water are claimed by the country of Russia," he announces bravely. "This area is known as Russian America now. It is a new time, and you need to accept the changes or accept the consequences. These captives will stay where they are for now. Also, I demand the return of four Aleut hunters that you took during your raid last year when many of my camping party were killed during the night."

Frog Clan leader responds, "That strike was in response to an attack *we* suffered by the Aleut the previous year. They deserved it. It is the only way to regain balance. They were sold to other tribes and used as sacrifice," he explains with satisfaction.

During all the talking, Ut-kart-ee's attention is drawn to the enclosure. Desperate to know if Do'ok is there, she gathers her strength and sends daggers with her eyes to the Cloud-Face leader and his guards as she walks with determination directly to the barrier where the prisoners are held, subdued rage emanating from her body. Two armed guards stand before the gate and take several steps back as she approaches. In the center front of the captives stands Do'ok, looking strong and defiant. He holds the hand of K'aan-at-shi who looks frightened, eyes glancing quickly from Do'ok to Ut-kart-ee and back again.

"We will get you out," Ut-kart-ee growls, "even if I must kill every one of these soulless dogs myself." She spits at the feet of one of the guards to keep him back. "You will be ready and do whatever you can from in there," she demands as she removes the bear claw necklace from her neck, secretly hiding her small knife inside and hands it to her son.

"Yes mother," Do'ok replies, feeling stronger for the small weapon, and he melts into the group like the head of a seal sinking into the sea.

When she returns to A-kadi who waits with the other enraged leaders, she whispers to him, "We must leave to plan our attack. *Now* before I cut this tiny wood frog to hear his mercy scream and accidentally get our People killed." She turns to show the Russian leader a broad, toothy Wolf sneer, an exaggerated smile, wild and threatening, and leads the group back to the war canoes.

Baranov stands in his place to watch the Tlingit leave, expecting that he will see them again and that the intense woman in the white feather robe will be an opponent of concern. As a precaution, he has the young man she spoke to taken inside to a more secure cell and retreats to his headquarters to dry off and pour himself a large, calming brandy.

Sea otter cleans herself, scrubbing her fur with her forepaws and bite-combing her brown, thick coat decorated with silvery strands. She feels alone since her pups recently grew old enough to be on their own. When finished with her bath, she performs a barrel roll, swishing herself clean. At lunchtime, she pries an abalone from the rocks and entwines herself in seaweed for stability, then holds the abalone on a flat rock on her chest as she floats on her back. She draws her favorite hammer-rock from her armpit and uses it to crack into her breakfast with relish. As she eats, she remembers swimming this way with her baby on her belly instead of a rock, but before she can finish her meal, she realizes that she's surrounded by People in boats.

Immediately, several arrows pierce her skin, the tips breaking away from the shaft of the arrow, but the lines confine her as she tries to dive. She fights and cries like a wounded child and snarls like a cat, but in time, becomes exhausted. A club smashes her head. On shore, her skin is detached at the tail and pulled off over her head, then hung to dry, and her bloody, naked body is thrown onto the beach.

13

Queen Ka'ahumanu (Cloak of Bird Feathers)

On ship, a Hawaiian messenger speaks carefully to Captain Vancouver, having memorized the words he is to say. "Queen Ka'ahumanu wishes the presence of your passenger Ana in her home. She wants to meet the falcon girl who helps the doctor. I am to transport her in safety and return her to the ship tomorrow."

Vancouver knocks on Ana's cabin door, realizing that he's concerned about her spending all her time in her cabin since Kualelo was called away by Chief Kamehameha. When he sees her in the entry of her dark room, he's reminded of a mole poking its head out from its hole. Her hair is tousled, eyes slightly sunken.

She's been curled on her cot, darkness, musty smell, rocking of the ship her womb-like hiding place. Only a sense of duty enables her to open her door.

"You have evidently made a name for yourself, Miss Ana. Would you like to visit Queen Ka'ahumanu? She has asked for you."

"What name?" she grimaces. "I'm actually a little afraid of her."

"She may also be interested in your falcon. Her promise of safety provides favorable circumstances for your visit, Ana. If you would like to go, you might benefit from learning about a new culture before your mission work in the North."

Reluctantly, she and Falcon join the captain and a few guards in a small boat to deliver her to the far west side of the bay where the royal families live. As they walk behind the messenger on shore, a light rain falls, and Vancouver explains that she would be wise to not violate any kapus. "It would create a most difficult situation for me. Food is prepared by men or boys only. It is kapu for women to make fire or to go into men's houses . . ." He sees worry lines on Ana's face and changes to, "You would probably be forgiven since you are a foreigner."

They walk inside the wall enclosing Queen Ka'ahumanu's residence, past a small guard house, food storage buildings, a shelter for the long, glossy-black boards that are ridden on the waves. Rhythmic pounding is heard as they pass the house where the tapa cloth for the royal family is beaten and prepared. The messenger tells Ana that the floral fragrance she smells is the flower nectar which is beaten into the bark.

She follows past a large home 40 feet long and 20 feet wide, a men's eating house, and a women's eating house, all with small, low entrances. Instead of being thatched in bunches of pili grass from the beach like the common homes in the village, these are thatched in banana or pandanus leaves or ferns, and the ends of some of the roofs are finished in black grass. Stalks of ti grow near the entrance to Ka'ahumanu's house "to keep out bad spirits, a sign of peace," the messenger explains.

Ana looks down at her ti leaf skirt, a sign of peace, a moment to calm herself, and she says a little prayer. Announced at the low doorway, she hears Vancouver say, "Until tomorrow." Taking a deep breath, she squats to her smallest self to duck-walk inside onto a mat-covered stone floor.

Sweet fragrance comes from freshly cut grass under the matting. After her eyes adjust to the darker space, she sees light from a whale-oil lantern in the middle of the windowless room and a few small flames from the darker corners, kukui nuts burning on sticks, sitting in hollowed-out stones.

Queen Ka'ahumanu sits near the center pole of the house on a raised platform of soft matting, wearing a brown tapa skirt and a feather lei around her neck, red feathers from the *iiwi* bird lie flat, pointed outward to form a flaming circle around her neck with an inner circle of fat brown kukui nuts. She sits with her legs to one side, stringing blue translucent glass beads, a gift from Captain Vancouver. The boar's tusk bracelet around her wrist clinks as she works.

A servant holds a feather standard over the queen's head, yellow with dots of black. Its handle is a human arm bone. At one end of the platform are folded stacks of tapa blankets and small pillows made of woven pandanus leaves. She seems calm, welcoming Ana with an offer of brandy, "from a Spanish man, Don

Marin, who came on an American ship," she explains, "much better than the drink made from our ti plants."

Ana has a few small sips, feeling it burn down her throat and causing a warm lightness to tingle in her toes.

"I can offer you poi, breadfruit, some fish, seaweed, black dog to eat, but it is kapu for us to eat coconut or pork or most bananas and some other foods."

Vancouver's warning flashes. "May I ask why some are forbidden?"

Ka'ahumanu thinks about her English words. "The spirits are our ancestors," she begins. "They created the balance of opposites, light-dark, rough-smooth. We keep that balance. Simple, really." She continues to string her beads. "Women come from earth gods, so we represent dark. Men come from sky gods and represent light. Light from man of the sky penetrates dark of woman, from the soil. The balance represents life, so, women may not eat food from light, which is anything connected to gods from the sky." She sits back, smiling.

Ana's brows crumple. "Coconut is connected to light?"

"Coconut trees represent war god Ku," she explains, looking up. "Pork is kapu because it represents god Kamapua'a, part man, part pig. Also, shark is the symbol of a high chief, so it represents light." She leans toward Ana and whispers, "If we were on your ship, we would eat coconut and pork anyway," she smiles mischievously. "Do not tell anyone," she whispers.

Ana grins, speaking formally, "Queen Ka'ahumanu, may I invite you to the ship one day?"

"For mid-day meal perhaps?" she laughs.

It's a busy day, Ana showing how Falcon hunts, Ka'ahumanu

teaching Ana how to fly her largest kite with the assistance of her aides. It's 20 feet long and 7 feet wide. They're followed by a small boy with a withered arm everywhere they go. His job is to report to Kamehameha if his favorite queen should spend time with another man, especially if they are alone together. He hides in the bushes, watching. Ana sees his wide smile.

After their sunset meal, they play Ka'ahumanu's favorite sitting game, *no'a*. A smooth stone, the no'a, is hidden under one of five crumpled pieces of tapa cloth. As Ana watches, Ka'ahumanu mixes the tapa pieces and distracts her with stories and songs until Ana tries to guess the location of the no'a. As night replaces day and outside fires begin to mimic the stars in the sky, Ka'ahumanu asks Ana, "How old are you?"

"I have lived fourteen summers."

"Good enough," the queen nods, taking Ana by the hand and drawing her down the beach, her tiny guard hurrying to follow. "This is a grownup game called *'ume*. It is a favorite night game, especially during Makahiki when we celebrate love and fertility. I hope you enjoy it," she smiles playfully.

Ana looks nervously at a circle of people sitting around a beach fire, wondering what awaits her, and when she sees Kualelo sitting among them, her heart jumps into her throat. Instantly she drops down beside him, grabbing his arm for security. "What are you doing here?" she whispers.

He squeezes her hand. "I was hoping you wouldn't be angry, since we already said goodbye twice."

Ka'ahumanu sits out of the way, watching. One musician plays a nose flute, and another plays a fringed bamboo rattle as a director walks around the inside of the circle. When the music stops, the director flicks a wand over the nearest man. The music begins again and when it stops, he flicks the wand over the nearest woman, indicating that the couple may spend the night together. They must separate by dawn or violate kapu.

Ana panics, in terror of being matched with a stranger, and she launches prayers to God. She looks to Ka'ahumanu to save her, but the queen only shrugs. With a flick of the wand, the last couple, she and Kualelo, are chosen to be together. Still, she's unsure, her heart racing.

"Go!" the queen waves her hands toward the shadows. "Be back before dawn!"

They run hand-in-hand down the beach, laughing, amazed at their good fortune until they find a private place out of the breeze against tall, warm lava rocks and Kualelo lays out a grass mat. Nestled against the rocks, he holds Ana close, burying his face in her hair. "I was so afraid I wouldn't see you again," he whispers. "I couldn't find another excuse to come to the ship."

"This is cruel," Ana sighs, snuggling down under his chin. She feels the tropical breeze softly lift the hair from her shoulders. "I'll be leaving soon, and . . ." She loses her thought when he surrounds her with his arms and kisses her forehead.

He kisses her ear and whispers, "I'm sorry, Ana." His left-hand travels her back, causing tiny explosions to thrill her spine. "I couldn't stop thinking of you, knowing you were still on the island." He kisses her neck and feels her take a deep breath. "I was desperate to see you again."

"I missed you." She's overwhelmed by his warmth, his scent, his kisses.

"The 'ume game was Queen Ka'ahumanu's idea," he breathes.

His right hand touches a breast, and he hears her gasp. "I told her that I loved you," his mouth just below her ear, moving downward.

She's lost, wrapping her legs around him. He kisses her fully on the mouth as he lowers her to the mat, his hands moving to every part of her body, probing, grabbing, becoming frantic for her. His mouth follows his hands, tasting, absorbing her scent. She trembles, lying on her back, arching her spine, trusting him completely. Her breath gains a voice and she cries out as light enters dark. When there is pain, she welcomes it, devouring all of him, body and soul, as if she starves.

As they lie together, she's thankful for the crashing of the waves, the power melding with emotion, and she cries. He kisses her gently, "Did I hurt you?"

"No, I cry because I'm lost."

"I have you," he tightens his arms around her and strokes her hair, gazing up at the night sky. "The star straight overhead is *Hokule'a*, a star of gladness because it's the star that we find at sea to guide us home. Do you see it? It will bring you home to me if you go. Please stay, Ana."

Her soul twists and tears. She runs her hand up and down his arm, wanting to hang on. "Captain Vancouver . . . the padres . . . what if I have a mother in the North?" she stammers.

He breathes hot air into her ear, sending goosebumps down the length of her body to her toes. "I *will* be important here one day and have my own plantation," he continues. "Stay with me." He kisses her fingers and migrates down to kiss her toes. "I missed these last time," he mutters, making sloppy eating sounds as she giggles. They make love again, slower, gentler. To Ana, it feels like worship, and she prays to be able to stay, if she cannot stay, to be strong enough to leave.

The horizon begins to lighten, and he panics, "Quick! The kapu!" He pulls her by the hand.

"I do love you, completely. I'll always love you." Her words hit the back of his head.

He pulls, frantic to get her safely returned before kapu, knowing that violators can be killed. They take "a shorter path," Ana stumbling behind. Dark palm trees become silhouetted by a golden horizon. She hears a mewing sound that becomes a cry and it abruptly stops. She assumes a baby has been put to the mother's breast, then sees them, the mother's hand squeezing the neck of her newborn where it lies in a shallow hole in the ground. Kualelo sees it too. "Come away!" he demands, tugging at her.

"No!" she chokes, rushing back, taking the baby, still covered in birthing fluids. Its eyes are open wide, mouth gasping for air. Ana calls to Zesen in her mind for guidance as she feels the baby's throat is crushed. As it struggles, she cries, holding it close until it's quiet, her own silent sobs causing spasms throughout her body. *May the Lord in his love and mercy help you with the grace of the Holy Spirit.*

Kualelo takes the lifeless child from her arms, placing it back into the shallow hole, and turns her away, returning her to Ka'ahumanu's home. He holds her head with both hands and pulls her forehead to his forehead, nose to nose, looking longingly into her eyes. "Stay, *Ku'u aloha,* my beloved."

Exhausted, Ana finds refuge on a sleeping platform and after restless turmoil, falls deeply asleep. She dreams of Wolf running along a ridge line. He stops to raise his nose to the sky and howl a long echoing cry, and she knows he's calling her home.

Just before mid-day, an attendant wakes her to take her to Ka'ahumanu who's having her hair combed. "You had a difficult return last night, falcon girl."

Ana covers her face. "A mother killed her child!" She cries, rocking her head.

"*Umi ia, i nui kea ho.* Hold on and take a long breath," Ka'ahumanu replies in a soft voice. "I'm sorry it upset you, Ana. It's common here, do not judge the woman too harshly."

She looks through blurry eyes, "Why is it common? Mothers don't *want* to raise their children?"

"They do, just not so many. It is a custom our ancestors brought here from their home island of Tahiti. If there are too many people on an island with limited land, some will starve. Last night that mother was being a good example by not having too many children. Even so, I'm sure she grieves inside."

"I thought this is a large island, a land of abundance," Ana counters. "Captain Vancouver said a huge number of people have been lost due to the 11-years war between islands and disease from foreigners. Would it not help your island be stronger if your families raise many healthy children?"

Ka'ahumanu is quiet for a moment. "Something to think about, young Ana . . . Tell me, what does your Christian God say?"

"It's a Command: Thou shalt not kill," she recites bluntly. "What are the beliefs of your people?"

"We royals come from the original gods, can trace our lineage back to the beginning. We pray to Kane, god of creation and sunlight, Lono for growing crops, Pele for fire and many other spirit gods. Spirits inhabit everything: rain, war, rocks, people, and every family has their 'aumakua, guardian spirit that manifests in an animal like a shark or owl or hawk," she smiles.

Ana thinks of Wolf.

"Our 'aumakua helps our souls get to the underworld we call Po." Her hair is finished, and her attendant picks up every loose hair. "My hairs are buried in a secret place," Ka'ahumanu explains, "so a witch can't curse me to death, of course. You are not a witch, are you?"

"What? No! I don't believe in witches, but I know there are bad people."

"How do you speak to your bird then?"

"I've fed him that way since he was a baby. It's his habit now," Ana shrugs.

"You are very clever!" Ka'ahumanu points a finger accusingly. "I wish you to stay with me, Ana of the Falcon and tell me about other people and places and beliefs."

"Vancouver," she chokes, startled by the invitation. "He must deliver me to the North. Someone else, maybe, could come?"

"I would not like that person as much as I like you," she rolls her lower lip, accustomed to getting what she wants. "Come, I will teach you to swim."

At the cove created for Ka'ahumanu, they take off their clothes and hold hands to walk into the water. Ana tries to grab sand with her toes and brace her legs against the movement of the water. "Relax!" Ka'ahumanu urges. "Let your body move with the water! Bend your knees and let your arms float. You can stand up anytime you wish."

The saltwater feels warm and buoyant, caressing Ana's skin and lifting her feet off the bottom with the crest of each traveling wave. When Ana is relaxed, Ka'ahumanu tells her to lift her feet off the bottom and kick. "Now, push yourself along the beach to another spot," she instructs, demonstrating.

The power and movement of the water is exhilarating. Ana pushes and kicks, playing in the water, actually playing for the first time since she was a young child and her sister Teresa made her a doll of tule.

"You're swimming!" Ka'ahumanu announces, clapping her hands.

"I am?" Ana cries. In her excitement, she gets out over her head and panics, flailing to get closer to shore.

They sit on the beach, watching albatross ride the wind currents, and Ka'ahumanu breaks the silence. "Now tell me, how was your time with Kualelo?"

Ana's heart jerks. "Precious . . . Important . . . I will miss him forever," she squeaks, tears welling in her eyes.

"I'm sorry," Ka'ahumanu takes her hand. "Come to the house, I will distract you with a gift to kill your pain."

She presents Ana with a gold colored tapa skirt and a top that can be tied over one or both shoulders. "Now you will not look like a hula girl in that ti leaf skirt, and you can remove that dirty looking thing from your chest. Do not let these get wet. If you need to wash them, fold the cloth flat and swish it in water, dry it on a hot rock." She helps Ana put it on.

"I *love* wearing these!" She twirls, feeling better.

"A parting gift," Ka'ahumanu whispers. "*A hui hou,* until we meet again."

Vancouver replaces the plaited pandanus leaves with canvas for sails on one of Kamehameha's largest canoes. The chief proudly refers to it as his Man-of-War. "A cannon would make it more authentic," Kamehameha suggests. "You know, for my protection," he smiles.

"King George has a kapu on that," Vancouver explains. "I will bring everything you need for a real schooner next year, the first in the islands," he promises. "While I am gone, consider meeting with the high chiefs from the other islands and agree to each manage your own island, have peace. Other ships encourage you to fight each other so they can gain power here."

Ana is invited to see Kualelo one last time for the game of shooting rats. The rats have been herded onto a field, and he shows her how to shoot a bow and arrow. "Get as many rats on your arrow as possible in one shot," he explains.

Ana's eyebrows arch, unable to imagine the impossible, but he points out the success of the children nearby and she gives it a try. The first and second arrows cause sore bruises on the inside of her elbow. He offers encouragement, wrapping his arms around her from behind, laying his hands on hers for another try, and she's distracted, relaxing into him, closing her eyes, remembering.

"I want to stay here forever," she sighs, feeling him tremble.

"Vancouver says this might help you in the North—to learn a weapon, even though arrows are more of a toy here. We're more likely to throw stones in a fight."

"Maybe teach me to throw a stone," she mumbles.

"Ana . . . I need you to learn to protect yourself. That's why Vancouver allowed me to see you today. Please do it for *me*."

She tries again and one more time. Slight improvement encourages her to continue, and when the competition is over, she can shoot on her own, her arrow true.

Kamehameha bends to touch foreheads and rub noses with Vancouver, then removes his yellow cloak. "This is for King George. Tell him it is the most valuable thing in the island of Hawai'i and that he is the only one who should wear it. If you are my sincere friends, you will protect us from ships that would hurt us. We wish to be subjects of King George."

That night, Vancouver has fireworks sent into the sky as his parting gift. To Ana, every sizzling explosion attacks her heart like a hot, sharpened blade with the message "WE ARE LEAVING" until she feels lacerated into tiny shards.

The hull has been scraped of barnacles and Dr. Menzies checks the repair of the seams as the caulkers pound oakum between the boards on the quarter deck. He's distracted by a supply of live turtles being carried below deck. "What's this then?" he asks Mr. Bonner.

"They're good eat'n inside that shell, Dr. Menzies. Heard of turtle soup?"

Menzies just turns away, shaking his head, more concerned about the stores of water and fresh food. He goes below deck to check on the hogs and goats in the hold.

At Master Whidbey's instruction, the bos'n calls "All Hands!" At his command, they hoist the anchor, and fifteen men scramble aloft up the ratlines to the rigging so high that they become dark spots in the sky where they hang to untie the lines to free the sails from the yards. Excitement builds as the crew stands by, waiting to hear the order "Strike the Sails!"

The ship slowly pulls away in the morning breeze bound for Northern America. Kamehameha and Ka'ahumanu sail beside *Discovery* in his "Man-of-War" along with other canoes, some of which are paddled.

From the deck, leaning over the side, Ana is desperate for a glimpse of Kualelo. She sees him in a single outrigger canoe, paddling furiously to keep up. She waves, tears streaming down her face. The canoes and ship move together up the coast until a brisk wind arrives to fill *Discovery's* sails and propel them faster. Kualelo waves his paddle over his head as high as he can, and the ship pulls away.

Ana drags herself to her cabin, hoping to sleep through her misery. She sobs, another love, the strongest love she's ever known, is torn away from her. Her soul wants to erupt, screaming from her chest, to call Kualelo back to her. Instead, she's sucked into the abyss of aloneness where there's no feeling at all.

14

∽◈∽

Tatook-yadi (Cave Child without a Father)

As the ships *Discovery* and the smaller *Chatham* sail northeast across the Pacific, Captain Vancouver considers the well-being of Ana. He directs his steward, Mr. Bonner, to invite her to his cabin.

Ana grieves for Kualelo. She tries to sleep because when she's awake, she feels only the wound of his absence. She dreams of him, the depth of his eyes, his warm touch, his smell. Awake, it's like he's been with her, like a ghost whose memory makes the little hairs on her arms stand up. She's tried to wish herself less pain, but the ache of losing him is what keeps him real, and she will not let it go. Arriving at Vancouver's cabin, she's unable to mask her sadness. It clings to her like black feathers on Raven.

Captain Vancouver sees Ana's gloom and asks Dr. Menzies to

bring his magic remedy, his secret tin of Scottish cookies. Dr. Menzies is happy to oblige. Ana and the two men sip tea and crunch Scottish shortbreads, sweet, light, buttery crispness that is entirely new to Ana, and it causes her face to lighten with the taste. As they visit, Dr. Menzies notices a tied lock of hair on Vancouver's desk.

"Whaz with the hair?" he asks, nodding toward the desk, crumbles on his lips.

"A gift, even though it is my own hair," Vancouver replies. "I do not remember, but a chief asked for a lock of my hair fourteen years ago. It was returned to me just before we left Hawai'i because the chief had died. I was told that the chief had kept it with him at all times." Vancouver shakes his head, "For *fourteen* years! It causes me to be in awe at the steadiness of the friendship of these people after all these years."

Menzies chokes on his tea, sloshing it down his chest. "Friendship? There's noth'n friendly 'bout obtaining yer hair, cap'n!" he spouts as he wipes up the tea. "Only reason ta want yer hair is for witchcraft against ye!"

"No . . . I cannot believe that."

"Ka'ahumanu hides every hair that falls from her head so a witch will not get it," Ana remembers. ". . . I suppose it was friendly to return your hair rather than to use it, though."

"Hmmm," Vancouver sighs, looking disappointed. "Well, good thing I do not believe in witchcraft. So now Miss Ana," he begins, "How will you spend your time on board? We will need to survey along the North American coastline as we travel, so it could take us several months. Would you be interested in having some responsibilities while on ship?"

Ana looks at the deck beneath their feet. "Yes, of course," she forces her words.

"There will be some work with Dr. Menzies of course. Also, I wonder if you might be willing to read to the officers and crew from the Bible on Sundays. Of course, the Bible-fearing men on ship are of the Church of England, but the Bible is the same Bible for everyone. I have an English version here," he says, picking up the leather-bound book from the side table, "which you may use. That way, more of the men will understand it and you can enlarge your English vocabulary."

Ana's cookie has gone dry in her throat and she adjusts herself in her seat, finally saying, "Thank you, Captain."

"Good. You will provide an essential service that will soothe all onboard. Also, Ana, I would be remiss if I did not help you prepare for working among the Tlingit, especially your ability to protect yourself, in some capacity at least. I have asked Dr. Menzies here to give you a few lessons on how to handle a dirk," he pauses as if thinking aloud, "and Lieutenant Puget can prepare you for the use of a firearm."

"Captain Vancouver!" she interrupts. "Sir, I'm not going to hurt or kill anyone! I'm to spread the Word of God, of Love, of Faith and Hope, to raise the people up, not harm them!"

"These are only *precautions*, Ana. I am resolved to secure your welfare, even when you leave ship. Should you be confronted with treacherous or hostile behaviors, the simple act of being armed could provide protection, and you may need to protect yourself from a bear or a wolf."

Ana swallows, "Bear? Wolf?"

Falcon flies over water, searching for prey. He scans sky and surface within a mile from his location, enjoying his flight and strengthening his wings in the wind currents. He misses the tasty smaller birds from the island.

He has begun to mature into adulthood. His dark-brown wings are turning blue-gray and the stripes on his belly are becoming spots. Despite his fatigue during these changes, he pushes up through the air, circling and circling, higher and higher. Then he dives, plunging at 200 miles per hour, faster than any other creature, and comes to pounce on a rat that scampers across the poop deck of the ship.

Ana stands in Menzies' lab-quarters looking at a picture of a tree with fern-like leaves and red clusters of berries. "Is this a special tree, Dr. Menzies?"

"Yes, lass. The Rowan Mountain Ash, the badge of my clan." He puts a dirk in her hand. She feels the weight of it and the smooth, worn boxwood hilt, her eyes avoiding the long, steel narrow blade. "What does *'Alba gu brath!'* mean?" she asks, reading from the inscription in the wood.

"Scotland Forever!" Menzies replies. "Tis for stab'n or thrust'n, ye know, lass. Yer not hold'n it correctly."

"The blade is so long! Where am I supposed to keep it?" Ana moans. "Is there something smaller?"

"Well, there's the wee *sgian dubh* or black knife that ye can tuck against yer leg into yer stock'n, but ye dinna wear any stock'n, and there's the *sgian-achlais,* a wee bit larger, that ye can carry under yer armpit in the lining of yer clothing," he replies, taking the dirk from her. "Neither will protect ye as much as this lovely dirk here." He thrusts it through the air in a practice stab and admires its sharp edge.

"Something smaller please," Ana whimpers, shocked by the flash of the twelve-inch blade. "I could never *use* something like that. If someone sees me with it, might it cause them to want to *pick* a fight?"

"If they see ye helpless, lass, they could assume yer *ripe* for pick'n."

Sunday morning after breakfast, all on ship are dressed in their best. The crew wears their least torn, least worn, cleanest pair of trousers. Officers are in their most formal uniforms, boots, buttons and buckles shined. Mr. Bonner brings a chair for Ana to sit on the forecastle, the highest deck in the bow of the ship, so that she may project her voice out over her congregation, most of whom stand.

Ana says a silent prayer for wisdom to do a good job and begins reading, throwing her words to the stern of the ship:

The Word of the Lord came to Jonah . . . And the Lord hurled a great wind on the sea . . . He appointed a great fish to swallow Jonah . . . Jonah prayed . . . Salvation is from the Lord.

She looks up to see smiling faces, those who already know the story and perhaps those who are believers. "May we have compassion for each other as God did for Jonah." Then she leads them in the Lord's Prayer, the tenors and baritones of the officers adding power to the words as they rise from the vast ocean up to Heaven.

Later that afternoon, she's on deck for Falcon to hunt. A tall, lean Native in loin cloth, stands watch. "*Seew kooshdaneit yaay? Swallowed by a whale?*" he asks in Tlingit.

"Gwaa!" Ana spouts, shocked to hear Tlingit language. She stares intently at his face, looking for anything familiar. His hair is knotted on top of his head and a Raven tattoo decorates his chest. "*Da su see tee? What clan are you?*"

"Coho Clan of the Raven People," he grins, "from Naakee-ann of the coastal Tlingit. Name is Utah (Paddle)." He squats to see Falcon in his cage. "*Your* clan?"

Ana shrugs, "*Tatook-yadi,* Cave Child without a Father. I think I come from An-ar-kark." She sees the muscle flex in his back. "How did you get *here?*"

"Stolen by the Quileute and made slave, sold to an American ship, traded to this ship," he keeps his eyes on her. "How did you learn our language without a grandparent to teach you?"

"My brother," she says and turns away, uncomfortable with his stare.

Discovery and *Chatham* plow through the water for several months through all kinds of weather. On this day, the wind makes a pleasant hum in the canvas. Dolphins race the waves created off the starboard bow. Vancouver sits at his desk in his cabin finalizing his maps and notes and writing in his journal between occasional bouts of coughing. His cough seems to be getting worse with the cooler weather.

The officers and crew work their watch according to the ship's bell, the crew constantly adjusting the rigging to get the most from the wind, repairing the lines and scouring the decks as needed. Now they rub a heavy holystone back and forth on the main deck until it's clean and smooth.

Ana practices the flute that Chusen made for her to pass the time. She tries to make the birdsong that she remembers, and as she hears the holystones pound onto the deck above her, her song acquires its beat. Now she plays a work song following the rhythmic hit and scratch, hit and scratch, like the work song of Zesen and her friends crushing acorns. The anguish of losing Zesen returns, and her music stops.

Both ships continue north, passing additional familiar areas that were surveyed and mapped the previous year. The island that was surveyed by Master Whidbey was named for him, Whidbey Island, and the southern portion of the large ocean inlet was named for Lieutenant Puget, Puget Sound. Vancouver recalls his negotiations with Spanish Captain Quadra. They had failed to agree on a settlement during the Nootka Convention regarding the claiming of territories but had averted war and gained a friendship. Before they parted, they had agreed to name the large island at the entrance to Puget Sound, Vancouver-Quadra Island.

Ana watches from deck as the sights change, black and white orcas swimming with the ship one day, humpback whales the next, blowing water in the air as they feed, rising up out of the water to crash sideways down again, slapping the surface.

The further north they go, the more snow-capped mountains she sees, peaks and so many islands, one could get lost among them. She sees a green, treeless meadow at the edge of the water and a mountain of rock jutting straight up to the sky, then a wall of ancient ice, forcing them to go around. The old mineral smell and cold of the ice permeate the air. It's a world that she had never imagined could exist.

One morning *Chatham* goes its separate way to survey, and two small boats from *Discovery* work in thick fog and constant rain to survey Behm Canal. Six canoes glide silently toward them out of the mist, putting Vancouver on alert. His boats are quickly surrounded, spears pointing menacingly at Vancouver and his crew. They show sea otter skins, wanting to trade, pointing at Vancouver's guns and ammunition. Bravely, Vancouver says, "No," shaking his head, offering iron and copper instead.

All activity stops. The Natives look to one another and say a few words in their language, then reluctantly begin to trade. Just as tensions relax, a Raven call announces their attack, and instantly, spears are thrust, gravely injuring some of the crew. A Native produces his own firearm and shoots at Vancouver, a misfire. The surveyors shoot back, driving their attackers away, and only a few muskets are stolen.

Back at the ship, Dr. Menzies and Ana are able to save all but one of the wounded men as Vancouver speaks to his officers. "These people were sold defective firearms by those who consider gain to be the only object of pursuit, so they trespass on the laws of honesty to get what they deem their rightful property, and our patience may have been seen as weakness."

"What tribe?" Dr. Menzies asks.

"Tlingit," Mr. Whidbey replies, "the women were wearing labrets."

Ana stands on deck looking like she watches islands in the distance. In reality, she stares blindly, worried about her future. The Tlingit they have encountered are aggressive. Now she wonders about the people of An-ar-kark and whether she *wants* to know them.

Utah must decide if he will jump ship since they're close to his home. Doubtful that the British navy condones keelhauling as too many drown or are shredded in the process, he suspects he would be thoroughly flogged and forced to work in chains if he's caught. He sees Ana on deck letting her falcon hunt and moves closer to speak to her. "You know you must have a lineage to receive any respect from the Tlingit," he warns in a quiet voice, his gaze intense.

She looks away, not wanting to think about it, "I refuse to lie."

"Tell them you are Shaayaal (Kind of Hawk) of the Wolf People, raised by your brother, and you can name your prominent friends like Captain Vancouver and Kamehameha."

"My brother was not Tlingit. He was Haida, a Tlingit slave," Ana replies curtly, bothered by this man who stands too close. "Why do you want to help me?"

"Because I know what it is to live with people who are not your own," he explains, looking about the ship. "It's alright that your brother was Haida. The Tlingit respect the Haida, but do not say he was a slave." He climbs back up the rigging to work.

Vancouver's yawl is beached on the western arm of Behm Canal and a few friendly Natives paddle to shore for trade, engaging in peaceful negotiations. More canoes arrive and attempt to surround the small boat. Captain Vancouver immediately sees their plan, ordering the yawl to push off into the water and toward his other boat, the launch, hoping for added protection.

Five canoes pursue them, one steered by an elder woman with a large labret. She steers her canoe up across the bow of the yawl, stopping it, and grabs its lead line, tying it to her canoe. Just as fast, a young man wearing a wooden Wolf mask climbs into the bow of the yawl. Vancouver draws his musket to send the Wolf back to his own canoe, but the Natives throw spears, narrowly missing Vancouver, and immediately jump into the yawl with their daggers, critically injuring some of the crew and grabbing everything they can, including most of the firearms.

As the launch joins them, another woman in a different canoe steers across *its* bow to immobilize it as well, and Vancouver orders them to fire. Some Natives are killed, others wounded, and the lives of Vancouver and most of his party are saved. Once again, Dr. Menzies and Ana tend to the injured, and the dead are prepared for burial at sea.

"Tlingit?" Ana asks, afraid of the answer.

Lieutenant Puget nods. "Welcome to Tlingit Territory."

Ana's stomach turns. In her cabin, she trembles as she reads her Bible and says her rosary. Wolf sits, waiting for her in her troubled dreams, his tail flitting back and forth.

Lieutenant Puget arranges Ana's hand onto the grip of a Toby, a Queen Anne version of a pocket-size flintlock pistol. "No ramrod needed to push ammunition through the barrel," he looks down at her. "Just open the barrel, tuck in the powder and ball, and close her up, ready to go."

"It *is* small," Ana adds, enjoying the smooth finish on the curved, wooden grip.

"Remember, it's only for close up. Come and get the feel of it." Standing on deck, he directs Ana to aim out over the water and pull the trigger. "Be ready for the recoil," he warns.

Slowly, she squeezes, producing an explosion like fireworks

and instantly drops the gun as a great puff of smoke erupts, clouding her vision. She holds her right hand protectively against her chest as she hears boisterous laughter from the crew.

Puget also laughs, seeing the shocked look on her face. "Now you know what to expect," he encourages. "Keep ahold of it next time."

Discovery and Chatham enter Cross Sound together just north of An-ar-kark, and Lieutenant Whidbey departs in a small boat to map several bays. They row through the north passage of Icy Strait to survey and are blocked by a solid wall of ice. Confronted by the colossal frozen fortress, Whidbey realizes that he felt the cold of it, and smelled the old wet of it, and heard the crack of it, before he saw it: a mountain of ancient glacier that extends a hundred miles to the St. Elias Mountain Range.

Discovery finally sits in the bay of An-ar-kark, and Ana's heart thrums. She sees the village nestled in front of its majestic background of snow-capped mountains. There are many homes built of wood, some partially underground, most of them small with large buildings here and there. She sees a few tall poles painted and decorated with images of animals and a few groups of shorter ones with decorated boxes on the top. The beach in front of the homes is littered, and racks of drying fish and skins wave in the breeze. She sees only a few people. No one comes to the ship for trade.

She wonders if her family is in this place and if they will accept her and especially if her mother lives and if she was ever loved. As her anxiety builds, she reminds herself that her intended purpose is to bring the Word of God to the Natives, but it doesn't calm her stomach.

Utah finds her on deck at the end of his watch. "I will adopt you into my family and clan," he pleads, coming up behind her. "The People of An-ar-kark respect us, and my family has status, so you would do well to take our name."

"I don't understand why you care," Ana sighs, wrapping her rabbit blanket tightly around her shoulders against the chill.

"I know what is ahead for you," he declares. She stares at him defiantly to cover her fear, and he gives up, shaking his head, walking away.

Ana feels her legs begin to shake by afternoon. No matter how much she tries to reassure herself, Utah's worries and the wounded from Tlingit attacks have gotten to her. She goes to Dr. Menzies to learn more about a dirk.

She quivers in anticipation of visiting the village. Dressed in her deerskin tunic that Miguel had made for her in the Tlingit fashion, she hopes she will look like she belongs in this place. Captain Vancouver accompanies her in the cutter and the yawl comes alongside for additional protection.

As she places her bare foot onto the cold, wet beach for the first time, she wonders if she might feel her roots, maybe recall some inherited memory, wondering if her parents have walked here, maybe put their feet in this very place. She tightens herself, not knowing what comes.

The village seems empty except for some elders who wear rainhats and capes. The women have large labrets protruding from their lower lips. An elder approaches them dressed in his apron and woven rainhat, walking with the aid of a staff. He works his lips across missing teeth to speak to Captain Vancouver in English.

"Hello Captain. I am ambassador here while the clan leaders are at summer camps and visiting in the north," he points to the north with his staff. "We are not prepared to trade now." He stares at Ana for several moments as if lost in thought. "I can arrange trade for supplies if you need."

"That is perfectly fine," Vancouver interrupts. "We are here to return one of your own. This is Ana, taken from this place as a newborn. We believe she may have family here."

"What clan? Who are your parents?" the elder asks, continuing to stare at Ana.

"Tatook-yadi," Ana shrugs, feeling embarrassed.

"You have no family then," he says, turning away.

A few more elders slowly make their way to the beach having overheard the conversation, the women with pronounced limps. They see Ana, stop and stare at her, seemingly afraid to approach closer. One with a face of wrinkles and a labret of shiny abalone steps forward with dignity, head held high, *Da su see tee?* What clan are you?" she asks Ana.

"Wolf visits my dreams," she replies in Tlingit.

The woman steps back, making a quick inhale as if startled. Ana smiles to calm the woman, showing the dimple in her right cheek, but the woman and her companions moan and turn away, covering their faces as if to protect themselves.

Confused, Ana feels they must know something about her. "Please," her voice is kind, "can you help me? The man who took me to the Spanish ship was named Yahaayi."

All the elders turn to look, wide-eyed, at Yahaayi, the self-proclaimed ambassador who stands behind them. His staff drops as his hands fly up to cover his open mouth and he falls to the beach on his knees. *"Ke-an-kow a niyaa xat!* Spirit Above, protect me!" he pleads.

"Gwaa!" Ana shouts, stepping back. "What are you afraid of?"

Vancouver intervenes. "You," he demands, pointing at Ya-haayi. "Tell me *now*, what do you know?"

"Tatook-yadi," he replies, remaining on his knees and pointing at Ana, "found in the forest . . . I know nothing."

"And you?" he asks, looking down at the elder woman.

"Du kikyadi, twins," she mutters from behind her hands.

Ana sucks breath, knowing that Ohlone twins are killed.

"Kush-tar-ka, a sign of trouble," the woman continues, taking another step back.

Vancouver looks to Ana for interpretation. "Twins," she says, "I'm not supposed to be alive." Her eyes remain attached to the elder woman.

The elder's voice begins to shake. "I gave you to the Shaman to be carried into the forest," she confesses, fear mixing with tears that glisten in her eyes . . . "to protect the village. It's Raven's way." She remembers Ut-kart-ee's screams and mutters to Raven behind her hands, closing her eyes, *"What is this? Why do you threaten me?"* but she sees Wolf in her head, her brave spirit leader and protector. She peeks at Ana through her fingers. "I am your grandmother, Yake-see," her voice is weak, raspy.

Ana reaches for Captain Vancouver for support. "My grandmother," she chokes, looking for something familiar among the wrinkles and in the eyes.

"Your name is on your face," her grandmother offers as she

lowers her hands. "You are first-born of a respected family of the Wolf People. Your mother fought to keep you even though twins are forbidden. She is Ut-kart-ee." Yake-see stops, not knowing how much the girl wants to hear.

Trembling, Ana asks the question she has always wanted to know, "Does my mother live?"

Her grandmother nods. "She named you and called to the ancestors to watch over you. You are She-ee." She sees the girl's face become a crying one.

Through her tears, Ana watches the elder limp forward, a fierceness in her eyes, then feels the weathered hand grab hold of her arm as if to claim her.

15

Du-tlaa (Mother)

The old Wolf Clan Shaman of An-ar-kark shuffles down to the beach. His hips have been crying all morning, but with most of the village gone, he feels responsible to find out about the ship in the bay. He notices Yake-see from his own clan, an elder woman of the Wolf People, talking with men from the ship. As he hobbles on, he sees that she has her hand on a girl's arm. The girl looks up at him and smiles, showing a dimple on her right cheek, a familiar face, looking like Yake-see's grandson Do'ok, only this is a girl . . . Slowly, understanding dawns, and daggers stab his heart causing enormous pain. He whispers, "*woosh yaayi,* two of them," and falls into unconsciousness.

Ana notices a man with wild hair coming toward them. He falls and she rushes to him, putting her hands on him, listening to his breath. She feels his chest vibrate and forms a tight fist, beating him on his chest with all her might as she has seen

Sezen do. It takes several times before she can feel the heart begin again. Then she backs away, unsure if she should have intervened.

Grandmother is frightened by Ana's magic. As soon as she remembers this child was raised by other people with different knowledge and sees her with the same fierce determination as her daughter Ut-kart-ee, fear changes to pride. She points a shaky finger at the Shaman as he regains consciousness. "She saved your life, old fool. You've named enough witches for one lifetime!" Then smiles to the others, "I'm so old now I'm not afraid of him anymore."

Ana feels herself float like a thin piece of parchment. "May I see my mother?" She looks beyond her grandmother as if her mother stands nearby.

"She is away, child."

"And my father?"

"He lives in the sky now."

Vancouver sees Ana's face go ashen and grabs her arm, "You will come back tomorrow."

"Please, I need to know," she cries. "Does my twin live?"

"We think he's a prisoner of a Cloud-Face Tribe north of here," Yake-see's brows furrow. "Your mother and uncle went to get him back."

On ship, Ana trembles, unable to rest. *He,* she thinks to herself. *I have a brother . . . if he lives. Someone who looks like me . . . and neither of us should be alive.* She wonders if he is the one always in her dreams who knows her so well and makes her laugh, and she prays for a chance to meet him. Her worry digs into her chest until she goes to Vancouver. "What if I never get to meet them?"

she cries, her voice shaky. "I'm so close, and they could get themselves killed!"

Vancouver is also concerned. "If they do not come back tomorrow, we will go and see about them."

Relieved, she brings Falcon out to hunt. He winds higher and higher and out of sight. As she waits on deck for his return and breathes the fresh, cool ocean air, she imagines meeting her mother, a mother she did not think she would ever know, a mother who believes that she died in the forest. She wonders if her mother will be happy to know that she lives . . . or maybe she will be afraid that she is a witch, returned from the dead.

While exploring his new terrain, Falcon strikes a small bird in mid-air and clenches it in his talons as he flies to a rocky bluff to eat. An adult falcon soars at him, telling him that he is in claimed territory. Falcon moves away and perches on the edge of a nearby cliff to watch the other bird, the first he has seen of his kind. He sees the other bird's nest and the family that resides there. He would like to stay but returns to his keeper before dark as usual.

That night, Ana cries. From what her grandmother said, her mother may have loved her. Unable to sleep, she climbs the stairs to the main deck and finds Bear in the sky. Pulling her rabbit blanket tightly around her, she thinks of Miguel and her family at the mission and sweet Teresa in Heaven, sending them her love with the next flying star. The memory of her night on the Hawaiian beach with Kualelo warms her, and she wonders if he also looks at the stars. He had said, "We've more danger from internal trouble than external. The wave near at hand is the one to watch." The night breeze calms as her worry quiets. She feels the comfort of his love surround her and returns to her cabin to sleep.

Huddled around the night fire at Naakee-ann, Wolf Clan Leader A-kadi tells other leaders the story of Ut-kart-ee's husband, Chark Cough-ye of Raven Clan, also known as Bear Killer. "The last words he spoke before he was killed were, 'This fight cannot be won against their weapons!' That is why we need iron weapons that smoke. So how do we get our children back without getting killed?"

"We pick them off quietly, one at a time, one here, one there," Leader Takl-eesh of Raven Clan responds. "It will balance the lives they have taken and the livelihoods they have stolen by hunting our areas. If they threaten to hurt our children, we attack regardless of the danger."

"*Aaa,*" he hears agreement among the leaders.

Alexander Baranov is losing people. They are being found dead in the early mornings at their guard posts in a pool of blood, minus their heads. His Aleut hunters have become as afraid as mice in a wolf's den and are likely to bolt even though their daughters are imprisoned. He has his remaining guards doubled so they are never alone and reduces the space they patrol as he strategizes what to do next.

Lord knows his problems, he tells Him often enough. His orders to create a farming community with prisoners and destitute families sent by Russia are difficult since they know nothing of farming! Impossible in this dark, cold wet weather. Now with violence from the local Tlingit, he questions his ability to stay.

Ut-kart-ee waits impatiently in Frog Clan House at Naakee-ann while her brother A-kadi recruits men from An-ar-kark to fight. She wants to scream like a sea otter watching her pup being clubbed as she imagines the abuse her son must be enduring. Unable to wait any longer, she sneaks from the village in the misty rain, through the forest toward the Russian camp. The whispered voice of her husband tells her to be careful. An eagle lights on a limb overhead, watching with a piercing eye.

"I have no choice," she tells him and continues.

The guards are on alert when she arrives, but they don't stop her approach. She walks purposefully, boldly into camp and stands in front of Baranov's building, waiting. Eventually, he comes out to meet her, accompanied by an Aleut interpreter and two guards with guns.

"I did not learn your name last time you were here," he begins.

"I will not give you my name," Ut-kart-ee replies. "I save it for those I trust."

"I am very trustworthy," Baranov assures. "I always do what I say I will do. You can be sure of that."

"In that case, I will offer myself as hostage in place of all the Tlingit in the pen over there." She points to the people in the fenced prison. "You can keep the Aleut slaves."

"In exchange for the Tlingit in the enclosure?" Baranov asks, thinking of the boy that was moved to a more secure building.

"Yes, they go in exchange for me as hostage," she repeats, wondering if this Cloud-Face does not hear well.

Baranov is suspicious. "How are you worth as much as *all* those sons and daughters over there who are important to the people I wish to control?"

"I am sister to the leader of Wolf Clan, the most powerful clan in An-ar-kark, and wife to the nephew of Raven Clan leader. I am mother of Ka-hu-ish, an honored leader known by all Tlingit. Many of my cousins from Naakee-ann are in your pen, and their families will act honorably, respecting my sacrifice. Would you *not* like to stop attacks on your people?"

"Yes, *of course* I would."

"Then let us stop killing and take me as hostage instead!"

Although he's concerned that she could be trouble or part of some secret plan, he can't resist. "Please accept the hospitality of a cabin while I consider your proposal." He motions to a guard and she is led to a sturdy plank building and locked in.

Before dark, she hears the Tlingit captives being released. She tells herself to relax, she has endured isolation before and could use a good rest, settling into a corner and arranging her robe around her for a long nap.

Ana stands on deck in her deerskin tunic and cape, watching large war canoes arrive at An-ar-kark, each about one-third the length of the *Discovery* with a carved spirit animal on the bow. Although the weapons, masks and armor look frightening, she hopes her mother and brother are with them. Tentatively, she steps on the beach with Captain Vancouver. Yahaayi is there to meet her. "Your mother and brother have not returned, but I told your uncle about you." He motions with his staff toward a broad-shouldered leader who stands with his feet apart as if poised for battle.

The leader wears an apron and deer-skin cloak tied at his neck. His thick hair lies past his shoulders, greased in red ochre, and there is a Wolf mask over his face. A heavy sheath hangs off his shoulder holding a double-sided dagger at least five hand-widths in length. People gather around him, expectant.

Ana's heart beats in her ears as she waits with her eyes down like a good Tlingit woman. She concentrates on keeping her lungs breathing, waiting, feeling intimidated by this important person, her uncle. As her wait continues, she begins to tremble.

A-kadi steps toward her, cocking his Wolf mask with a question. He removes the mask to get a better look, and with his finger, lifts her chin to see her face. It's as if Do'ok stands before him, and he struggles to maintain his composure. The others who see her face take several steps back.

"This is your uncle, your mother's brother, leader of Wolf Clan of the Wolf People," Yahaayi explains.

"Do not speak for me," A-kadi grunts. "What do you want?" He turns away from her to cover his confusion, wondering what trick Raven plays on him.

She speaks meekly, keeping her eyes down, "To meet my family . . . and to bring the Word of God to your village."

"We have *seen* what comes with your Cloud-Face god!" A-kadi erupts. "The crosses on the hills, the mistreatment, the murders, theft of our food and sea otter skins. There is no honor in your god!"

Yahaayi interprets for Vancouver. "There are bad among every People," Vancouver replies. "We wish to survey the coastline and learn the names of the places here, not to profit from you. We will trade for supplies needed to sustain ourselves, fresh water and food."

"Guns to trade?"

"No," Vancouver shakes his head. Then wanting positive relations with this leader and for Ana's sake, he adds, "We do have guns to use on your behalf, if necessary."

Surprised, A-kadi looks closely at Vancouver, never having heard of a Cloud-Face taking sides with the Tlingit before. "Prove your words by helping us *now*," he challenges. "Our people are hostage in a Russian Cloud-Face camp. We need them back."

"Why are they held?"

"To stop us scaring away our own sea otters, to keep them from being hunted," A-kadi spits, enraged.

"Who are the hostages?"

"My sister and nephew." He turns toward Ana, "her mother and brother."

Do'ok looks through the space between timbers of his cell to see K'aan-at-shi and the others released, and he suspects it has something to do with his mother. He wonders if his separation from the group also has something to do with her, and since she would not sacrifice *his* freedom for the others, he knows something has gone wrong. His stomach tenses, and he feels the spirit of his father build within him. When he asks a guard about his mother, the Aleut slave looks toward another building and shrugs, walking away.

From her small cell within the plank house, Ut-kart-ee can

see men tromping through the mud and only Aleut prisoners in the corral. Relieved that Do'ok has been released, she now hopes that A-kadi will do nothing stupid, feeling that in time, things will calm down and she will be released.

An Aleut slave comes in with food. "Do you know Do'ok?" he asks in trade talk.

She is alarmed. "Why?"

"He asked about you."

"Before he was released?"

"He is still here."

Instantly, Ut-kart-ee is seething. Her words come like jabs of a knife. "You tell your slime-covered leader that he has no honor, like all the other Cloud-Face filth! He might think the clans will let *me* stay here since I volunteered, not *both* of us! He has no idea how much trouble he has brought on himself now!"

In An-ar-kark, Vancouver ponders the situation. He thinks that as a British diplomat, he will be able to introduce reason. "I will talk to the Russian leader," he offers. "If I am able to bring both hostages home, will you stop aggressive behavior toward them?"

"Yes," A-kadi answers easily. "The People of Naakee-ann may not. It's *their* lives at stake. They will starve before the Cloud-Face are finished hunting there." He looks toward Ana, "She comes as my interpreter."

The next morning, Ana begins with hope and prayer and worry. Her gruff uncle A-kadi and a few of his friends come on board, displaying their spirit animal crests and dressed for war.

A-kadi watches Ana, so much like his nephew Do'ok, with no one to speak for her. A tiny seed of pity begins to grow within him because of her aloneness, and he feels the spirit of her father, Chark Cough-ye, hovering about him, encouraging him to watch over her. "Yake-see says you grew up in a Cloud-Face school of Ke-an-kow," he says to her.

"Yes, with my Tlingit family," she answers quietly, eyes down. "Actually, they were slaves."

"Ahhh, yes," A-kadi remembers. "Crane Clan sold slave children to the Cloud Face. They thought it was secret, but nothing is secret in An-ar-kark . . . At one time, I would have been expected to kill you and your brother, you know."

Shocked, Ana takes a moment. "Thank goodness it is a *different* time."

"Your mother may be sent away from the village because of you." He stares at her. "Keeping Do'ok was tough enough, and now, you. If the Council decides she must go, there's nothing I can do."

Ana tries to hide the choking in her throat, thinking she may have destroyed her mother before she's met her. She feels Wolf within and lifts her eyes to her uncle's for the first time. "Your trouble has nothing to do with my mother or my brother or me. In reality, they sacrificed themselves at the Cloud-Face camp for others. Perhaps you can present *that* point to the Council . . . if necessary."

A-kadi's mouth becomes something between a grimace and a smile. *Lekwaa, fighting spirit,* he thinks to himself, *like her mother.*

Baranov is surprised to see two British ships, *Discovery* and *Chatham*, emerge through the white fog in front of his rough settlement. Four small boats start for shore and he prepares to meet them, getting back into his mail for protection. Once he has assembled as many Russians as possible for security, they walk in formation showing the Russian flag. He notices that both ships have their cannon pointed at him.

As the smaller boats arrive, he sees that the same Wolf man who was there previously comes with a girl and some other natives along with two British captains and about twenty navy officers who are armed. After introductions, Baranov asks why they have come in such an aggressive manner.

"In the navy, sir, we know that if you want to have peace, you must plan for war," Vancouver responds.

"What may I help you with, captain?"

"We need the release of two of your prisoners. I may be able to help you solve your problems without further bloodshed."

Baranov shakes his head, thinking how naive this captain is. He has no idea how many problems he has. Seeing no other choice, he invites Vancouver into his building, announcing, "The prisoners stay where they are for now."

Vancouver motions for A-kadi and Ana, along with an armed guard, to accompany him while the others wait outside.

Ut-kart-ee sees a crowd on the beach, including her brother A-kadi. Since Baranov has broken his word and keeps Do'ok, she feels she must create a disturbance, then she can help them find Do'ok. She strains to get a better look.

Do'ok knows his mother would never let him be a prisoner for long and thinks they probably have her as well. He's prepared to attack the next person he sees in order to free her. He quiets his mind and regulates his breathing, ready to act swiftly like the eagle grabbing its salmon in mid-flight.

Inside Baranov's building, Ana and the leaders come to an agreement. Ana will provide religious instruction once a week at Baranov's camp in exchange for her mother's and brother's freedom. Baranov will travel further south in search of friendlier neighbors and a richer supply of sea otters, especially since he admits that hunting has become slow in this place. In that new area, he will ask permission before camping or hunting or fishing and will trade so the Natives will be compensated for the food and furs that are taken. Vancouver will provide Baranov with some trade goods to get him started since Russia provides little assistance.

Exhausted, Ana enters the first small boat to return to the *Discovery*, not wanting her mother to meet her in this place of imprisonment and in the presence of her captor.

On *Discovery*, A-kadi stands with Ut-kart-ee on the main deck as Do'ok examines the ship. "Sister," A-kadi says, "I wish you would do what I say some of the time. Your husband can only do so much to watch over you from his place in the sky."

She is fascinated with the ship, almost like a floating village, all the rigging and sails and the people working together, some of whom climb high into the lines. She's heard her brother's words before and has responded before, not feeling it necessary to respond now.

A-kadi takes her hands into his to get her attention. "I have news," he says hesitantly, wondering if it's the right time.

She looks at him expectantly.

"Your daughter lives," he says softly.

Ut-kart-ee looks confused, "I hope so, I left the children with Tinx."

"Your first-born daughter, your twin who was taken into the forest, she lives."

She stares, "Your words play tricks on me, I think."

Ana watches from the shadow of the stairs. Her mother is beautiful, dressed in a long, white feather robe and wearing jewelry. She looks like a Tlingit queen except without a labret. Seeing her uncle A-kadi holding her mother's hands, she steps forward, unable to stop the tears that flow down her face.

The woman turns a shocked, pallid face in her direction, and then she's there, grabbing Ana with unnatural strength. Ut-kart-ee's mind is flooded with the memory of her own screams as this baby was taken away from her, and she can't let go. Her heart beats so fast that it floods her head and she can't hear. Fiercely, she looks around to protect her child like Wolf defending her pups. "She-ee," she whispers to Ana, clutching her. "I tried so hard to keep you! How?"

"*Du-tlaa,* my mother." Ana feels her mother tremble and holds her to keep her from falling. They stay bound together, each afraid the other is not real, smelling scents, feeling hair. Ut-kart-ee's grip begins to weaken, and they separate enough to share faces, familiar faces.

"It took all of me, *all of me,* to keep the child I had in my arms," Ut-kart-ee whimpers. "I kept *you* alive, here, in my heart."

"I have longed for you, Du-tlaa," Ana sobs, and they hold each other again, one unable to stand without the other. "I was afraid I was a slave."

"*Never* a slave!" Ut-kart-ee declares. "You are *aanyadi*, of noble birth!" She looks at Ana's face and combs her fingers through her hair. "You are She-ee (Limb of a Tree) of the Wolf People, first-born of Ut-kart-ee (Root of a Tree) and Chark Cough-ye (Eagle Lowered from the Sky)."

Do'ok appears over Ana's shoulder. He looks distraught, and Ut-kart-ee's breath catches. Looking beyond, she sees shock and fear on the faces of her People on the ship. She becomes silent, drawing her daughter close again as if to protect her. Her voice shakes as she whispers, "You shouldn't be here. You put Do'ok and yourself in danger."

16

Du-eek (Brother)

Do'ok is enchanted by the enormous ship *Discovery* and is thinking about using sails for his canoe when he notices his mother rush to a young Native and grab her. He watches, seeing a glimpse of the girl's face and his heart shocks as if struck by lightning. Her face is familiar somehow. He moves closer to get a better look.

A-kadi watches the fire of life return to Ut-kart-ee and wonders how he might keep Ana for his sister's sake, at least for a while. If Ana is killed or sent away, Ut-kart-ee's life spirit could be lost forever. On the other hand, if Ana stays, she and Ut-kart-ee could be sent away and they would not survive away from the clan. The bones of those who have tried still rest in the forest, not burned and sent to the Land of the Dead.

Do'ok watches them together, this girl and his mother, so intense in their greeting. When his mother notices him, her face changes from wonder and joy to worry, and he steps back. She waves him over and he sees *his* dimple on the girl's face. He freezes, coming just close enough to whisper, "I thought she was in the Land of the Dead."

"I was wrong, son. This is your brother," she says to Ana, "Do'ok."

"Do'ok," Ana repeats tenderly, turning toward him.

Confusion becomes anger. "Why are you here?" he chokes. "I just learn I'm a twin, the reason I've been feared all my life, and now you come to remind everyone? To put the final arrow into my chest?"

Ana bursts into tears. "I've always loved you," she sobs. "You're my best friend. You visit me in my dreams, with Wolf and sometimes Eagle. You warned me of an earthquake that nearly killed me!"

Do'ok can only see the alarmed faces from his village, igniting his fear. He feels like walking poison as he moves to the other end of the deck to stand alone, always alone, turning his back on his twin. Memories of the Shaman's torture return. *A-kadi will reject me now, send me from the village, he'll have no choice.*

Ana lets Falcon fly, wishing she, also, could soar over the village to see her family without upsetting their lives. The thought that she's brought hardship to them squeezes at her heart. She grips the rail as she relives her brief encounter with them over and over, still wanting more.

Falcon hunts expertly, having watched the falcon family attack their prey. He flies toward their area now, but Raven is there, attempting to feast from their nest. The adult falcons defend their nest and territory, diving at the big black bird and creating chaos in the sky. The flutter and noise alert an instinct in Falcon and he charges, joining the fracas, diving at the raven time and again until it flies away hungry. Falcon returns to his perch on the cliff nearby to watch the falcon family as the sun dips down to the horizon.

Ana sags from the emotion of the day as she waits for Falcon.

"*Not* a slave," Utah says quietly from behind her, the full moon reflecting from his kukui nut necklace. "So what's your plan?"

"I'm a twin, so my future here seems unlikely."

"Maybe it's better to be a twin, though, than a slave since you haven't been *killed* as a twin?"

She realizes that he *has been* a slave, away from his family against his will. His attention to her seems to be a kindness now, and she becomes compassionate. "Please, don't worry about me," she says warmly. "Take care of yourself."

Morning brings fog to reflect Ana's muddied mind since she spent most of the night imagining "What if's," trying to create possibilities for herself to stay, and Falcon has not returned. She doesn't ask to be taken to the village for fear of putting her family in danger. Sitting alone in the galley, she loiters over her oatmeal, stirring more than eating and wonders what her mother and brother and uncle are thinking. Going on deck, she notices an increase of activity, preparation for departure, and her stomach knots. She has no idea if she will go or stay.

Vancouver comes to tell her that he has sent Lieutenant Puget to Baranov regarding the importance of her safety if she is left behind. "Baranov will realize, Ana, that your education makes you valuable and it will enable you to achieve a high station here. You would be able to assist him with negotiations and calm inevitable contentions between people as he creates a new settlement south of here. In fact," he ponders aloud, "you could become important to Russian America. If you stay with Baranov, you could still be near your family."

Being at the Russian camp is not what Ana wants. It's harsh and hostile, and she doesn't trust Baranov. Worst of all, being there might turn her mother and brother even further away from her.

A-kadi meets with the councils on Ana's behalf, but they will not accept her. Her existence is unexplainable, a trick from Raven, something to fear.

"I put her into the forest myself!" the Shaman declares.

A council member speaks up. "We must stay true to our *shagoon*, our heritage, not change who we are by accepting twins!"

"Ana is a healer," A-kadi argues. "She saved the life of the Shaman here. She could help us deal with Cloud-Face tribes."

"Or change us slowly over time like a worm in our bellies," another replies.

Ana moves swiftly through the water in one of her uncle's canoes paddled by him, his friend Kookenaa, and her mother. Vancouver suggested that her family escort her to the Russian camp to give her first Bible lesson as part of the agreement that was negotiated. She sits in front of her mother, wanting to turn and stare, to touch her, to say she's sorry, to ask about her brother, hoping her mother will tell her what to do.

Her first time in a canoe, so close to the water, she tries to remember how to swim just in case she needs to do it. The memory of swimming with Ka'ahumanu brings her a moment of calm and warmth. She begins to use the paddle she was given, mimicking the motions of Kookenaa in front of her as they glide through the water.

They turn toward shore at Naakee-ann to leave Ut-kart-ee to wait during the lesson, not wanting her to be at the Russian settlement. As they approach, Ana thinks about Utah's offer to take her to his family here, but her being a twin could change that. She sees severed Russian heads mounted on poles along the beach and gasps, turning away, shaking her head to rid it of the image of withered heads, missing eyes and tongues, and the idea of living with Utah's family in this place flies away on Raven wings.

Baranov has a rain cover and platform prepared at the Russian camp for Ana to present her message. It's about compassion from *Corinthians*. She hopes it will soften Baranov toward her Tlingit people. Her English is interpreted by an Aleut and delivered to the rough Russian settlers by Baranov himself. They grin and smirk as they hear Baranov speak of love.

A-kadi arranges with Captain Vancouver for Ana to stay the night in her family's little house on the edge of Raven Clan for the sake of his sister. It will give the family time together before Ana must leave.

Her younger siblings take her hand and tell her about their father Chark Cough-ye and his battles and show his personal belongings. By the time they're finished, he seems so alive that she can feel him with her, and she feels part of the family.

At storytelling time, Do'ok comes into the house as if on cue. His unexpected arrival causes Ana to tighten, and the younger children climb all over him. "A-kadi said I should be here," he explains "as storyteller." They settle around the fire and he tells a few traditional stories, sneaking peeks at Ana during the telling.

In the beginning, before the great flood, Raven was Power. He created the world and brought us the sun and the moon and water and taught us many things. Now he is a spirit helper that we respect for all he has done. We treat him well and are thankful for the gifts he has given.

Raven used to have a straight, beautiful beak. A story of how it became curved is that he hung by his beak from the dome over the earth to hold his mother up out of the great flood to keep her from drowning . . . Who would not do that to save their mother?

They all look at their mother who smiles back, her eyes glistening. She watches them together as if it has always been that way while Do'ok's voice washes over her, cleaning away much of her grief from the death of her husband. Her heart feels full, and her family seems complete now that Ana is there.

Ana wiggles her toes near the fire, surrounded by the sweet smell of cedar and the warmth of her siblings, thanking God for this moment. Her favorite story is about the night that Do'ok and her father faced the bear and her father earned a second name, Bear Killer. The children proudly show her the bear claws as evidence of the story.

"I'm grateful to know this story of my father," she smiles, "and to meet my family living here in An-ar-kark."

"You've been alone?" Do'ok asks.

Ana nods.

"I know about feeling alone," he confides, siblings hanging onto his arms.

"You have a mother and family and had a father! How could you feel alone?"

"Because I am a twin." He wonders if she also had a difficult life as he hugs his mother before returning to Wolf Clan house and A-kadi.

Ana falls asleep in the furs with her siblings, feeling at peace. Wolf joins her in her dreams, leading her into the forest. Eagle arrives and folds his enormous wings to sit on a tree limb over-head while Falcon waits for her further down a green path.

The morning tide and wind are good for *Discovery* and *Chatham* to depart, fresh water and food stored for the trip. Captain Vancouver asks Ana to speak with him in his cabin. He must have her decision whether she will go with them or stay. She finds Dr. Menzies and Lieutenant Puget there as well.

"We will travel down the coast and can stop at your Spanish mission, Ana. We can easily take you back if you wish," Vancouver offers.

"Now that you have met your family, maybe you don't feel so compelled to stay?" Lieutenant Puget suggests.

"I *must* stay," Ana replies, "to fulfill the purpose that saved my life as an infant, and I need more time here, to know my family, to try to make it right somehow. I suppose I will stay at the Russian camp though. It seems to be my only choice."

"At least you should be safe there," Vancouver says with relief.

"Weel, let's have a drink to tha' then, young lass!" Dr. Menzies speaks with fervor in an attempt to distract the tear that wants to form in his eye. He produces his prized Scotch whiskey *and* his tin of shortbread cookies. "Could be the last time yer able to enjoy such a treat." He pours each of them a dram into Vancouver's China cups and passes the tin. "Dinna inhale when ya drink, lass."

"Smooth," Vancouver smiles, savoring the drink. "Why can't *this* be your prescription for my cough?"

"I dinna want a tipsy captain," Menzies replies, pouring himself another drink. "You'd probably start fake'n yer cough ta get my supply."

Ana touches her lips to the amber liquid and feels the sting of Scotch. Tears form instantly as she realizes that she's saying goodbye to these men who have kept her safe and taught her so much and have seemed like fathers to her. She wonders if her life will ever stop being a continual process of saying goodbye to people she loves. She has been so focused on her Tlingit family that she has not, for even one breath, considered saying goodbye on ship. She has no idea how to go about it as she continues to sip her drink. Soon, the pain in her heart is dulled.

"I will never forget you," she announces loudly. "If the world were filled with men like you," her words come freely now, "we would all enjoy Heaven on Earth!" She smiles, wondering if her tongue is swollen, making it more difficult to speak.

Captain Vancouver calls his steward, Mr. Bonner, to help Ana to her quarters and assist her in packing her things. "Dinna forget yer weapons, lass," Menzies warns as she gets up to go. She turns and gives each of them a loving embrace. Uncomfortable with the sentiment, they pat her gently on the back saying words like, "Take care" and "Be careful."

Vancouver tells Lieutenant Puget to send word to Ana's family that she will be taken to the Russian camp on *Discovery*. "I want to deliver Ana myself," Vancouver says, "so that I can be sure of the arrangement. Also, if A-kadi or Do'ok want to come with us, we can bring a small canoe on board for them to paddle back to An-ar-kark because we will continue on."

Finished packing, Ana stands on deck with her belongings when she hears Do'ok request permission to board. "Your captain sent word that this is a good time to talk," he says, his eyes wandering about the ship. They sit together in a corner out of the way of the crew, and Ana feels like she's awake in one of her happy dreams with her best friend, except that he's real.

"I thought I was wishing for my mother all this time," she tells him. "Now I know that I was also longing for you, brother."

"I didn't know I had a twin, that *I* am a twin, until recently, after our father died," Do'ok confides. "I guess I looked for you too without knowing it."

Master Whidbey calls "All Hands!" signaling crew to go aloft up the ratlines and Do'ok watches them climb. "The Eagle in your dream is our father," he explains tenderly. "He died protecting our village."

"Was he a good father."

Do'ok feels the emptiness within her question. "The best," he says, "I would help you know him." He seems to instinctively understand her without all the words.

She tells him about growing up in the mission and her Tlingit slave family there and the Ohlone people. He tells her what it was like to grow up with her mother and father as parents, and she sits back, closing her eyes, imagining herself to be there too. "For some reason, now that I have met you, I feel more whole, like I have all my arms and legs," he admits, waving his arms and legs in the air.

She laughs and grabs his hands to kiss his knuckles and touches them to each side of her face to wipe away her tears. They gravitate toward each other like magnets, and when they arrive at the Russian camp, before he leaves to return to An-ar-kark, he gives his promise to see her again. As she sees him go, his absence is quickly filled with her awareness that she is alone, again.

Her room in the stores building at the Russian Camp is larger than her berth on ship and very cold. She worries about not having a fire. The food in storage must be kept cold, and the ammunition stored there makes a fire too dangerous. She's thankful that she has her deerskin clothing and boots and her rabbit fur blanket and will need to find something even warmer for winter.

"I grew up in a mission," she tells Baranov the next morning. "I know what it is to work. I can process and cook food, make soap and candles, clean, plant and harvest, but I know nothing about fishing or hunting."

Baranov tells her to help with food and cooking and serve as a teacher. "We have a few children and, God willing, there will be more, so plan to add Russian to your repertoire of languages."

"May I ask what compels the settlers to live here in such difficult surroundings? Why do they choose a life of hardship?"

"Well first of all, it is a life," he explains. "These people were either starving on the streets or criminals in prison. They are willing to work hard and take chances in order to have *any* kind of life. So you might want to be cautious around them, although there are a few good people here. That's why it's important for them, for all of us, to hear the Word of God and to be reminded of moral living, to give hope for a better future."

"So you intend to stay permanently in Anaaski?" she asks, hoping for "No."

"We'll travel further south as Vancouver requested," he replies. "The Aleut call it Aguanalasksh 'Where the sea breaks its back,' but it's Russian America now. We have a settlement northwest of here and we'll continue to establish ourselves in the territory."

That evening in her room she burns a candle and stares at Falcon's empty cage. Wind blows in the trees outside, invading her room, and the flickering candlelight makes shadowed fingers through his cage that seem to claw the wall. She wonders if she'll ever see him again. The ghost of his house and the constant rain make her aloneness even worse.

She wonders how she ended up in this cold, muddy camp full of people who either hate her or whom she can't trust. Some of the settlers seem more dangerous than the Aleut. The memory of their aggressive eyes on her make her shudder. As she tries to sleep, she reminds herself that Do'ok left her a small canoe so she could leave if need be, but she doubts she could make it through the rough surf alone, and she has nowhere to go anyway.

In her dreams, Wolf is angry, standing in front of her, locking his eyes onto hers. He snarls, his nose wrinkles up the sides, showing his menacing canines. His feet are spread as if preparing to fight, head slightly lowered. Ana isn't afraid. Instead, she feels emboldened. She wants to *join* him in the fight, against what, she doesn't know. She feels like Wolf wants her to be strong.

Her first work in the Russian camp is to prepare fish for a stew. The Aleut women who work with her speak between themselves, making sideways glances at her, and she remembers Dr. Menzies' parting words, "Dinna forget yer weapons, lass." That evening she sews a long pocket inside a flap of her tunic where she deposits her dirk and the tiny pistol becomes her bedmate.

The next day she asks to speak with Baranov, and a rough, grizzly-faced man tells her in his own version of English that Baranov has left the camp. He himself is the new commander. Ana's heart races. She knows that Baranov is the one who keeps order in camp, and she doesn't like the too interested way this man looks at her. She feels like a rabbit in a trap. The voice in her head says, "Get out!"

Quickly to her room, she gathers her things and carries them to Do'ok's canoe. A hand juts out, grabbing her wrist too firmly, hurting her. "Where are you going?" the new commander demands.

Ana is held firm, unable to move, "Let me go!"

The man's jaw drops, and his eyebrows lift in surprise as Utah steps out from behind him holding a gun. "Let go of her," he demands.

Instantly, the new commander releases her arm.

Staggered, she tries to cover her fear, "I am going to see my family. Baranov would not want me to be detained." She and Utah push the boat into the water, and she climbs in, saying a quick prayer, hoping to get away without being shot or having to swim.

She paddles hard against the current and wind while Utah paddles efficiently, the strength of his arms and back propelling the canoe forcefully ahead. They travel several miles, sure they aren't followed, and she turns to him. "Utah! What are you *doing* here?" she screams over the wind. "Did you jump ship?"

"No," he calls. "Vancouver *released* me from duty in exchange for my promise to watch after you if you can believe it! Only Vancouver would do something like that."

Sobs erupt from Ana. She didn't realize how intently she had been trying to be strong, control her fear. "Only Vancouver," she repeats, shaking her head. "I was feeling so alone and afraid." She smiles through bleary eyes at Utah. The back of his hand wipes her tears away.

The weather slows their trip, and sea spray soaks her face, hair and clothing as they keep paddling. Her shoulders stiffen from the repetitive pull on the paddle, hands become tender with blisters. She notices tiny bundles of flowers tied together, lying in the bottom of the canoe, miniature yellow suns surrounded by dainty blue skies.

"What are these?" she asks, holding a bouquet up to Utah.

"Forget-me-nots," he replies. "I meant to leave them in the canoe for you, but it seemed you needed my help."

She wonders about this man who seems to care about her.

The sun lowers to the horizon as they reach Naakee-ann, and she looks away from the ghastly heads on posts as they reach the beach. Residents keep their distance, meaning that she's not welcome. "I've already had my homecoming," Utah explains, "so they're not surprised at *my* being here. It won't help your reputation if I stay with you, so I'm going. If you need me, I'm at Coho Clan."

As Ana's grandmother said, her name is on her face. The villagers know Do'ok well and instantly recognize her as his twin. She asks for the only name she knows here, the one who Do'ok spoke about, "May I speak to K'aan-at-shi?" she asks in Tlingit.

Soon, K'aan-at-shi and her family come to the beach, shocked to see Do'ok's twin. K'aan-at-shi's father turns to those nearby. "This one's brother and her Vancouver saved our village from war. We must balance their generous act by welcoming her for the night." He and his family usher Ana into their home.

"Thank you," Ana says, keeping her eyes down. "I was afraid at the Cloud-Face camp."

"You are Tlingit," K'aan-at-shi says. "You shouldn't be there at all. Is that not correct, father?"

"It's a matter for Wolf Clan of An-ar-kark," her father replies. "We can provide help when needed. It would dishonor Frog Clan to ignore their family member when we know Wolf Clan would always help one of ours."

Inside their home, Ana is shown to a place on the platform near the family's fire as the evening meal is prepared. "I'm happy to meet you," she says to K'aan-at-shi. "I understand why Do'ok wants to spend time with you."

The pink of K'aan-at-shi's cheeks blooms. "I like him also," she says, looking to her parents.

"I wonder if I might be able to stay in the village a few *days*," Ana asks, "while the Russian leader Baranov is away."

"I will speak to the Council tomorrow," K'aan-at-shi's father replies.

The next morning, Ana is outside to greet the day and Utah approaches, dressed in apron and cape. Highlights of auburn flicker in his hair as it freely floats behind him. He walks smoothly, swinging his arms with ease, arms and legs used for climbing the rigging of a ship. His skin has already paled a bit since it was toasted by the tropical sun of Hawai'i. "I just wanted to check on you Shaaya-al. Where is Falcon?"

"Falcon didn't return from hunting before Vancouver left. You can't watch over me like Vancouver planned, you know. He doesn't understand Tlingit custom. It's wrong for me to talk to you." She lowers her eyes, "unless we were married."

"Someone must speak for you since your family doesn't. What will you do?"

"I don't know," she sighs, walking away.

Utah turns, watching out the corner of his eye and his brows squeeze together. *Did she say 'married'?*

17

Taakw (Winter)

Do'ok arrives at Naakee-ann to see K'aan-at-shi before going on to see Ana at the Cloud-Face camp, but as he walks through the village, he sees Ana talking to a man. She explains that she left the Cloud-Face camp because she was afraid and that Utah helped her.

"*Da su see tee?* What clan are you?" Do'ok asks.

"Coho Clan of the Raven People." Utah moves closer to Ana, protective. "Vancouver released me from the ship to watch over her."

Do'ok's eyebrows rise in surprise.

"I told him that Vancouver doesn't understand our customs," Ana adds.

"In truth, you shouldn't be talking with *me* without a chaperone," Do'ok agrees. "Do you wish to marry her, Utah?"

"Maybe," he replies, surprising them all.

She looks up at him, eyes wide.

"I'm not afraid of your Power, and I might like to be needed. It seems my family was fine without me." His eyes linger on her face.

"What power?" she asks.

"The Power that allows you to be alive and to return to the home of your birth, of course. It would help, though, if you don't remind others that you are a twin," he continues. "You and your brother shouldn't be together."

Do'ok and Ana look at each other. "I *just* found him!" she cries.

Ana is allowed to stay in the women's house at Naakee-ann although her presence makes the other women uncomfortable. That night, she's revisited by Wolf in her dreams. Again, Wolf is angry, and it fills her with determination. In the morning, she asks Do'ok to take her to An-ar-kark.

In An-ar-kark she finds Ut-kart-ee at home, and her worries pour out, "I don't feel safe and my deepest wish is to live with you! I'll go to the Council myself, but not if it causes harm to my family. Please mother, tell me what to do!"

Ut-kart-ee holds her daughter, a sly smile on her face. "I've never shied away from trouble, daughter. You should do what *you* know to be right. You'll spend the night here, with me."

At Wolf Council, Ana looks directly into the eyes of each of the house leaders and the Shaman, knowing it is ill-mannered, wanting them to see the Power that Utah says she has. "I did not come here to disappear," she begins quietly. "I am here to make a difference, to tell about the Christian God, and to help you be strong to face the Cloud-Face tribes. They are everywhere. I've seen it." Her voice enlarges as she continues. "More and more ships and settlers will come and change Wolf Clan's *shagoon*, fate. I can help protect you!"

The Council is stunned by Ana's brazen speech, especially since it comes from a female, a twin they have the right to kill. "What do *you* have to gain?" a Council member asks.

"I wish to be with my family . . . and to know why twins are kush-tar-ka."

"I can explain," the Shaman offers. "In the beginning, all the People were happy until twins were born. One was good at hunting and fishing, the other was always hungry. When the hunter drank water, the hungry brother hit him on the head with a rock and pushed him into the water. An elder came up from the vapor and said, 'You have killed your brother; now, wherever you drink, the waters will become bitter,' and so it is. One twin will be good, the other will always be bad."

"So it is a twin that gave us our hot springs where our elders go to soak their aching bones!" A-kadi interjects. "How many have said those waters are a gift from the spirits?"

The Shaman and other Council members are quiet, never having been asked to question the meaning of a legend handed down from the ancestors.

A-kadi continues. "There is a difference among the Cloud-Face tribes. Like Ana's Vancouver, some are worthy of our attention. Others should be kept away. She would help us know the difference and speak their languages."

"She brings healing powers we've not seen before," the Shaman admits.

White flakes silently float down from the sky like eagle down as Ana walks back to her family's little home. Startled, she stops, trying to examine the tiny designs before they melt on her skin. When the flakes enlarge and come faster, filling the sky, she panics and hurries home but is unwilling to go inside. The snow is new and magical, and she can't stop watching it fall, seeing it accumulate, turning the world white. She picks it up, squishing it in her fingers.

The door-flap of the house opens, and her younger siblings run outside. They scoop the snow, squeezing it into balls and throw it at each other, laughing. Ana is hit in the face with a cold, wet, slushy splat, and she throws handfuls back until her fingers are numb. Inside, she experiences the greatest contentment she's known, sitting between her siblings, warmed by the fire.

The next morning, she squats on her haunches at the shoreline to watch a *dulth*, crane. It stands unmoving on one leg, the other tucked up against its body for warmth as it looks out over the water. Time stands still as if an entire day could pass without a distraction. Its wings extend, longer than Ana is tall and a great down-push with a few steps launches the regal bird into the air. As it flies, Ana hears its throaty, rattling call, and time begins again at the same moment that an arrow whizzes past her arm, leaving a bloody slash. Shocked, she turns to see her Uncle A-kadi coming toward her.

"I have news from the Council . . . What's wrong?"

She rocks, holding her arm. "I'm not sure."

A-kadi removes her hand to see, then goes to find the arrow on the beach. "I'll speak to this person. He wasn't trying to kill you, or you'd be dead. Now that the decision of the Council is made, you should be safe."

Trembling, Ana washes her arm in sea water.

"You may stay through *taakw*, winter."

"Thank you!" She wraps her good arm around him. "I'll earn their trust! I promise!"

A-kadi is taken aback by her embrace, realizing that she doesn't have the reserve of someone raised in their culture. "They don't want you to die alone during the cold winter, that's all. They're afraid Vancouver would come to take his revenge."

Ana has learned to manage one of her uncle's small canoes, and she bravely takes herself to the Russian camp for her weekly Bible message, not wanting to burden her family. She's allowed to spend the night with K'aan-at-shi at Naakee-ann, hoping that Utah is secretly watching out for her because she imagines another arrow at any moment.

At the Russian camp, she's relieved to see that Baranov has returned, but he seems unwilling to admit that she was in danger during his absence. "My man was watching over you." He waves the matter away with his hand.

She feels the hackles of Wolf stand just behind her ears and dismisses *him*. "Well I live at An-ar-kark now."

"Good, our new location is not far beyond. You can continue your lessons there."

She wants the Russians to be far away from her village. "Do you have permission from the leaders there? Are you prepared to trade?"

He seems unconcerned. "I haven't asked yet. You need to interpret for me."

His smug over-confidence churns in her stomach. For ten heartbeats she thinks she might let him get what he deserves. "If I translate for you, what will you offer to avoid war?"

Winter is a relatively quiet time. Most food gathering and processing is complete. Time is spent making clothing, baskets, and gifts to prepare for the ceremonies, marriages, and memorial potlatches which occur in winter. No ships enter the bay for trade in winter.

Ana feels the wet chill penetrate her deer-skin clothing and boots, and she keeps herself wrapped in her rabbit-fur blanket most of the time. The rain seems relentless with brief moments of snow as the days shorten. She relaxes into life with her mother who teaches her how to create baskets in her Wolf design, and the Shaman allows her to assist in healing and births while he attends to spirit. She gets to know his son T'aay.

A-kadi sees Utah walking through the village and steps in front of him. The two men stand eye to eye. "You may not see Ana without supervision."

"You treat her like *family* now?" Utah asks, disregard in his voice.

A-kadi ignores the attitude. "It's obvious she's ours. She has permission to stay through winter. Why are you interested?"

"Do'ok didn't tell you? I wish to marry her. Is it you I ask?"

A-kadi tells him to wait a few days for an answer and goes to find Ut-kart-ee. "You can't stay in this little house any longer," he declares.

She looks up from her baskets. *Now what?*

"This house is for Raven Clan. If you insist on being so stubborn as to not marry again, you will move back to Wolf Clan House where I can speak for you."

"I need no one to speak for me, brother," her chin is held high.

"It's not just for you," he explains. "A Raven from Naakee-ann has offered marriage to Ana. Who will speak for her?"

Ut-kart-ee stands, preparing to argue and realizes that what A-kadi says is true. Slowly, she looks around her little home with love for all its memories, knowing she feels closest to Chark Cough-ye here. "Please send slaves tomorrow to help us move" *for my daughter's sake.* She returns to her basket-making, her head hanging a little lower than before.

Living at Wolf Clan House with her family and other clan members reminds Ana of the mission. Utah arrives to ask for her and stands with pride, wearing his ceremonial tunic decorated with Coho and Raven designs, his hair twisted into a knot. A-kadi intervenes, "Wait until spring for a decision about your proposal. If Ana must leave then, it would not be wise for her to marry."

"If we marry," Utah argues, his hands forming fists, "she would live with me in Coho Clan at Naakee-ann. Your Council has no voice there."

"The decision of *our* Council may affect whether she wants to stay *anywhere* in the area," A-kadi explains with irritation. "Find someone else, for your own sake."

"I wish to speak with her," Utah demands. A-kadi raises his eyebrows as he walks away.

Ana continues health care during the winter, attending births with the Shaman when the family allows. On the edge of the village, twins are born, and attitudes instantly change from joy to guarded and somber. The elder aunt who cares for the new mother looks to the Shaman to take over.

Ana sees the moment when her own newborn fate was chosen and can't let them die. "We'll keep these babies," she says firmly, knowing it will be trouble.

A-kadi learns of her decision and is furious. All decisions within the clan are made through the Council. The family with twins will be shunned and forced to move away. Ana has created an impossible life for them because of *her* choice.

Several days later, Ana returns to check on the mother and babies and finds the mother distraught. At the insistence of her relatives, the babies have been taken into the forest.

"Maybe I can save them!" Ana barks, heading to the doorway.

"Days ago," the mother replies, waving Ana back into the house. She looks away, the back of her hand pressing against her mouth. "They're gone."

At home, Ana thinks of the tiny innocents alone in the cold forest. She cries, cuts her hair, covers her face in charcoal and prays for them, asking the Lord for grace through the Holy Spirit.

Ut-kart-ee sees Ana's acts of mourning and remembers painfully her fight to keep just one baby. "I was angry with Ke-an-kow over the years," she admits to Ana. "Now I'm thankful that He took care of you!"

Ana shakes her head. "I just can't let those babies be forgotten. I know change takes time, especially when there's fear and beliefs involved. Maybe I can try again with the Council . . ."

"Thank you for allowing me to speak. I'm here to say that twins are not trouble. My brother Do'ok has helped Naakee-ann Village avoid war with the Russian Cloud-Face. I have helped as a healer and brought Vancouver to you. Ke-an-kow says that all children, even twins, are a heritage, part of our shagoon.

"Life is always changing. Wolf Clan's treatment of twins can change. The salmon berry bush will become taller next year unless the deer trim the new, tender leaves or there is a drought or insects take it. Change is constant.

"Change will come from Cloud-Face tribes. More and more will come. We need all babies, and twins, to increase our numbers against them. I have been to a place where twins are sacred. Let them live. Learn their potential."

A Council member is tired of waiting, tired of listening. "The family of the woman who had twins demands compensation for the great distress you caused. They ask for five blankets."

A-kadi gives Ana a stern look. "I will provide payment," he states gruffly.

Days get shorter and colder and a Wolf Clan memorial potlatch is scheduled. Guests come from many villages including Utah who has been looking for an opportunity to see Ana. He assumes she will be expected to participate.

She's pleased that some of her baskets are used as gifts for the Potlatch and impressed by the speeches and ceremonies, the chanting and dancing, the beautiful regalia and crest clothing. To her great surprise, Tinx brings her a beautiful deer-skin tunic decorated in tiny shells that have been sewn into rows of Wolf ear shapes. "This is to demonstrate my place as the sister of your father," she says, helping her to put it on.

"It's beautiful!" Ana squeezes her aunt and wears the new tunic to the evening celebration. After watching the dancing for a long while, she stands to join in, lifting her feet like the others, but they move away, so she stops and joins A-kadi and Utah where they stand watching.

"He wishes to speak with you," A-kadi says. "He's been bothering me for weeks." Then he goes to stand a short distance away, arms crossed.

Utah moves close in front of Ana, looking down into her face. "What's stopping you?" he asks quietly.

"What?"

"How long will you wait for Wolf Clan Council to determine your fate? It's very traditional to wait for a Council, the spirits, your dreams, or whatever to tell you what to do, but you have seen enough of the world to know that you can make decisions for yourself. Do you wish to stay here or not?"

"Yes, I want to be with my family."

"Well, it doesn't depend on any Council," he trembles with frustration. "If you *want* to stay, I am asking you to marry me. We will live at Naakee-ann and you can see your family often."

Ana looks to the ground, shaking her head from side to side. "I don't know. Maybe I need to *feel* accepted by the Council of my own People, and I don't think the councils of Naakee-ann will want me either."

Utah is silent, also looking at the ground as he watches his toe make an X in the dirt. "Then I release myself from my promise to Vancouver to look after you. I've tried my best. You have your uncle and mother now." He walks away into the bouncing crowd of dancers.

Ana's chest tightens, surprised by his abruptness. She wonders if she's made a grave mistake. She's felt safe with him, the one who would find a life for her somewhere no matter how difficult, and she immediately wishes him back. Her wait for Council decisions among people who do not accept her begins to feel like she sinks in thick, murky water, and suddenly, it's difficult to breath.

Sharpness of winter softens, north winds calm, and rain comes even harder. The world is on the verge of spring. Having hardened herself during the coldest months, Ana is able to collect new underwater plants and seaweed from the rocks with her younger siblings, her feet slipping on the frigid stones. The men go hunting for fresh meat to revive them from their winter diet, and the work of processing and storing begins again.

Ana watches the feeding frenzy that occurs with the arrival of the spawning herring: gulls and eagles overhead fill the air, and seals, sea lions and whales stir the water as they gorge themselves. Seeing the activity breathes new life into her. She helps her family place hemlock boughs on the shore to gather fish-eggs and is surprised at their delicious, light taste. The village is once again filled with fish and fish-eggs hanging to dry and everyone is busy.

Although she has not traveled to the Russians during the coldest months to give Bible lessons, now she paddles with an elder slave to the new camp which lies south, her gun and dirk hidden inside her tunic and cape. She wonders what this new camp will be like. As they manage through the waves, she thinks of the little knife that Dr. Menzies showed her that she could have kept in her boot now that she *has* boots, and smiles, thinking of him.

She realizes that she's become a different person since Dr. Menzies and Captain Vancouver left her at An-ar-kark. In spite of being uncertain of her future, she feels more self-confident, that both Zesen and Queen Ka'ahumanu would be proud of her because of her courage. She knows her mother and grandmother are proud.

"What's your story, Kit'aa (Stick for Prying)?" she asks the slave who paddles with her. "Who are your People, and how long have you been here?"

Kit'aa is surprised that this young woman would be interested and would ask such personal questions. "My people are from Eagle Clan of the Wolf People in the North. I've been here ten years."

Ana is confused. "A slave at the hands of your own People?"

He shrugs, "There was a battle between your clan and mine, and I was captured."

"Why have you not tried to escape? or escape now?" She knows she'd let him go.

"The slaves who cause trouble are the ones who are sacrificed," Kit'aa explains. "I think it's best to be a good slave."

"I'm sorry." She wonders if she is putting herself in danger by befriending this man. "Is there not someone from your Eagle Clan who has the ability to trade you back?"

"There was sickness in my village, and few survive. Maybe one day I will be released. I'd like to be a free man before I die, to have a soul and go to the Land of the Dead rather than left on the beach like a dog."

Ana is learning that being a slave is a life of neglect. She wonders if people who are treated as non-persons eventually *believe* they are nothing and is thankful her brothers and sisters at the mission are no longer slaves. "There's a way for you to go to a beautiful Land of the Dead called Heaven where you can be with Ke-an-kow," she says softly. "Would you like to know about that?"

Before Kit'aa can respond, she sees the Russian camp and is shocked by the many sturdy wooden buildings, one with a second level on top, surrounded by a thick barricade of upright logs, and she realizes that the word "camp" is no longer appropriate.

Baranov comes to greet her looking healthy and excited. "Welcome to New Archangel!" he calls.

"Have you permission from the locals for all of this?" she waves her hand to encompass the entire settlement.

"They actually *sold* me the land!" Baranov declares, his eyes alight. "We even invite the local Tlingit to dances! . . . even though we need to remove their weapons at the door."

Ana feels uneasy but gives the Bible lesson, telling the story of God commanding Raven to bring food to Elijah each day, morning and night after years of no rain.

Returning to An-ar-kark, Ana tells A-kadi what she's seen at the Russian settlement. He looks away as if he already knows and soberly tells her that the Council has decided her fate. "It's spring. You must leave."

Ana's spirit hovers above her body.

A-kadi sees her face go pale and tries to explain. "The trouble you caused with the delivery of twins showed the Council that you will always interfere. Your determination to do as you wish, like your mother I might add, causes problems."

"What did the Shaman say?" Ana asks faintly.

"He said you have Power and it's not wicked, but he sees trouble ahead with you."

"Where am I supposed to go?"

"The new Cloud-Face settlement would probably be best, even though it may not be entirely safe."

She remembers her discomfort at Baranov's comment about the dances and covers her face. *My father would protect me.* "Uncle, what would my father have me do?"

He shakes his head toward his feet, "I don't know."

Alone again and afraid, she wanders away from the village and into the forest looking for solace. It's dark and quiet, the thick canopy above protecting her from rain, and the only breeze is high in the treetops. Standing still, she hears the forest creatures begin their songs. She sits on a moss-covered log, closing her eyes, just being, feeling, smelling the rich, ancient dirt and the sweet and pungent growing things. An unexpected "guffaw" erupts from her mouth when she realizes that just hours before she'd been feeling strong and confident, and now she's unwanted and lost. *Nothing is certain.*

She prays for protection and a clear path ahead. Instead, she sees her father's face, torn by the claws of a bear, and he smiles at her. Tears flood her eyes and drip down her face. She hasn't taken time to really think of him, and now she can feel him with her. She blinks, trying to clear her vision and through the mist, she sees a large gray wolf with golden eyes. The sight causes her stomach to grip.

She hears Falcon call and looks up just in time to see him settle down onto her arm. "Falcon!" she cries. "You've come when I need you most! How did you find me? Oh how I've missed you." She strokes his head. Falcon's piercing eyes look at her and at her surroundings. "Looking for a nice rat from a ship?" she asks. "Will you stay with me now? Or do you have a family of your own?" She hears another falcon call, and he becomes agitated, squeezing one set of talons, then the other. He looks at Ana for four breaths of time and pushes off to fly through an opening in the canopy.

"Come back some day," she calls after him, relieved that he's okay and that he has a friend. She looks for Wolf, but he's gone.

Gifts, she thinks to herself. *I've been given gifts . . . to feel my father with me, to know that Falcon is well, to know my family . . . I should be thankful.* She accepts what's been given, feeling it renew her and walks out of the forest and back to An-ar-kark, planning to send word to Utah, asking if he will visit her one more time.

18

An-ar-kark (Village on the Shore)

Ships come in spring, many of them American ships from Boston, the "Boston Men," trading guns for sea otter and other skins. A-kadi and Wolf Clan are ready. They've been hunting sea otter and other game with seriousness, knowing that trading their skins is the best way to attain guns, and guns are the only way to keep the unwanted Cloud-Face tribes at a distance. With the first American ship of the season, Wolf Clan is able to trade skins for two dozen muskets and extra ammunition along with a small cannon and canisters of grape shot. Other clans trade for guns as well.

A-kadi and Ana work together. He bargains for weapons and lessons on their use. She uses her English skills to ask the captain about what might break and methods of repair, making sure the moving parts are not faulty like the ones Vancouver encountered. Many of Wolf Clan, including some women, are trained to use a musket, practicing with them for hunting. Ut-kart-ee asks to be trained along with the others, but A-kadi is afraid that her temper will cause the death of someone without sufficient cause, so he doesn't arrange it.

At the same time, Ana is nervous about the increased activity in the bay and wants to be liaison between her People and the ships. Thankfully, the Council seems too busy to enforce their decision for her to leave the village right away. She still hopes to prove her value and change their decision.

Village Council strives to keep control, requiring that the Boston Men stay on their ships at night. The clans of An-ar-kark don't drink the rum they receive as gifts knowing it weakens them. Instead, seeing the power it has over Cloud-Face tribes, they put it into storage houses for later trade back to them.

Wispy ghosts float and hover just above the water. The Shaman can see them, the spirits of those who have already died from a Ship of Sickness just arrived. At his direction, green, six-foot spikey stalks of devil's club are attached to every doorway and window in An-ar-kark. Their large, maple-shape leaves hide the thorns on their undersides, doing their best to keep the dark shadows of sickness away. Ana hopes the devil's club will also keep people inside their homes.

"The last time this happened," Do'ok shudders, "most of Crane Clan was taken by the sickness." His stomach tightens, remembering his torture from the Shaman, being *blamed* for the sickness. "The few of Crane Clan who survived were adopted into our clan."

Ana goes to the Shaman. "The people from Crane Clan who recovered last time may not get sick this time. They're the ones to help us care for the sick now."

The Shaman grinds his jaw, remembering how powerless he felt last time. He speaks to the few remaining Crane Clan to ask for help, but they are controlled by fear, remembering the pain of losing their family. The only person who volunteers is Yahaayi.

"It's time I earn some respect," Yahaayi tells Ana, pounding his staff on the ground as if to convince himself.

Ana sees fear on his face and touches his hand, wanting to encourage him. "Thank you for saving my tiny life in the forest."

He grins, enjoying the pleasure of being thanked for something. "I guess I was moved by Power to do it," he says, though he knows he was motivated by greed. "I hope your Power will protect me now."

"My power?"

"Yes!" He's surprised she seems unaware of her Power. "The fact that you've come *back* to us and have not been *killed* shows you have Power! Also, you have Ke-an-kow's book and you know His thoughts."

"Well, I can't promise you'll be safe, but we'll be careful. Ask Raven Clan to send slaves to each house, tell everyone to stay inside, not go to any ship for trade no matter what."

Wolf Clan slaves are sent for medicinal plants. They gather bladderwack seaweed from the beach and pound the inner bark of spruce on hot rocks, mixing it with oil in case of skin eruptions. They make poultices of devil's club for the pain and swelling and collect willow-bark and rose-hip for tea.

Ana, her mother and Aunt Tinx cut and tie English cloth, making something like a mask. Dr. Menzies had described them to Ana, beak-like, stuffed with fragrant herbs used during a plague to cover doctor's faces. Simple cloth masks to cover nose and mouth are the best they can do. She's thinking of the safest way to proceed when Utah arrives. He seems irritated, distracted.

"I've been away . . . just received your message," he mumbles.

"Utah! I'm so happy to see you! We *do* need to talk, but you have to leave!"

Abruptly, he stands straighter, angry. "Do you think this is a game?" he shouts, "because I do not! You've played with my offer to marry long enough!"

"We have sickness! See the devil's club?" she points. "Please, go back, keep your People at home!"

The green warning causes his eyes to enlarge. "What about you?" he softens.

"I need to help. I'll send word when this has passed." She pushes him away.

Ana is paddled to the Ship of Sickness with her face cloth securely on to talk with the captain, calling to him from her canoe. "Please understand, captain, that you will not be allowed to come ashore or to put your sick or your dead on our beach. We will deliver fresh water to you, and you must release your dead to the deep, out into the sea, far away from our bay."

"Who are *you* to speak for this village?" he asks, having noticed she speaks English with a Spanish accent.

"I am niece of the most powerful chief here," she replies. "We will shoot anyone who comes ashore."

"You know we can destroy your village from here, yes?" the captain calls back.

"Yes," Ana replies, "and other ships and our benefactor, Captain George Vancouver, would learn of it, and you would face a courtroom and judge for any deaths you cause!"

With that, the captain disappears from the side of the ship, and with the support of A-kadi, she has their casks filled with fresh water and delivered twice a day.

People who had been on ship to trade before the Shaman announced the sickness become ill, and Ana declares those first houses to become quarantined, the healthy inside helping the sick. Slaves are told to take fresh water and food to their doors. The People feel there is hope with Ana at work, wearing her mask. She seems to know what to do and acts with confidence. Even so, those who were already sick, some elders and children weaken and die, and Ana knows it's time to build the funeral pyres.

When sickness enters Hawk Clan House, she holds the fevered hand of her grandmother Yake-see, and puts a cool damp cloth on her forehead. "Will you drink tea, grandmother?" She holds her grandmother's treasured English cup, a gift from Vancouver, as encouragement.

"If it will please you," Yake-see's voice is faint. "I wish to see your grandfather Al'ooni. He waits for me in the Land of the Dead. You're strong, granddaughter, and good. I thank the spirits for the gift of meeting you."

"I am thankful it was you I met on the beach, grandmother."

Ana prays and tearfully sends word for the family to say their goodbyes, letting them come a few at a time using the masks and sending them to the river to wash. Ut-kart-ee stays, refusing to let go of her mother's hand until her spirit has flown.

"She was a loving mother," Ut-kart-ee says, sitting on the raised platform. She bites the inside of her mouth to keep from sobbing, wanting her mother's path to the Land of the Dead to be dry, not muddy from her tears.

Even though Yake-see seems to sleep, her eyes flicker at Ut-kart-ee's voice and she forms faint words, "I'm sorry I gave the baby to the Shaman." Ut-kart-ee gently squeezes her mother's shoulder.

"May the Lord in his love and mercy help you with the grace of the Holy Spirit," Ana prays. With a long sigh of release, peace consumes her grandmother.

Shouk waits outside for Ut-kart-ee. "My second mother," Ut-kart-ee says when she sees her childhood caregiver. "Do you remember that painful bath after my rite of passage?"

Shouk pats her hand. "A different sort of pain. This will wash away in time."

When the sickness is battled in only two remaining houses, the weary Shaman and his son T'aay continue to scare away dark spirits. Wearing spirit masks and carrying animal charms, they fast and drink a little sea water. They shake rattles as they chant and dance, dance and chant, over and over and again until the Shaman falls to the ground, quivering in a fit. T'aay knows his father battles the spirits. He's seen it before, and T'aay continues with his chanting.

The Shaman becomes quiet, and T'aay knows he's sleeping.

His father needs more sleep in his older years, and they've been working to exhaustion every day for weeks. T'aay continues the work on his own, chanting and dancing until he is nearly asleep on his feet. Needing to return home for their own rest, he kneels beside his father to wake him, taking his hand, and it's cold. He turns his father's face toward him, and it's gray.

"Gwaa!" T'aay falls backward. He sits, staring, as if in a dream until he feels his father's spirit surround him. He forces himself back onto his feet and begins to chant again, this time for his father's spirit, but he chants alone, and his one voice sounds hollow, ragged. He dances alone and his movements are rigid from grief.

The body of the Shaman is carried by his brothers-in-law of the Raven People to his home where he is wrapped in deerskin and strapped to a plank. His dagger is placed into one closed hand which is held against his chest and his rattle into the other. His hair is wound atop his head and held in place with a bone pin, topped with his headdress. Finally, his face is covered with a small spruce-root mat, and he is placed in one corner of his house while his family call his spirit helpers, beaver, otter and bear, to be with him in death.

Each day his body is moved to the next corner of the house, moving like the sun, while his Raven in-laws build his grave house away from the village in a burial site for shamans. The grave house is longer than the length of the Shaman, made of logs with a plank roof, and the floor is raised one foot off the ground. The door faces the water and is decorated with the carved and painted images of his spirit helpers to guard him in death. On the fifth day, he's laid inside with his head toward the rising sun on a mound of devil's club, a box of his spirit tools with him, his canoe alongside the house.

Women cut fresh spruce branches seven feet long and tie blue and yellow and red woven strips to the top of the branches to attract the Shaman's spirit helpers. They wave the branches high overhead, left and right, trailing colors behind them as they walk through the village, through all the places where he has ever gone, wherever his spirit helpers have gone with him. As colors float, the women ask for the Shaman's spirits to protect them, to help them be healthy and live long. The protection of his spirit helpers is the Shaman's last gift to Wolf Clan.

From the beach, Ana is enthralled as she watches the colors move, fluttering banners dance behind long branches in and out between houses like the play of porpoise diving in and out of a turquoise sea. Wondering if she will still be there for potlatch in winter, she asks her mother why the Shaman is not cremated. Ut-kart-ee explains that it isn't possible for fire to burn the body of a Shaman. "He will be guarded by his spirit helpers, remembered and thanked for his service. People will send small tributes of tobacco from the water whenever their canoes pass his grave house."

When the sickness has passed and the funeral pyres are gone, and some of the People whisper about Ana being the cause of the sickness and wanting her to be gone, Ana of the Wolf People agrees to marry Utah of Coho Clan of the Raven People who is from Naakee-ann. Wolf Council decides to overlook the customary wait times in order to expedite Ana's move away from An-ar-kark.

Without a priest, she conducts the ceremony herself. The

wedding takes place on a warm day in Wolf Clan House, the couple standing in the place of honor in front of the painted Wolf Clan partition that separates A-kadi's space from the others. Bunches of late purple lupine gathered by Ana's siblings bow from a tall basket. She wears her special tunic from Tinx, and around her neck hangs her cross from the mission along with a bear claw from Do'ok. Her face is decorated in red wolf ears by her Aunt Tinx, her hair parted down the middle, shining down her back.

Utah wears his best ceremonial tunic showing a coho salmon on his back, deer hoofs clacking from the bottom. His hair is knotted inside a crown of ermine curls held by a ring of copper like a crown. They face each other, Ana holding the Bible in her left arm, rosary beads dangling from fingers, and Utah's hand in her right. She turns to see their families who stand to watch along with some men from Raven Clan who are there to honor her father.

"Utah, do you enter into marriage with me freely and wholeheartedly?"

"Yes, it is my choice . . . completely."

"Are you prepared to love and honor me as long as you live?"

"Honor?" Utah asks.

"Respect," she explains. "Treat me like I have value."

"Yes, of course I value you."

"Utah, do you take me for your legal wife according to the rite of our holy Mother, the Church?"

Utah slants his mouth, confused.

"Do you accept me as your wife according to the statements that you just made, which are from the Church?"

"Yes, but how many times must I say 'yes'? When do *you* say 'yes'?"

"Right now," she laughs. "I take you, Utah, as my legal husband according to the rite of our holy Mother, the Church." Then she speaks in Latin to hear the words as they would sound from the padres, *"Hoc ut matrimonium benedicat Deum.* May God bless our marriage and what He has joined, let no one break apart."

Her mother, uncle and siblings are expectant, wondering what's next. Do'ok stands, looking eager, perched next to a giant wooden drum that hangs from the rafters. His wrapped beating stick is held in the air, ready to pounce.

"Ok," Ana smiles, "we can dance now," and the drum booms. After the chanting and dancing and gift giving, Ana requests one gift from her family. It's for the slave Kit'aa to be released from slavery and allowed to stay at Wolf Clan House as a free man. Her uncle A-kadi does so without hesitation, relieved that Ana has found a husband, and he's from another village.

After feasting, there is more dancing, and Do'ok is relieved from his drumming duties to dance, remembering how his young-child feet followed his father's when he was learning. He glances at K'aan-at-shi out the corner of his eye and dances close to her, watching her ebony hair shimmer in the firelight like liquid.

A-kadi arranges for the married couple to spend their first night in the little house at Raven Clan. To Ana, it feels like home, surrounded by her ancestors. As she and Utah come together lying under the furs, it's as if she's filled with the essence of her Tlingit People. The chanting of the evening vibrates through her head and in her mind, she sees the shadows of dance reflected in firelight. She imagines herself to be a shadow danc-ing with the ancestors, becoming part of Wolf Clan's shagoon. She senses the deep roots of her Wolf clan's shagoon, its origin and heritage and vows to have a positive influence on its destiny.

The next day, they paddle to Utah's new house in Naakee-ann. She was hoping to be accepted by Coho Clan in time, but there is no reception. The house is solid, well-built and Ana is im-pressed. She tells him she's proud to be his wife. It's just enough encouragement for Utah to lower her to the furs. "What if the People here don't want me?" she worries. He wraps his arms around her and looks into her eyes. "I am strong here. No one will cross me. You're safe." He begins to examine the contours of her body again, happy for married life.

"I'll make you happy," she whispers, her fingers combing through his hair. "Be patient, though. I haven't been raised in a home, especially a Tlingit home. I've much to learn."

"You'll do well," he mouths against her neck, getting dis-tracted. "We . . . will . . . do . . . well," he mumbles against various parts of her body.

Within a few days, Do'ok arrives to stay at Frog Clan in Naa-kee-ann in preparation for his marriage to K'aan-at-shi. He must show his worth as a provider by working for her father and com-pensate her family for the loss of her help when she moves away with him.

Ana loves seeing her brother, and K'aan-at-shi helps her orga-nize her baskets and foodstuffs, becoming a good friend. When

Do'ok has proven himself worthy, his joining ceremony to K'aan-at-shi is scheduled for late winter.

Ana imagines having children and realizes that K'aan-at-shi will be an important aunt to her future daughters, and Do'ok will be the one to raise her sons. That is if she stops drinking the special tea that helps her avoid getting pregnant. She doesn't feel ready to have babies yet, especially because she doesn't know how others would respond to her children since she is a twin.

Fall hardens into winter and every household is busy preparing for memorial potlatches, weddings, naming ceremonies, and every other type of celebration. Ana cuts and dries meat that Utah and other hunters bring in and listens to chanting and drumming practiced as she works.

Most of Wolf Clan arrives at Naakee-ann dressed in their ceremonial regalia, singing Wolf Clan songs for Do'ok and K'aan-at-shi's wedding. Do'ok asks Ana to read from Ke-an-kow's book, and she chooses from *Corinthians*. *"Be humble and gentle; be patient, bearing with one another in love."* Her words seem perfect, and the couple gaze at each other, happy in love as the dancing begins.

Sweet signs of spring erupt all around at the perfect time. The celebrations are over, and the women are weary of collecting beach food. Birds return to their warm-weather homes, the river runs higher and faster, fishing increases, and everyone watches for precious moments of sunshine, but the most exciting part of spring is that K'aan-at-shi has developed the beginnings of a tight, round belly.

As he beds her, Utah wonders why Ana hasn't gotten pregnant since they've been married longer than Do'ok and K'aan-at-shi. He wonders if Ana's Power is too strong for his seed and decides he will bed her more often until he overcomes it.

Ana doesn't feel ready to take care of babies, still trying to find her place among the People. Her promised weekly trip to the Russian Fort takes longer now that the Russians have moved south, and she lives north at Naakee-ann, requiring her to spend the night at An-ar-kark each way. Preparing the lessons and doing her at-home chores leaves little time for her husband and the attention he expects. She knows his patience grows thin, and she doesn't blame him.

Do'ok and K'aan-at-shi ask Ana to be at the birthing because of her healing Power even though her aunt will deliver the baby, as is custom. Ana has talked with them and they all agree that if the baby is a girl, her hips will not be dislocated as in the past.

Young Shaman T'aay dances and chants, shaking his animal spirit rattle to clear away negative spirits and make way for an easy entry into the physical world for the newborn. K'aan-at-shi squats like Frog in front of a young tree bearing down hard, gritting her teeth, growling to the tree like a bear, and falls back to rest. Time to push again, Ana helps her into position while the aunt positions herself to catch the baby. Finally, a healthy baby boy is born. K'aan-at-shi lies on her back to rest while her aunt cuts the cord with a stone knife and wipes the baby clean with absorbent moss.

"Do'ok will be a proud father," Ana smiles.

"Yes," K'aan-at-shi breathes, relieved.

"Now, bear down again to rid your body of the after-birth."

K'aan-at-shi gathers her remaining strength to squat one last time, trying to push out the unwanted matter. It's hard work, and she's so tired. Ana begins to worry that there may be a problem and helps K'aan-at-shi sit up, rubbing her back. The after-birth finally arrives, it comes with another baby.

Everyone is stunned. Ana's Wolf spirit presents itself, and she grabs the newborn from the afterbirth, holding the slippery bundle firmly. Her own birth, as told by her mother, plays quickly through her mind, how the Shaman was given the first born to be taken into the forest, and she puts the baby she holds into K'aan-at-shi's arms and immediately takes the first baby away from the aunt who has not yet recovered from the shock of two babies. "You may cut the cord of the second baby," she directs the aunt.

The aunt seems befuddled. "Is it girl or boy?" she asks faintly.

"A boy," K'aan-at-shi interjects, pushing strength into her voice even though her face shows shock. She looks at Ana and grabs her wrist with one hand, holding her unexpected second gift in the other arm. "We have twin boys," she announces with a shaky voice as if trying to accept what has happened. She locks wide eyes with Ana.

Do'ok anxiously waits with his mother and uncle. When at last K'aan-at-shi and Ana come out of the forest, *each* holding a baby, all three feel the air suck from their lungs and their legs weaken.

Ana watches their reaction. "Do'ok, help your wife and your second-born son get to the women's house, and I will bring your first-born son, unless the grandmother would like to carry the first born?"

Ut-kart-ee immediately puts out her arms to accept the baby, making cooing sounds to her grandson as she follows the birth parents.

"How do you feel about twins?" Do'ok asks K'aan-at-shi as he supports her walk. "Tell me the truth."

"I love you," she replies easily, gazing at her second-born. "How could I not love our babies? I will do *anything* to keep them, both of them," she turns to see their first-born. Her mouth widens into a satisfied smile, "They're *perfect*."

"You can ask my mother," he cautions. "She can tell you of the hardships ahead, and so can I. They make our future uncertain."

"It doesn't matter," she whispers, tears already forming in her eyes.

Ana walks with A-kadi, tremors traveling up her legs. "You look angry, uncle. How will you respond?"

"Head on against the Council," A-kadi declares, already distracted with planning. "They can fight like bucks in rutting season and I will stand firm like a mountain of rock," he grinds his teeth. "I will not let others tell me how to lead Wolf Clan any longer!"

K'aan-at-shi settles onto a bed of furs with one baby, while Ana holds the other. "Your babies will have Power because of the change they will bring," Ana encourages. "Rest now, I'll watch over them. Do'ok has sent a runner to tell your parents."

"My parents! And now you expect me to rest?"

19

Shagoon (Clan's Origin, Heritage and Destiny)

Wolf Clan Council calls a village-wide meeting, shocked by A-kadi's decision to keep the twins. A crowd gathers around the 65-foot memorial pole for Ka-uh-ish, the sun peeking out between white flying clouds illuminating tense faces. A-kadi stands with Ut-kart-ee and asks Ana to stand next to Do'ok and K'aan-at-shi, each of them holding one of their twin boys in his cradleboard. "I want the People to see the ones who cause their fear."

Raven Clan Leader Takl-eesh begins. "A-kadi, some say if you and your family break with tradition, you should take your Wolf Clan elsewhere, away from the village."

A-kadi addresses the People. "You're right to be worried. We've been wrong all these years. We have not understood our ancestors. Like the Wolf pups here on the memorial pole, our vision has been clouded by Fog Woman. Twins are not wrong. Aren't we brothers to the animals? They have more than one off-spring at a time. Why should we be different? We must correct our error. Wolf Clan stays. Those who disagree may go!"

Chaos erupts overhead with great fluttering and bird cries, *rrehk, graak*. Raven flies with a young falcon in his talons. Falcon chases, diving at Raven, hitting him hard again and again, swooping waves in the sky until Raven releases the juvenile to defend himself. Falcon charges even harder, injuring Raven. Hurt and exhausted, Raven flies away in search of easier food. As he leaves, one large black Raven feather floats slowly down and lands at Ut-kart-ee's feet.

She stares at the feather, unable to look away, knowing she's seen it before. *My Spirit Dream! Ana of the Wolf People brings Falcon to battle Raven. Ana is the Wolf that drops the black Raven feather, symbol of a break from tradition, a change of shagoon.* She grabs her brother's arm for stability, imagining all the tiny lives who will be saved because of this moment.

Falcon circles, seeing his master below and flies down to set-tle onto Ana's arm. The People gasp, feeling the Power of the mo-ment. So happy for Falcon, Ana cries, petting his breast, kissing his head, talking to him like they share a language. "I've missed you so, my Falcon friend. Do you have a family now?" She sees the fear of the People and turns toward her mother who seems stunned, as if touched by Power. Utah stands behind A-kadi and whispers, "her pet falcon, raised on ship."

Eagle soars in from his hunt over the beach *ssseeeuu* curious about the scuffle in the air, his wings glide nearly flat before he slows to settle atop the memorial pole. "Eagle Lowered from the Sky," A-kadi mutters. "These twins are his children and grandchildren," he announces, grabbing Ut-kart-ee to keep her upright.

Ana feels Falcon's distress because of the nearness of Eagle and raises her arm to send him off, watching him fly until he's gone. People stand dazed until Eagle loses interest and flies off as well.

"What is this witchcraft?" someone calls.

T'aay, Wolf Clan Shaman since the death of his father, steps forward. "There's no witchcraft here. I've grown up in this clan and know these twins."

"Maybe they bewitched you."

Another joins in, "How does that twin have Power over Falcon?"

"Falcon carries the spirit of my father Al'ooni of Hawk Clan," Ut-kart-ee says, her voice shaking. "He's come to support our change from tradition."

"Be thankful for Wolf Clan," T'aay announces. "We are strong, with the most guns to protect the village. Your concerns are in our hearts, but we will have twins, that is the way of it." He walks back into Wolf Clan House, and the family follows.

Inside, A-kadi pats T'aay on the back. "You've done well, T'aay, a worthy leader."

"Except that you're a better Shaman than paddler," Do'ok teases. "I let you win that canoe race when we were eight years old, you know."

"I know," T'aay laughs. "That was when I knew you were a good person."

After their meal, Ana sits with Do'ok, "Is it true, our ancestors are always with us?"

Do'ok thinks for ten heartbeats. "Our uncle Ka-uh-ish said that our ancestors are part of our *shagoon*, our origin. Their beliefs and accomplishments are what we inherit, and they lead us toward our destiny. We're continually influenced by those who came before, and what we do will influence those who come after us. We're never truly alone."

"How did mother get the idea that Falcon carries the spirit of her father? my grandfather?"

"She might believe it, especially with his name Al'ooni (Hunter). Why would he *not* come to join his spirit with ours?"

She wonders if Falcon has carried the spirit of her grandfather all this time so she wouldn't be alone during her long journey home. She imagines her part of Wolf Clan's shagoon, tendrils of roots winding through the village and into the sea.

Glad to return home with Utah, Ana hopes for a moment of peace. When they arrive, people turn away, whispers of her Power over Falcon having arrived before them. She notices Coho Clan Shaman nearby and wonders if he's thinking she's a witch. In the evening, she tells Utah that she's uneasy and sad. "I was hoping I might be accepted here one day."

"They don't know about your relationship with Falcon," he wraps his arms around her. "Why not tell them the real story?"

She burrows her forehead into his neck. "I would, except that maybe their fear adds to our Power? Maybe it protects my family and the twins?"

Utah moves away. "I guess that you, that we, need to endure it then. It's difficult for me too, you know."

"I'm sorry husband," she moves closer. "Maybe it was a poor choice to marry someone like me." She smiles mischievously, grabbing him around the waist.

"*You* will be the sorry one," he pulls her all the way down to the furs as she shrieks and laughs, pretending to get away but not too hard.

Ut-kart-ee finds a musket at Wolf Clan House and hides it for herself, determined to learn to shoot, hunt, protect her family. Having watched the others, she collects shot, black powder and a ramrod, then sneaks into the forest to the base of a steep cliff where she can shoot into its wall and do no harm. Carefully, she takes the pouch of black powder and pours it into the barrel, although not certain of how much to pour. She wraps a round of shot into a tiny piece of cloth and adds it to the barrel, then inserts the ramrod and pushes it all firmly in as far as it will go.

Lifting the gun to her right eye, looking down the barrel to line up the sightline like she has seen others do, finding the trigger, she pulls slowly, preparing herself for the kick-back she knows will come, but the musket itself explodes. The blast comes slowly, almost gently, into her face and hand and she thinks of her family, how they still need her, how she just met her first-born, then there's nothing but white.

On the ground screaming, unable to see out of her right eye, she tries to feel her face and realizes her thumb and two fingers are missing, blood everywhere. She's afraid of her injuries and even more afraid of the overwhelming pain she knows is coming. She screeches, calling for help, knowing she won't be able to make a sound much longer.

Do'ok races his canoe to Naakee-ann, pounding through the surf to get Ana, the vision of his mother's ruined face filling his mind. "Mother needs you! A gun has exploded," he cries. She grabs her medicine bundle and hurries off. "Prepare yourself, sister, the injuries . . . they are severe. No one knows what to do for her."

At Wolf Clan, Ana gasps at the sight, patting her mother's left hand, "I'm here, mother."

Ut-kart-ee moans, trembling in pain, squeezing Ana's hand.

Ana shudders. Her mother's beautiful face has been blown away on her right side, and what is left is raw, wet flesh outlined in burned remains. Her right eye is burnt and out of the socket and the outside of her right ear is missing. With these injuries and the missing fingers and thumb, she's lost a lot of blood and fluids.

Shouk comes with willow-bark tea to be sucked through a hollow bone. "This is how she drank during her right of passage when water could not touch her lips," she explains, holding the bone to the left side of Ut-kart-ee's mouth, but she cannot suck.

Ana puts her finger over the end of the bone to drip the tea into her mother's mouth. Thinking of Dr. Menzies, she asks for a bottle of rum from storage, switching rum for the tea. She does her best with the scalpel he gave her to cut away the burnt, dead flesh and the injured eye, impossible to repair.

As Ana gently cleans the wounds, Ut-kart-ee cries and moans until she's left to rest while Shouk gives more rum, telling her it will be finished soon. Ana continues, pulling skin up over the wounds of the missing thumb and fingers, stitching them closed and closing the wounds to her face where there is skin to work with. She lays absorbent moss over the missing eye and face wounds that remain open, then covers the area with a triangle of cloth tied around her head, hoping to provide her mother some sense of comfort.

Ana sits, holding her mother's lifeless left hand, trying to hide her worry. She knows it will take a strong person to recover. Her mother's face will be horribly scarred and deformed, and there is nothing Ana can do. "You're strong, mother, you will recover," she reassures as her mother lies in the numbness of rum.

A-kadi comes to kneel beside her. "Sister, I should have known you wouldn't stay away from guns. I should have arranged for you to have lessons with the others, as you asked."

"No yer fault," she tries to speak.

A-kadi takes her hand, silently mourning the sister she was. "Remember your fighting spirit, sister. You'll be strong again, maybe stronger than before."

Most of Wolf Clan believe that Ut-kart-ee's injury is punishment for bringing twins into their village. It makes sense. It provides the balance that the spirit world requires. The women talk about it as they work, licking their labrets as they visit, forgetting they wear the labrets to remind them to *refrain* from gossip. "I knew she would cause trouble, and she let her *twin* daughter stay with her. She was asking for something to happen."

"Well, if anyone must pay to regain balance, she's the one. She started the whole thing when she kept Do'ok. I've never seen a child receive as much attention from a mother as that boy, too much attention."

"Now she insists on keeping the twins of Do'ok! It needs to stop! Or something will happen to all of us!"

Utah stands inside their house, grinding his teeth when Ana returns home. "Why didn't you leave word for me before you left?" he demands.

"I had no time! My mother! I thought she would die!"

"You're supposed to think of your husband first now that you're married."

"I should put you ahead of my critically injured mother? Do you even care how she is?"

"Of course, how is she?"

"She *might* live, horribly scarred, missing an eye and several fingers."

"Sorry," he mouths, his face hard.

Ana feels irritated. Between the furs that night she resists his attempt to bed her. Offended, he wonders if he should show his strength, his power over her, and he forces her legs open with his knees, holding her wrists hard against the sleeping mat as he takes her by force. She doesn't cry out, refusing to let him know he's hurting her. When he's finished, she's sore and shaky, feeling smaller and weaker than she's ever felt. She can't sleep, wondering how their relationship could change so quickly, wondering if he has ever really cared for her.

In the morning, Utah seems a bit happier than he has for

weeks. He feels he's regained some of the Power he lost when he married Ana, and if he stays strong, they could still have a good life together. Ana is relieved to travel to the Russian Fort and check on her mother on the way. At An-ar-kark, she finds that her mother's condition is unchanged.

Her Bible lesson is of Noah's Ark and the Great Flood, a flood that all cultures know. It's a story that includes Raven and Dove and an olive branch which is the Holy Spirit offering hope and salvation. The message is that there is *always* hope, so she thinks it will be meaningful for the Russians and the Aleut and herself.

After the lesson, Baranov tells Ana his problems, looking distraught. Their supply ship sunk in a storm. It was full of the provisions they needed to live through the winter, and a new ship is not coming. "The only thing I can do is take the sea otter skins meant for Russia and trade them instead to other ships for food and supplies. I hate to do it."

Ana wonders why this Russian leader is telling her his problems. She already feels overwhelmed with her own worries. *What does he expect of me?* "I'll pray for you," she says. "You should do the same."

Despite Ana's care and T'aay's spiritual work, Ut-kart-ee's wounds do not heal as they should. "Please mother, let me ask for help," Ana pleads. "I can't take care of you like a doctor from a ship."

"No!" Ut-kart-ee cries. "I'd rather die!" Her rape, A-kadi's beating, her husband's murder, she wants nothing to do with them. "This is my punishment to restore balance for the hardships I caused Wolf Clan, and I accept it."

Ana is shocked. *I'm the one to blame. I shouldn't have come home.* She takes her hand, "Shouldn't the pain of losing me be balanced with joy now?"

"I *do* have joy because of you. The balance I create now is for Wolf Clan, for our change of tradition. I'm the one who started it. I'm the one to pay."

Ana cries. "Please choose life, mother. I've just found you. I need you to be strong."

"Enough," Ut-kart-ee pats Ana's hand. "Let me rest."

That evening Ana sits on the sleeping platform next to her mother who stoically hides her pain while Do'ok and K'aan-at-shi tend their twin boys. Ana's concerns seem to melt away at the sight of the little family together in soft firelight, a perfect vision of love and contentment. Silently, she prays for healing and protection for them all.

As the family fire dances the shadows of the listeners, Do'ok tells the story of a man named Katz who marries a grizzly bear. *"The man Katz didn't mean to do it,"* he begins. With great detail, he tells how Katz was hunting and found a grizzly in her den, becoming confused when she decides to keep him as her husband. They have three bear cubs together! When Katz begins to remember the family he left behind and worry for them, his bear-wife warns him to forget them. Not knowing his cubs spy on him, he checks on his family anyway and hunts to provide food because they are starving. So the she-bear has her cubs tear him limb from limb.

"What an excellent story for a new father!" K'aan-at-shi grins, poking her finger into Do'ok's stomach. "Provide for your family or pay a terrible cost!"

"Do not be concerned, wife," Do'ok squeezes her cheek. "I wish to show my devotion in *many* ways," he smiles, directing her to their furs for the night.

To Ana, the story speaks of love for lost family. As she waits for sleep, she wonders if Utah will turn against her like the she-bear in the story. *Should I put the needs of my family above his if theirs are greater? Could the stories about balance be true? Since Do'ok is so happy, must I be miserable?*

Sleep finally comes. Wolf waits for her on his haunches at the entrance of a trail into the forest, his golden eyes look illuminated in the darkness. She can still feel his eyes on her as she begins her journey back to Naakee-ann.

The weather is rough as she paddles her way home, working hard to break through the crests of choppy waves under a dark gray sky, the wind her constant adversary. As she works, she wonders about Wolf. It seems she dreams of him just before something significant happens. She hopes to rest before facing the chores of married life, but Utah waits for her inside their home.

"This is not working," he declares.

"What?"

"Us, together. You've no time for me, no time for this house," he waves his hand. "You don't try to be part of this clan and fulfill responsibilities to your in-laws." He looks away, "You don't accept my seed. I can't think of a reason to keep you."

Ana stands, not knowing what to say. Everything he says is true.

"I'll get another wife, and you become a useless dependent since you do nothing. Why should I keep you?"

"I'm sorry I'm not what you expected, but what can I do? I have duties as a healer and a teacher . . . I'm doing my best . . . Do you wish me to leave?"

"If you go back to your family, we're no longer together," he warns.

She answers softly, "I'm married with words from the Church."

"I guess that's *your* problem!" He nearly tears the door flap off to get it out of his way.

Ana finds herself lying next to her mother at Wolf Clan House, worried for her, sad about her marriage, wondering what to do. *Do my healing skills have value here? Do they remember that I'm paying off their trade agreement that got their children back?* She feels like Wolf in her dream sitting at the beginning of a path, not knowing where it leads.

After five days, A-kadi takes her aside. "A problem. You must be married! Why are you so like your mother? I have asked all over the village, and no one will take you, not even the old ones!"

"I believe I *am* married, according to my Church."

"Well your *family* and your Tlingit *People* say you are *not* married, or you would be living with your husband in *his* clan. It is our way, Ana. I will not let a member of my family be a burden to Wolf Clan! Our status is at risk because of the twins. You don't understand how hard your mother and father worked to build the wealth of Wolf Clan to be allowed to raise Do'ok. That is the same determination you need now to find a husband!"

She feels hopeless. That evening after stories, she remains near the fire to search her Bible for the next lesson. Thinking of the lost Russian ship and their lack of supplies, she hopes to focus on abundance. She finds, *"If any provide not for his own, and especially for those of his own house, he hath denied the faith."* Her stomach clenches, knowing she's not lived up to her promise to Utah.

At the Russian fort, she finishes with Romans, *"May the God of hope fill you with all joy and peace in believing, that you may abound in hope, through the power of the Holy Ghost."* Once again, Baranov approaches her in great seriousness. *"Please* ask Wolf Clan to provide us with food! If we don't get supplies, we'll starve! Some Aleut resorted to eating strange black mussels last week and died horrible, painful deaths within hours! We're desperate! Please speak for us!"

Ana travels back to An-ar-kark thinking of Baranov. She won't ask Wolf Clan to feed the Cloud-Face since her People already think she's a burden and knowing how her mother and uncle feel about them, she doesn't think her words would make any difference.

That evening, she finds her mother with high fever and thinks there is infection behind the eye socket. Gently, she probes into the space to clean away a yellow discharge and applies a few maggots, knowing they will consume only dead flesh, become flies within a few days and fly away. Exhausted, she lays kelp leaves in the bottom of a spruce root basket with water and drops in heated rocks from the edge of the fire to boil, adding willow bark to steep, hoping the tea will reduce her fever. Waiting for the tea to cool, she asks her mother what her greatest wishes were when she was younger.

"I wanted to have many babies," she smiles slightly on one side of her face. "I did that . . . and I wanted to be with your father. I did that too . . . as long as he lived. I wanted to know you were okay in the Land of the Dead." Her one-sided smile grows as she looks at Ana.

"And what do you want now, mother?"

"Now I want to die."

Ana's heart sinks. She'd hoped her mother's spirit was strong enough. "I *need* you to get better, *please* mother. I just found you! There are *many* people who need you . . ."

"First-born, I wish to speak to you. You affect Wolf Clan's shagoon as much as I. You teach us we must change, not slow like the rain changes the mountain, but quick like the tides change the beach . . . and we taught you what it is to be Tlingit . . . and that you are loved, have *always* been loved."

Ana looks at her mother through blurry eyes and kisses her uninjured cheek.

"I see you . . . your spirit. It shines with love, not as brightly as before. It's time to make choices for *your* destiny."

"I don't know my destiny, mother. I've always tried to fulfill expectations from others . . . except that I've always wanted to find *you*."

Ut-kart-ee pats her daughter's hand. "I will die soon and when I do . . ."

"You will *not* die!" she cries.

"We all die," her voice is calm. "I'm not afraid. I'll see my ancestors, be with your father. I'll come back one day . . . full face, both eyes, all fingers, happier than now."

"Are you in pain, mother?" Ana lifts an alder cup of the willow-bark tea.

"I'm fine," she waves it away. "When I go, think about leaving this place . . . You have saved the twins to come. It's the greatest gift to know you, but your destiny is not here. The glow of light from your face has faded."

"Mother, you will get better," she sniffs. "We will pick berries together and you will help me become a better basket maker . . ."

"We will do that one day," Ut-kart-ee interrupts. "Have them burn me in my ceremonial tunic from my rite of passage." Her words become softer. "You keep the robe of white swan feathers, a gift from your father." Her mouth is tired. "I will sleep now. Remember I love you forever . . . and you are stronger than you think. Ke-an-kow takes care of you . . ." Her hand relaxes as she sleeps.

Her mother's forehead radiates heat. She sends a slave for cold water from the river and asks Do'ok to come, remind their mother why she needs to live.

Do'ok lifts his mother's hand, hot against his cheek and sends a runner for Shaman T'aay. "You need to be grandmother to my children," he squeezes words through his tight throat. "The twins need a *fierce* grandmother like you, and I need you." He tucks Ut-kart-ee's tiny rock Wolf charm from A-kadi into her steaming hand.

Ana fights her mother's fever into the night but cannot save her. Just before dawn, she puts her mother's spirit into God's hands as Shaman T'aay dances and chants. She and Do'ok hold hands and gather their younger siblings to say goodbye to their mother.

Ut-kart-ee hears the wailing of her children and the Shaman's chanting to clear her path and doesn't try to wake. As the voices begin to fade, she focuses on other things.

Wolf sits on his haunches, waiting for her with softened eyes near the cool, snow-covered clearing of her Spirit dream. Winter sun's golden rays are just coming up from the east, reflecting shards of brilliant light from her iced rock. Wolf stretches up to his fullest height as if he's waited for her a long time. He turns and his large paws pad down a rough, broken path toward the East. She follows over rocks and through the brush until he leads her all the way home, into the arms of Chark Cough-ye.

Her husband smiles at her out of both sides of his mouth from a perfect face, the eagle feather twirling in a lock of his hair. She smiles back with both eyes. "I thought I'd see you holding our first-born daughter," she says as if in a cloud. "I was able to meet her sooner than expected."

"Yes, I know," Chark Cough-ye's voice sounds like liquid gold. "I was there. I'm proud of her."

"Was that your spirit with Eagle sitting on top of the memorial pole in the village?"

"Impressive, huh? A-kadi did well, as did you, my *chuck-har-nut*, right by me, always ready."

Ut-kart-ee's face becomes a glowing smile, showing the dimple on her right cheek.

From a distance, Wolf howls. They find themselves together on a beautiful island surrounded by vast green water, a canoe waiting on the glistening beach. Together, they continue their journey.

20

Abundance

Ana's heart is heavy, sitting at the bottom of her chest like a rock. *"Taok wu-gootz. I am broken,"* it tells her.

Despite Do'ok's protests that his babies will be spoiled, she releases her tiny twin nephews from their cradleboards to hold them in her arms, sitting near the warm fire as K'aan-at-shi tends the family meal.

"They give me relief," she murmurs, warm, squirming bodies against her own a welcome distraction from the pain of losing her mother. "How will you cope when they're eight years old and go to Naakee-ann with your brother? Won't you miss them terribly?"

"Of course," K'aan-at-shi admits, stirring the stew, "but it's our way, and I'll have more children, and Do'ok will have nephews to teach. I'll be busy and they won't be far away."

"You put Do'ok and your family in danger!" Her mother's words

come back to Ana again and again like waves of cold water crashing against her. She rocks the babies, trying to block the tremendous regret that surrounds her, and it grows into self-loathing. She gives the babies back to K'aan-at-shi and holds her head, trying to squeeze out her mother's voice.

"Get out for fresh air," K'aan-at-shi suggests, wrapping the twins.

She walks the beach, finding her worries again among the shells. Raising her face to the rain, she's drenched and cold and trudges back to her spot on the sleeping platform under her furs, next to the empty space that was her mother's. Unable to sleep, she sifts through her Bible looking for scripture on death, grief, the afterlife, hoping for comfort.

Freed slave Kit'aa goes with Ana to the Russian fort, "to be with you after the spirit of your mother has gone." She's glad for his company in her darkness. Standing on the platform, she sees about thirty Russians and at least twice as many Aleut waiting in a light, misty rain. She calls out words from Psalms, her cadence slower, heavier today. "God is our God forever and ever. He will be our guide even to the end. His kingdom is everlasting and endures through all generations. It's a promise," she says. "God will guide us in this life and the afterlife. We are never alone."

Before she can walk back to the canoe, Baranov stops her. "Have you spoken to Wolf Clan yet about getting provisions for us?"

"They won't supply your needs unless you have something to trade, and they can get their own otter skins, so skins wouldn't bring you a good return."

"Ana, forget about 'return'! I'll agree to whatever trade I can get, or we'll starve! *Two* of my ships have sunk now, one with provisions and one full of sea otter skins, and there will be no additional ships during winter. I *need* a local trade, Ana."

The next day she walks a path upriver described to her by Do'ok. The dripping needles and leaves light up as the sun clears the clouds, encouraging noisy bird calls. Broad leaves splat with drips of rain from trees above. She finds her uncle A-kadi sitting alone on a rock at a quiet spot near calm water. Stopping, she notices a buck nearby raise his head in alert. He lowers his young antlers and continues to graze, moving away into the forest.

Her uncle's bare back is topped with the red ochre on his hair from the naming ceremony of yesterday. Hearing her approach despite the roar of the rapids nearby, he turns toward her with a piercing look, clearly annoyed. "How did you find me?"

"Do'ok said you like to be alone here."

He continues to stare, one eyebrow raised.

Ana looks at him innocently, feeling like a child. "Sorry for interrupting," she mutters, lowering her eyes. "They won't survive without help, their provisions sank."

"The Russian Cloud-Face? Maybe we should *let* them starve, maybe Raven clears out intruders for us. After all, they steal, bring sickness, won't trade guns. Why help them?"

She feels guilty, as if *she* brings trouble. "I don't believe they would let *us* starve."

He turns, scanning the riverside, "The Aleut would let us die." Turning back to Ana, his face looks like he's eaten something spoiled. "You know you have no status here? You should be speaking through your husband."

Wanting to argue, she lowers her eyes again. A-kadi turns

back to his river in silence, she bravely tries again. "Vancouver felt Baranov was a man of his word. What if a worse leader comes to replace him?"

A-kadi sighs. "You're lucky that your mother was my sister and that I see her in you. I will talk to Baranov. If he can trade, we could help for a few months, then we are *finished.*" He wades chest high, across the river and into the forest.

On her way back, Ana watches two wolf cubs play in a distant patch of tall, purple lupine. The flower tops bob as they roll over the stems. One nips at her brother and zips away, wanting to be chased. *Just like a girl,* Ana thinks. The brother rolls lazily in the lupine, pushing his nose and ear across the ground and through the blooms, sneezing a great, wet ejection of pollen. Not interested in chasing, he continues to roll in the grass. *Oh to be so carefree!* Mama wolf returns from a hunt, watching from the tree line, looking at Ana. *I pray your hunt was successful. I don't wish to be a lesson for your pups in how to kill.*

The mother yips, alerting her cubs of her return, and they tumble in her direction, jumping on top of each other as they make their way to her. She smells them each carefully, checking for any unusual scents. Gazing briefly at Ana, she leads them away to their dinner.

Thinking of her own mother as she walks back to An-ar-kark, she remembers their talk about her destiny. "Your light fades," her mother had said. "The light," Ana shouts to the sky, "was the excitement of finding my family! It would still be here if you were still alive!"

She begins to work, collecting food, preserving food, making baskets, one task after the other, before dawn and into the night to prove she doesn't need a husband and will not be a burden. She tries to include her younger siblings to distract them from their mourning, but it doesn't seem to help. They seem happier with their Aunt Tinx and K'aan-at-shi.

One morning while cleaning fish for drying, wondering why the children aren't as comfortable with her, a horrible thought surfaces. *Do they blame me for their mother's death?* The idea strangles her. *Why shouldn't they? I blame myself!* Her world stops and she sits, stunned, until Do'ok comes to see her.

"Sister, I wish to speak with you." She continues to look to the distance, controlled by her thoughts. He lowers himself to sit beside her, "Ana, listen to me. You are working too hard . . . *exactly* what our mother did."

Her eyes move to look at his face.

"It was hard for her, and she still found happiness. I want *you* to find happiness, to have a husband you love, and to have children."

Ana's eyes fill with tears, this kind of talk from her mother maybe, not her brother!

"You must have a *good* life!" He shakes her shoulder. "Don't you see? It's the only way to honor the lives of our parents, all the hardships they endured for us! It's what they would want."

"You are my greatest treasure, brother."

"Please tell me you will pray to Ke-an-kow for your own happiness," he squeezes her hands. "I can't bear to see you suffer."

Her dream that night begins with a light sensation on her arm, just a hint, barely there, persistent. It makes the hairs on her arm stand up, and there is warmth. Delicious heat spreads up her arm to her shoulder and throughout her entire body, getting warmer until it feels like it might burn. She smells sweet coconut and opens her eyes in her dream to see the light brown eyes of Do'ok very close, then the eyes change to Kualelo's, his endless, dark, liquid eyes. She lifts her hands to grab hold, and there is nothing to grab.

"Ana, what sustains you?" Kualelo's smooth, rich voice.

She replies faintly, like under water, "Love, all kinds, everywhere."

A new voice loud inside her head, bringing her awake, *"Ana, Love Thyself."*

She gasps, sitting up with a start, the voice so loud that she looks around to see if others were wakened, her senses filled with Kualelo like warm oil on her skin. Her heart receives a stab, a knife inserted into her beating, wide-awake heart when she realizes she's without him. *He can't still be waiting for me,* yet she can't stop thinking about him, the smallest possibility giving her hope. She takes herself outside where her frantic heart won't wake everyone. In the full moon, she sees the crashing of the night waves and the canoes sitting on the sand, asking to be used, go south to the blue waters that surround Kualelo. She remembers the bliss of feeling completely loved and accepted and wonders if the light her mother saw was the remnant of that love, and she realizes she will mourn for the rest of her life if she doesn't find out about Kualelo.

Dropping to a driftwood log, she closes her eyes, searching for a glimmer of future. Her mind plays with visions of Kualelo, Do'ok and his babies, her mother's ruined face, and she's left looking at the Russian Fort, hearing Baranov's words, "We will starve."

"We need a place of abundance!" She gasps.

At dawn, after breakfast, she paddles through the fog to speak with Baranov.

"You've helped me already, Ana," Baranov rises from his desk. "A-kadi came and we agreed on a trade."

"Good, I thought you had no plan for *after* that."

His eyebrows rise in surprise. ". . . and?"

"If you send a ship south to the island of Hawai'i, I believe I can have it filled with food and returned to you in less than two months from departure."

Baranov finds it difficult to believe she could accomplish such a thing and he's reluctant to send out his last ship, especially on such a long voyage.

"You must have skins to trade," she continues. "They have an abundance of food so you will get more for your trade there."

Baranov's mind is racing, "You surprise me, Ana." He shakes his head thinking of who he could spare for captain and crew.

She sees his thinking. "I know High Chief Kamehameha," she sputters, trying to repress her excitement. "He'll give you fair trade!" She quivers, hoping her words are true.

"It would be dangerous, Ana. Ships go down all the time . . ."

Back in her canoe, she's incapacitated, her mind frantic, feeling she could explode like the weapon that killed her mother. *What if Kualelo is married? Or dead? Or doesn't love me? How do I say goodbye here? especially when my family is broken? Should I risk going with people who sink their ships? What if Kamehameha won't trade? What if I fail?* Trying to keep a question long enough to think it through is like trying to catch a fish with her hands in the rapids. As she launches her canoe for home, she remembers her mother telling her that her destiny is not here, and she feels desperate to know where and what her destiny is.

Do'ok watches Ana pack her things, looking distraught. "I want to support you. I want you to be happy, of course. I want you to be safe, *but I don't want to be without you!*"

She sees her brother's face has tears. "Do'ok," she holds his hands, "if *you* weren't so happy, I wouldn't even *think* about leaving, and I may be coming back. Kualelo probably has a wife and a family by now. I need to find out or I'll never rest."

"You'll be on another uncertain voyage, not knowing what lies ahead again," his dimple appears in the tight grimace of his face.

"This time I go to know my choices for my own life." She stands motionless, unwilling to move without his blessing.

"It shouldn't surprise me that you create your own destiny considering who our parents were. I should admire your courage since I had the same parents." His chin begins to twitch, and his jaw clamps shut holding back new tears. "They would be proud of you."

Ana sees his struggle and her vision blurs. Until now, she has concentrated on the journey rather than the goodbyes.

"And if you don't come back," he grinds his jaw, "what will I do then? What happens to *our* life? the one we share?"

"You'll visit me in my dreams like you always have, little brother, and we'll laugh together like we always have, and *I* will be there wherever *you* look, wherever you see a reflection of yourself. We've known each other since birth! We'll always be connected."

He straightens, hardening himself. "Will you let me be the one to take you to the ship then?"

"I'd rather say goodbye here in An-ar-kark," her heart twists. "I need my last vision of you to be with K'aan-at-shi and your twins and A-kadi and the whole family, or it will break my heart, and I want to say goodbye to Falcon before I leave, if he can find me."

Like Falcon soaring on a wind current, Ana stands with her arm-wings extended wide in the bow of Baranov's little sloop. It tears through the surf, three sails filling with a brisk wind. She's removed her rain cape and boots and stands barefoot, bare-armed and bare headed in the wet, bracing wind, hoping for relief from loss, anxiety, uncertainty. The cold feels good, the colder the better, hoping it will numb her heart because leaving her family is breaking it.

"You must go inside to your cabin, now," Kit'aa touches her icy wrist.

"Just a few moments more, Kit'aa," Ana turns toward him, showing the tears that have traveled her face. "It helps me."

He stands next to her, patiently pulling his cape tighter around him.

She sees the elder shiver with cold. "You didn't need to come with me, Kit'aa," bending to pick up her tunic and boots from the deck.

"I need to know that you make the voyage safely."

The sloop is a little more than half the size of Vancouver's with only three decks: the surface deck, the hold, and the bilge.

Kit'aa was told by the captain that he will need to work and sleep with the crew as an able seaman, and Ana is worried. He has no idea what a seaman does, and he'll be living with the Aleut who hate him. She'll be working in the galley and suspects it will be difficult for her to watch over him. In the morning, she nearly trips over him at the entrance to her cabin. "Kit'aa! Why are you sleeping here?"

"I want to be sure you're safe through the night," he replies, rubbing his face, "and I don't fit with the crew."

"Maybe I talk with the captain to find you a place with the Russian crew, would that be better?"

"I'm not sure. I don't want to be any trouble, and Do'ok said he would take my scalp if anything happens to you."

As she stands on deck, the wind covering her face with hair, she recalls her last day at An-ar-kark, how she had stood on the beach for the longest time trying to mimic Falcon's call and lifting her arm to get his attention, attracting onlookers. About to give up, he had come. She'd recognized his white throat and breast first, his long, talon toes landing on her arm, a communal gasp from the watchers. "Are you glad that I saved you from the rabbit hunt and brought you here to find your family?" She'd noticed how gray his upper feathers had become, his piercing eyes taking her in, black pupils opening and closing as she talked to him until dusk. He'd looked around for a bit to eat, then flown away, calling back to her as he left.

Her goodbye with Do'ok had been much more difficult. After hugging everyone else, he'd been last. Her throat tightens remembering how he'd grabbed her arms, panic in his eyes, nearly bruising her, refusing to let her go. "You're tearing my heart in two," she'd told him, but it wasn't until his uncle A-kadi stepped closer, putting his hand on Do'ok's shoulder that he'd finally let her go. She'd taken his head in her hands, put her forehead to his, her nose to his nose and said, "I *will* see you."

"I will see you too," his last words, in a husky voice.

In her last vision of him, he held both of his babies and K'aan-at-shi's arms were wrapped around them all. *Maybe he will be leader of Wolf Clan one day if I'm not there to remind people that he is a twin.*

Baranov's ship, *Ermak*, weathers a few storms, soaking every-one and everything. The little sloop bobs through the squalls like a duck, and when the sun shines and the air warms, the captain calls for the bilge pump. Kit'aa helps, raising the handle up and down, sending down the air, causing water to come up the pipe and into the sea. He sleeps hard that night, rolled in his fur at the entrance of Ana's cabin.

When the weather becomes too warm for her deer-skin clothing, she changes into her tapa cloth. The breeze cools her skin and she thinks how nice it is to wear less, causing her to re-member the silky comfort of her swimming lesson. She stands on deck as the sun nears the horizon, the wind relaxing just before it drops, she smells something fragrant like ginger and her heart begins to flutter. Her mind races most of the night, planning the trade for food, and she wonders about her future, trying to con-trol her hopes for Kualelo.

The next morning she keeps herself busy, scrubbing the galley and head, doing laundry and sewing for a few of the crew. She helps caulk the areas of the deck that are dry and begins to look for more work until she hears "Land Ahoy!" from the crow's nest, islands in sight. She can see the tips of a volcano in the distance. Her heart drums so hard, she thinks it will shake free.

On deck, she approaches the captain, "Now that we're close, I suggest that the crew not be allowed to leave ship. I know it seems cruel, but it's likely some will desert, and I don't believe you have the means to pay for new crew." The captain tightens his jaw, but she continues, knowing it must be difficult to take a young Native female seriously. "If you needed to take islanders by force to serve as replacements for deserted crew, Chief Kamehameha would certainly have you all killed, so it would probably be better to avoid all of that."

One of the captain's eyebrows rises, and he turns away.

At Kealakekua Bay, Chief Kamanawa, one of the Sacred Twins, is the first to come aboard. He wears a yellow and red feathered cape and is followed by an aid who carries a yellow-feather standard to indicate his status as chief. Kamanawa speaks to the captain to determine his intentions and directs the ship to a place where they can drop anchor.

Ana suspects that soon the ship will be buzzing with islanders bringing fresh water and food, and negotiations must be made to *fill* the ship with food that will be edible at the *end* of the journey home and for months afterward, so she approaches Kamanawa herself. He notices the pale woman in tapa cloth and wonders how an islander boarded the ship before he did. "Aloha. I'm Ana, a friend of Vancouver, also of Queen Ka'ahumanu. I was here three years ago."

"I remember you!" he says. "You left a story behind when you went away with Vancouver. You are the Girl Who Talks to Falcons and Heals! You were with the Red-faced Man Who Collects

Grass and Cuts Off Limbs!" he adds, grinning. He takes her by the shoulders and touches his forehead and nose to hers. "Aloha, E Komo Mai, welcome, Ana."

She smiles, tears forming in her eyes, remembering this place where she was welcomed, not knowing until now how important that time would become. "I'm afraid my falcon stayed home with his family," she smiles, showing her dimple.

"And what have you done with Vancouver?"

"Sadly, I've not seen him in three years. Has he been here?"

"No, and Kamehameha has wanted him. We've battled hard and lost many people, and last year he captured the island of Oahu and its port, Honolulu.

"I hope Chief Kamehameha is well?"

"Yes, of course!"

"And what of Kualelo?" She tries to ignore the hammering of her heart. "Do you know Kualelo from Molokai? He was hoping to be helpful to Kamehameha."

"Yes, of course! He is very well! Come with me, I will take you to Queen Ka'ahumanu. I'm sure she wishes to see you!"

Ana sees Ka'ahumanu sitting on her beach. "Ana Falcon girl! You have come back to me! Did you bring your Christian Bible? Will you stay with me now?" the golden ferns on her head and the lei over one shoulder vibrate with excitement.

Ana relaxes with the warm welcome and smells the sweet fragrance of ginger flower in the queen's shampoo.

"I want to know, Ana, how did you keep this tapa cloth you wear that I gave you so long ago in such good condition?"

"I didn't wear it," she shrugs. "It was too cold and raining in the north. I wore animal skins to keep warm."

The corners of Ka'ahumanu's mouth turn down. "Then it's good you have come back to me! Now why have you cut your hair?"

Ana tells Ka'ahumanu about her life in the north, the death of her mother, and the reason for the Russian ship, as well as her concern that the crew not be allowed off the ship.

"Don't worry. I will send word to the local chief. He will put a kapu on contact with these crew people. Also, Kamehameha is home now. He may want to get involved in this trade for animal skins. You've lost weight. Come. Eat."

After they eat, Ana's breath begins to slow, matching the lazy repetition of the surf caressing the beach. Stress falls away, and for a moment, her mind fills with calm until she sees Kualelo walking toward her. She thinks her heart will jump out of her chest, yet she's frozen, holding her breath, waiting for a sign of his feelings. His face spreads into a wide grin. She jumps to her feet and runs to him, stopping an arm's length away. Cautiously, she steps forward to put her forehead on his. He rubs his nose on hers and squeezes her so hard, she can't breathe, lifting her feet from the sand.

"My Ana Falcon Girl!"

"How did you know so quickly that I was here?"

"I've had a man posted on the beach for the last two and a-half years to watch for you," he says proudly.

"We've been placing bets on who would see you first," Ka'ahu-manu laughs. "I knew it would be me. I did a good thing getting you together with the 'ume game that night." She notices Ana's blush and moves to the shadow so they will feel alone.

Kualelo wears only his loincloth, and she longs to touch his chest and sink her face into the crook of his neck. "I have missed you," she says touching his arm.

"And I, you." He holds her head to touch foreheads again. "Why has it taken you so long to come back to me my ku'u 'i'ini, my heart's desire?"

His words soften her fear. "I'm a twin, and twins are killed in the North. And I found my family . . . but my mother was injured. I couldn't save her." She sobs, covering her face with her hands.

Kualelo pulls her close. "We have much to talk about," he whispers into her hair. "I've been busy getting ready for you."

"You have?" She looks up at him, wet eyes wide. "You expected me to come back?"

"I asked you to come back. I told you I loved you, so I thought that if you loved me, you would come back . . . I admit I was beginning to lose hope."

Ana feels guilty for being so consumed with her family that she didn't keep Kualelo in the front of her mind. "What do you mean 'getting ready'?"

"Well, I've been working for Chief Kamehameha and he's been good to me. He's given me a nice piece of land and I've built an English-style house on it. Now I manage some of his men and 200 of his war canoes. My life is good except that I need you."

Ana trembles, lowering her eyes, "I *do* love you, Kualelo, but there's something I need to tell you."

He takes her hand, waiting.

"I'm afraid that I am . . . married," she speaks to the ground.

He lifts her chin, looking into her eyes, seeing deep sadness there. "Do you love him?"

"Not like I love you. He made me feel safe for a while, but we were not a good fit. He sent me away."

"What a fool he must be," he wraps his arms around her. "Really Falcon Girl, you are worried about an ended marriage? You know *I* am your true love. Remember, I live on an island that plays the game 'ume," he smiles.

Heat travels up her neck and face as she examines her toes.

"In the islands, if you come home with me and decide to stay, we are married. We can complete traditional ceremonies if we want to. If you left your husband, though, why do you still feel married?"

"I used words from the Church for the ceremony, even though we didn't have a priest."

Kualelo takes both of her hands, "You would not be married according to the priests anyway. I think you're hurting yourself for no reason. If you want a proper wedding, we can find a ship captain to perform the ceremony in whatever language you choose." He kisses her mouth, long and tender, and she melts to her toes.

"Alright," she swoons, her eyes still closed, absorbing his heat and smell and touch she's missed for so long. Her eyes pop open, "Never play that 'ume game again!"

Kualelo laughs. "No additional wives, I suppose?"

"What do *you* think?" she pushes hard against his shoulder. "You don't have one *now* do you?"

High Chief Kamehameha and Chief Kamanawa talk with the captain of the Russian ship. Within a few days, the *Ermak* is loaded with pigs, taro, breadfruit, bananas, yams, and coconuts.

On ship, Ana tells the captain she will stay. "Part of the agreement for this food is that Kit'aa has my cabin for the return trip. He has an important message for my family."

The captain nods.

"Kit'aa, tell them that Kualelo and I are together, and I'm happy. Will you?"

"Of course," he says, "but who will look after you if I go back?"

"Kualelo will. Don't worry, your scalp is safe," she smiles. "You be safe too, Kit'aa. Have a long life." She puts her forehead to his, then turns to leave ship. "Find a wife!" she calls back.

Kit'aa waves her last remark away with one hand and goodbye with the other.

Ana practices her swimming at the Queen's beach while Ka'ahumanu coaches from the shade of her favorite tree. "You should know I have been encouraging new mothers to keep their babies since you were here. I have found tradition is difficult to change."

"Yes," she tries to relax her body in the water and float. "I have personal experience with that. I think it can take many years."

"I was thinking that you and Kualelo do not have children yet and you have a large house and knowledge of languages, reading, writing, healing. You are the perfect person to take care of the babies who are allowed to live and unwanted by their mothers."

Ana stands up in the water revealing her mother's tiny carved wolf charm and bear claw on a strap around her neck. She looks at Queen Ka'ahumanu, "might I also attempt to reunite them with their families?"

"If you wish."

"Is this an actual request? Or a command? Or just an idea?"

Ka'ahumanu tries to keep a serious face, "What do you *wish* it to be?"

"A command!" Ana shouts with an excited grin.

Kualelo runs toward them on the beach, his feet barely touching the sand. "I found a ship captain who knows Latin!" he calls. "It's time to be married! Come on Ana Falcon Girl!"

She grabs her clothes from the shade. "I need my mother's white swan robe and my Bible!" she squeaks, feeling fire in her heart. As she runs toward Kualelo, her mother's voice seems to bounce with the charm against her chest, saying "be hap-py, be hap-py, be hap-py," and Do'ok's dimpled grin pops into her mind.

21

Epilogue

Do'ok of Wolf Clan of the Wolf People gains status for his clan and himself as Master Storyteller, practicing nightly around his family fire, his children wide-eyed. Like all stories of any clan, Wolf Clan's stories *belong* to the clan, not to be told by anyone else without permission, to do so would require compensation of the offending clan or even the possibility of war. Among his stories are "Chark Cough-ye, Bear-Killer Warrior," "Ut-kart-ee, Basket-Maker Fighting," and "Ana Falcon Woman, Saves Twins and Heals." These loved ones will never die.

Several times a year, he sees Falcon circling overhead around and around above An-ar-kark, looking for Ana Falcon Woman. Wrapping several layers of deerskin over his arm, he stands with it extended, waiting. Falcon circles several more times, then comes down to land and stay awhile. As soon as Do'ok speaks, Falcon flies off, wondering what's happened to his master.

Ana tells stories as well, to all the children of E Komo Mai House (Welcome House) of the Island Hawai'i. All the children, including her own, sit together in the evenings with the golden glow of tiny kukui nut lights. In addition to Hawaiian and Bible stories, and Tlingit stories of Raven, she tells her version of "Bear-Killer Warrior," "Basket-Maker Fighting," and "Lost Twins Found," which is her right since she is of Wolf Clan of the Wolf People.

Wolf visits her dreams sometimes, often with Falcon, and when she wakes with a giggle or laugh, she knows she's been with her brother, the one who knows her so well, the delight of him bubbling up from her chest.

From time to time when she reflects on the events of her life, she wonders about choice and destiny and her influence on Wolf Clan's shagoon. When regret from her mother's death returns, she sends it away on her love for her mother and remembers the words she heard so loudly inside her head, "Ana, love thyself."

22

Author's Note

My intention with this writing is to pay tribute to the Tlingit people by creating interest in their culture and character through the love and interaction of family members. Hopefully, it also presents their courage and the support they felt from their traditions and community. My apologies for several things: for any misrepresentation of the culture during the 1700's, for giving this simplistic representation of an intricate, complicated heritage of traditions and proper behaviors and for omitting the symbols that should have accompanied many of the Tlingit words which were borrowed from Emmon's *The Tlingit Indians* and Edward's *Dictionary of Tlingit*.

It is partly because of the Tlingit people's fiercely independent, daring, and industrious nature, along with their intelligence and cleverness that the United States may refer to the bold, breathtaking wilderness of Alaska as its own. They traded with the invading Russians from 1743 to the 1860's while maintaining independence, and their resistance undermined attempts at colonization and inhibited Russia's southern advancement down the Pacific Northwest Coast.

Each member of Tlingit society belongs to one of two large groups based upon the mother's lineage: Raven or Wolf (or Eagle as adopted in the North in later years). The complex structure between the two large groups provides a brilliant social organization of interdependence that guides the functioning of the community. A village typically consisted of a variety of independent clans, each with its own heritage, from each of the two large groups or lineage. One may only marry a member of the opposite lineage. Although the lineage is passed through the women to her children, the family lives within the father's clan. When a boy reaches eight years old, he lives with his uncle (his mother's brother) for upbringing.

The Tlingit had no chiefs. The most influential person within a village was usually the leader of a clan with the most wealth, but he had no control over other clans. Although wealth was important to status and rank, so was generosity and proper behavior aligned with Tlingit customs. Strictly honest, they had a need for revenge if treated unfairly or ridiculed, and they valued their *Shagoon*, their ancestors, origin, heritage, traditions, reputation, and future at the highest level.

23

Facts within the Fiction

This is a work of fiction based on researched people, events and cultures of the 1700s.

Twins were killed in many Native American cultures in the 18th Century. By the late 19th Century, twins and their families were still being shunned in the upper Puget Sound area. Twins were not allowed to go near water for fear the fish would be frightened away. Their father was forced to stay home to protect them, so providing for his family became impossible.

Twenty-one Spanish missions were founded between 1769 and 1833 by Franciscan Catholic priests along the California coast to evangelize the local Natives as part of Spanish expansion. *Ohlone* is a term given to generalize 40 different Native groups of the San Francisco area, 10,000 people who spoke 12 distinct languages, each with its own territory and its own chief.

Captain Bodega Quadra and Friar Riobo arrived at Sitka,

Alaska, in their Spanish ship *Favorita* in 1779. Friar Riobo purchased five children for the purpose of raising them in the Christian faith, and he worked at several of the missions.

British Captain George Vancouver surveyed Hawaii and Alaska during three annual trips, 1793-1795, visiting the Spanish missions in California enroute. During one trip, he transported kidnapped girls from the merchant ship *Jenny* back to their home in Hawaii. His officers were Peter Puget, Joseph Baker, Joseph Whidbey, Archibald Menzies, and William Broughton. Dr. Menzies and Lt. Joseph Baker were the first Europeans to reach the top of Mauna Loa. Vancouver's third trip from Hawaii to Alaska was his last, dying at home from illness related to his cough in 1798.

Kualelo was the most widely traveled Hawaiian of his time, the first Hawaiian to visit Europe, returning to his home on Molokai aboard Vancouver's ship *Discovery* after study in England. On ship, he worked with Dr. Menzies. His later success was due to Kamehameha giving him land, control of 200 vessels and the marriage of a chief's daughter.

The named Hawaiians were real people, including the "Sacred Twins." Ka'ahumanu was King Kamehameha's favorite wife. She outlawed infanticide in 1824. The close relationship between Kamehameha and Vancouver was accurate, and Kamehameha did pledge himself a subject of King George. A copper plate was created as evidence, but Britain did not respond to the pledge. Today, a modification of the British flag is included on the Hawaiian State flag.

Alexander Baranov's Russian America was established by the forced labor of Aleut to hunt sea otter at his settlement at

Kodiak followed by others including one at Yakutat and New Archangel founded at Sheet'ka Kwaan, known as Sitka, Alaska today. According to one source, disease and harsh treatment decimated the Aleut population by 80 percent between 1741 and 1799.

Two of Baranov's ships sank, and he sent his little sloop, Ermak, to "his friend" Kamehameha in Hawaii for food. The ship was returned fully loaded.

The Russians felt it was because of the "Boston Men" providing the Tlingit with guns that enabled them to successfully repel Russian colonization. The United States purchased Alaska from Russia in 1867.

24

Resources

Most informative or influential sources

Borneman, Walter R. (2003). *Alaska: Saga of a Bold Land*, New York: HarperCollins Publisher.

Edwards, Keri. (2009). *Dictionary of Tlingit*, Juneau, Alaska: Sealaska Heritage Institute.

*Emmons, George Thornton, edited with additions by Frederica de Laguna. (1991). *The Tlingit Indians*, Seattle: University Washington Press.

Ewing, Susan. (1996). *The Great Alaska Nature Factbook*, Portland, OR: Alaska Northwest Books.

Gear, W. Michael and Kathleen O'Neal. (1990). *People of the Wolf* (and the entire *First North Americans* series), New York: Tom Doherty Associates.

Gulick, Bill. (1996). *Traveler's History of Washington*, Caldwell, Idaho: The Caxton Printers, Ltd.

Grinev, Andrei Val 'Terovich. (2005). *The Tlingit Indians in Russian America, 1741-1867,* Lincoln, Nebraska: University of Nebraska Press.

Handy, Emory, Bryan, Buck, Wise, et. al. (1999). *Ancient Hawaiian Civilization: A Series of Lectures* Delivered at The Kamehameha Schools, Honolulu: HI: Mutual Publishing.

*Kan, Sergei. (2016). *Symbolic Immortality: The Tlingit Potlatch of the Nineteenth Century,* 2nd Ed., Seattle, WA: University of Washington Press.

*Kāne, Herb Kawainui (1997). *Ancient Hawaii,* Captain Cook, HI: The Kawainui Press.

Keithahn, Edward L. (1963). *Monuments in Cedar: The Authentic Story of the Totem Pole,* New York: Bonanza Books, p. 156.

Keremitsis, Eileen. (2003). *Life in a California Mission,* San Diego, CA: Lucent Books.

La Pérouse, Jean Francois de. (1989). *Life in a California Mission: The Journals of Jean Francois de La Pérouse,* Berkley, CA: Heyday.

*Margolin, Malcolm. (1978). *The Ohlone Way: Indian Life in the San Francisco-Monterey Bay Area.* Berkley, CA: Heyday.

Milliken, Randall. (2009). *A Time of Little Choice: The Disintegration of Tribal Culture in the San Francisco Bay Area 1769-1810,* Ballena Press Publication.

Moore, Susanna. (2015). *Paradise of the Pacific: Approaching Hawaii,* New York: Farrar, Straus and Giroux.

Museums: Bailey House Museum, Wailuku, Maui; Hulihe'e Palace in Kailua-Kona, Hawaii; San Francisco de Asis Mission Museum in San Francisco; San Jose Mission Museum in Freemont, California; Southeast Alaska Indian Cultural Center

Museum and Sheldon Jackson Museum in Sitka, Alaska; Alaska State Museum and Juneau-Douglas City Museum in Juneau, Alaska.

Salisbury, O. M. (1962). *The Customs and Legends of the Thlinget Indians of Alaska*, New York: Bonanza Books.

Sheet'ka Kwaan Naa Kahidi, Traditional Tlingit Dancers in Sitka, Alaska, 2018 on-stage presentation.

Speckman Jr., Cummins E. and Hackler, Rhoda E.A. (1989). "Vancouver in Hawaii," *The Hawaiian Journal of History*, Vol. 23, p. 31-68.

Thornton, Very Rev. Walter, S. J. (1918). Translated from an unpublished manuscript of Father John Riobo of the voyage in 1779 to Alaska, printed in *Catholic Historical Review* 4(3): 222-29.

Wallis, Velma. (1993). *Two Old Women*, Kenmore, WA: Epicenter Press.

http://collections.dartmouth.edu/arctica-beta/html/ EA15-74.html (language samples for Vancouver)

25

Acknowledgements

My greatest thanks to my husband Dennis, most important advocate, resource and collaborator, and first reader extraordinaire, putting his degree in journalism and political science as well as a rich foundation in everything historic and Catholic school beginnings to much-appreciated use. The book would not have happened without him.

Thank you to family and friends for encouragement, reading and feedback, and especially to those who helped with editing: Carol Olsen, Michele Lynn and Jerry Raitzer, Karen Bailozor and Becky Keck. Their support helped calm my self-doubts.

Thank you to my mother for admiring my writing when I was a child and to Susan Mooring who said I had been a Native American twin in Alaska in a former life. She suggested that I write about that experience and said that my twin was still on the other side. I have woken in the night, laughing with someone I felt I knew well, "the joy of him bubbling up from my chest." Thank you to Michael and Kathleen Gear, archeologists and authors of *The First North Americans*—a series of novels about the peoples of prehistoric America--for helping me imagine life long ago. Thank you to Tara Woolpy, author of *Releasing Gilian's Wolves,* for publishing advice. Thank you to Allen Gardner for his 8th grade report on falconry.

Thank you to those who requested a copy before it was written: Lourdes Valdesuso, whom I met on an airplane from San Jose to Seattle; world-traveled, retired teachers Bob and Kathleen Prentice; my artistic, glass-blowing dentist Dr. Berner; and Carol Olsen's neighbor, who wanted ten copies for Christmas gifts. Their early interest and my husband's unwavering encouragement, "It reads like a book!" was the breath I needed to keep writing.

26

Questions for Readers/ Book Groups

1. **For any chapter,** what did you find interesting about a culture of that time period? (Tlingit, Aleut, Haida, Spanish Mission, Ohlone, Hawaiian, Russian, European, American)

   After reading:

2. Chapter 1: When Ut-kart-ee rubs her forehead on bark, creating a wound, what is meant by "the remembered power of choice"?

3. Chapter 6: What three foods do you suspect Crane Clan brought from the Cloud-Face ship that looked like "maggots, dry like tree fungus, a dark thick liquid"?

4. Chapter 8: How did clans benefit from a potlatch?

5. Chapter 9: Ana thinks, "Anger feels better than sadness and better than fear." When was a time that you felt angry? Was there some hidden sadness or fear involved?

6. Chapter 10: Should Do'ok's parents have told him at a younger age that he was a twin?

7. Chapter 16: Vancouver offers to take Ana back to the mission. What would you have done at that point in time if you were Ana?

8. Chapter 17: Zesen told Ana, "Your mind can be your worst enemy; think of something to be thankful for." Kualelo told her, "We have more danger from internal trouble than external." How did both Ana (in Chapter 17) and Do'ok (in Chapter 12) cope with problems by changing their ways of thinking?

9. Chapter 19: How does Ut-kart-ee's Spirit Dream come true?

10. Chapter 20: In Ana's dream when Kualelo asks her what sustains her, she replies, "Love, all kinds, everywhere." Considering her life, why would she answer that way?

11. Chapter 20: Ana recognizes that her original visit to Hawaii with Vancouver was more important than she had realized at the time. Is there a time or place or moment that you realize has been instrumental to your life as you reflect on it now?

12. Epilogue: Regrets can make it difficult to love oneself. How might one cope?

After reading the book:

1. When Ut-kart-ee prays that her future children will "never die," what does that mean in her Tlingit culture?

2. To what extent was A-kadi's roll important to Ana? How might the story have changed if he had never accepted twins into Wolf Clan?

3. What is a story like "Bear Killer Warrior" or "Basket-Maker Fighting" that could be named and told as part of your family's heritage?

4. Ana finds that change is hard, especially when beliefs and customs are involved. How might you relate that truth to present day?

5. An on-going theme is the desire/need to belong. Ana wanted to find someone-like-a-mother. Do'ok wished he could find a friend. Nevertheless, A-kadi jeopardizes his belonging in An-ar-kark to break tradition. How strong is your need to belong? Do you feel free to express a view that is contrary to your group's?

**Victoria Ventris
Shea**

After a career in education and writing online courses with video, Victoria presents her first novel for entertainment, a historical fiction adventure, SHAGOON. Having spent most of her life in the woods of Washington state, her writing usually includes experiences in the natural environment. She has had a passion for writing ever since her first serious boyfriend dumped her at a tender age. Her distaste for history changed when she realized that her interest was in the characters, not the dates and events that were taught in school. Now she indulges in research and the creation of real-life characters as she puts together bits of history in new ways.

She celebrates family, especially cooking together, and is interested in warm climates, sandy beaches, large bodies of water, palm trees, and plumeria. During breaks from writing, she helps her husband build houses, practices yoga and enjoys the mussels from Penn Cove where she currently lives on Whidbey Island.

Having always admired Native American cultures, when a psychic told her thirty years ago that she had once been an Alaskan Native American twin, and she learned that twins had been left in the forest to die in some Native cultures of the past, she felt compelled to investigate. The story of SHAGOON has been building ever since.

Earning a BA at Eastern Washington University and MA from Lesley College, Cambridge, MA, she taught in Washington and Hawaii, served as a professional learning facilitator and mentor for teachers, taught Professional Certification courses for Washington State University, and created online courses with video for schools as well as for the New Teacher Center of Washington state.